THE SOFTWIRE

THE SOFTWIRE
BETRAYAL ON ORBIS 2

PJ HAARSMA

CANDLEWICK PRESS
CAMBRIDGE, MASSACHUSETTS

First edition 2008

Library of Congress Cataloging-in-Publication Data

Haarsma, PJ.
The softwire : betrayal on Orbis 2 / PJ Haarsma. — 1st ed.
p. cm.
Summary: On his second rotation of service, Johnny Turnbull uses his ability as a human softwire to communicate with the Samirans and free them from their enslavement.
ISBN 978-0-7636-2710-2
[1. Computers—Fiction. 2. Science fiction.]
I. Title. II. Title: Betrayal on Orbis 2. III. Title: Betrayal on Orbis Two.
PZ7.H11132Si 2008
[Fic]—dc22   2007038285

2 4 6 8 10 9 7 5 3 1

Printed in the United States of America

This book was typeset in Utopia.

Candlewick Press
2067 Massachusetts Avenue
Cambridge, Massachusetts 02140

visit us at www.candlewick.com

For Skylar

"Here it comes!" Theodore Malone shouted.

"But we're not ready yet!" I yelled back, scoping the sorting bay for any sign of *it.* I snatched the hand laser off the floor and hid it inside my vest.

"Give me that," Maxine Bennett protested, and took the tool from me. She pointed it at the scavenger-bot now dissected on the metal floor in front of us. "This is the last one. If that thing gets its paws on this before we fix it, who's gonna clean this place up? Not me," she said. "I plan to do more on this ring than just pick up after Switzer."

I did too. I just hadn't figured what that was yet. I strained my neck to see past the huge cranes rooted on the inner dome at the center of Weegin's World. There was no sign of *it.*

"Fine, Max. Then you keep working, and I'll find some way to block the lift," I said, standing up and tearing back toward the other kids.

"Better hurry, JT," Theodore said from across the sorting-bay floor and to my far right.

"You could help," I told him, but Theodore shook his head. He was safely out of the way, perched atop one of the electric-blue sorting belts. The belts were placed every meter or so inside the curved factory. Theodore waved me over to join him on the gaseous device, but I needed to make it to the second-floor lift, located between him and the last belt.

Our roommate, Randall Switzer, was dozing on that farthest belt. I could see a portable O-dat clutched in his oversize paw. It was a weak attempt to prove his intelligence, but I knew the lazy malf only wanted to nap.

I heard the lift squawk into action. Theodore stood up on the belt. "It's on the lift! Forget about the bot, JT—just run!"

I froze. From where I stood, I couldn't see the lift, but I could definitely hear what was on it.

"Work! Work! Now work!" *it* screamed over the machine's metallic hum like a distress beacon.

"It's getting off the lift—now," another kid said.

I turned back toward Max. "Leave it," I shouted at her.

I took my chances and charged toward Theodore.

I hadn't even broken stride when my feet were knocked out from under me. Before I hit the floor, a heavy, clawed foot (the worst kind) thumped against the lower part of my vest, knocking the wind out of me.

"I see you with tools. Where you get tools?" *it* screamed at me.

"I'm fixing the scavenger-bot," I shouted back. "You broke

them all!" But I knew speaking to him was useless. The bald little beast just tilted his head whenever I spoke, as if amazed I could make sounds with my mouth. It was worse than trying to reason with Switzer.

"My tools!" he said, and pushed down on my chest.

When I was first assigned to Weegin, almost one complete rotation ago, my Guarantor always cradled a yellowed larva in his thick, three-fingered hands. He nursed that puffy thing phase after phase, and I never once bothered to ask him what it was. No one did. Weegin answered most questions with a twist of your nose or your ear, or even a painful yank on your hair. If he had wanted me to know what it was, he would have told me. But the mystery was gone now. Two phases ago, right after I fought the Belaran, Madame Lee, inside the central computer, that puffy lump of flesh hatched into the little monster that stood over me as I gasped for air.

"Who gave knudnik my tools?" he demanded, and lifted his disgusting foot off my chest.

Previous confrontations with Weegin's offspring taught me to give up early since he never understood a word I said anyway. I simply curled up on the floor, clutched my stomach, and waited for the oxygen to find its way into my lungs. Looking satisfied with my condition, the undersize monster set his beady eyes on Switzer.

The alien was not exactly a miniature version of Weegin, as you might expect. His hands were far more muscular, and his legs appeared thicker and stronger than they should for a Choi from Krig. The bald protégé stalked the corridors of Weegin's

World with his lower jaw thrust absurdly forward, the result of a severe underbite. A row of pointed teeth curled up and over his top lip as he marched around barking orders at everyone. Somehow this pink little maggot thought he was in charge.

He ran straight at Switzer and slammed the operation button next to his head. The sorting belts hissed into motion.

"Work. You. Big thing. Work now!" he yelled, and stood guard so no one could get at the controls.

Theodore had jumped to the floor. Switzer, however, remained soundly asleep. Even the clatter of the awakened cranes did not stir him.

"Maybe he's deaf *and* dumb?" Theodore said.

"Switzer!" Max shouted, but he did not move. Switzer kept right on sleeping as the blue mist holding him up headed for the chute. The chute was a hole in the wall that led to a furnace burning deep beneath Weegin's World. It was a drop Switzer would not survive. Max and another kid tried to get to Switzer, but Weegin's hatchling snapped his large, protruding snout at anyone who moved.

I pulled myself off the ground. "Distract that thing," I told Max, and she chucked a wrench at him. The alien turned on his heels and stomped straight toward her, his lengthy claws clacking on the metal floor.

"Tools are expensive!" he screamed.

I stuck my hand in the greenish-gray radiation gel used to protect our skin when there was junk to sort. I slid over to Switzer and reached my hand under his nose. The ghastly smell—rotten meat mixed with crusty socks and a touch of recycled toilet water—did the job. Switzer wrenched his head away and fell to the floor as Weegin dashed out from his glass bunker. I ran to an O-dat at the other side of the bay and accessed the local computer network with my softwire. I shut the cranes down instantly.

"Is it here? Speak. Is it here yet?" Joca Krig Weegin shouted from the second-floor balcony that jutted out over the sorting-bay floor. He hoisted his knobby body onto the railing and canvassed each one of us with his bloodshot eyes.

"Is what here, Weegin?" said a voice from the tall glass doorway.

I spun around to see the Keeper, Theylor. His purple velvety robes swept the floor as he entered Weegin's World.

"You're not welcome here!" Weegin screamed at the regal alien, raining spit on anyone below him. "They're mine. Every last one of them!" With that he turned and scrambled back into his office.

I saw Theylor's left head frown while his right head turned to all of us and said, "Hello. I hope everyone is fine?"

"We're a little bored," I said.

"No, *really* bored," Switzer added.

Switzer was right. There was nothing to do at Weegin's anymore. Our Guarantor's junk business was in shambles ever since his dealings with the disgraced Trading Council member, Madame Lee, had failed. Most cycles, I simply roamed around the complex while Weegin barricaded himself in his office. It was nowhere near the life I had imagined for Ketheria and myself before we had arrived on the Rings of Orbis.

"Hello? Hey! I need a little help here, anyone?" Max said, jumping from side to side using an even larger wrench to swipe at Weegin's offspring.

"Weegin hasn't even named that thing," Theodore said.

"His name is Nugget," said my sister, Ketheria, as she entered the sorting bay. She noticed Theylor immediately. "Hi, Theylor."

"Hello, Ketheria," he replied.

"Come here, Nugget," Ketheria said, and the creature immediately stopped harassing Max and marched over to Ketheria, sticking his chin out and up. For some reason he never bothered my little sister. Ketheria tickled him under his chin while he reached up and played with her light brown hair.

"Ooh, ooh," the alien moaned.

"Freak," Switzer said, sneering.

"Which one?" Dalton Billings said, and Max shot Switzer's friend a steely look.

"Why does she like that thing?" Switzer asked.

"Jealous?" Max teased him.

Switzer snarled at her but caught Theodore grinning. Theodore was easier prey for him than Max, and he moved toward my friend, fists raised. I stepped forward, too.

Nugget saw this and sprang to his feet, charging at us with his ridiculous lower jaw smacking against his upper lip.

"Work. Now. More work!"

"There is no work, you little rat," Dalton shouted at Nugget as he stomped past.

"He doesn't understand anything we tell him, Theylor," Max said.

As Nugget got close, Theylor raised his long right hand, and the alien was frozen in midstride. I could see a soft, warm glow from a bronze device wrapped around Theylor's arm. I'd seen him silence someone before, when we first arrived on the ring, but I'd never noticed that gadget before.

"*Thank* you," Max exclaimed.

"This may help," he said, and made a sweeping motion with his slender arm.

The blue translucent skin on his fingers peeked out from underneath his velvet robe as he pointed to an R5 that now entered Weegin's World. "Right there will be fine," he told the robot.

I hadn't seen an R5 since we first arrived on Orbis 1. The robot was used to implant neural ports behind everyone's left ear allowing them to link up with the central computer. Everyone but me, that is. I don't need a neural port. I am a softwire—a leap in human evolution that allows me to interact with any computer using only my mind. Some of the other kids, especially Max, think my ability is really golden, but I find it just makes most Orbisians very nervous. The Citizens think their precious computer is some kind of all-knowing sentient being. It doesn't make them very happy knowing I can get inside it whenever I want.

"Who's that for?" Theodore asked.

"Who do you think, split-screen?" Switzer said, rolling his eyes and snickering with Dalton.

Ketheria stepped forward and said, "That's for Nugget."

"You are correct," Theylor told her.

"But why didn't Weegin take him to get this done earlier?" I asked.

"Yeah, it would have made life around here a lot easier," another girl said, frowning.

Theylor looked up toward Weegin's office. "It seems your Guarantor has been avoiding contact with us for quite some time."

I looked up and saw a mound of unanswered messenger drones stacked outside Weegin's office. They waited patiently to uplink the screen scrolls they carried with Weegin's neural implant, if he ever let them.

"What are they for?" I asked.

"First we must deal with . . ." Theylor began.

"Nugget. His name is Nugget," Ketheria reminded him.

Theylor looked at my sister and smiled. He placed his long, slender hand on her head without touching the strip of metal now physically attached to her skull. When Madame Lee exposed Ketheria's telepathy, Keeper decree required that she be fixed with a prosthetic to diminish her abilities. Ketheria didn't seem bothered by it, though, and her hair had grown back nicely, almost covering the sculpted metal that banded her head. My sister said she even liked the large amber crystal placed in the metal over her forehead. I asked her once if it hurt. She just shrugged and said, "Not anymore."

"How are you, Ketheria?" Theylor asked.

"I'm fine."

"I'm glad," the Keeper replied. "I am also glad Nugget has a friend."

"He's different from his father, isn't he? Weegin is a Choi, but Nugget is a Choisil," she said.

"I am afraid you are right," Theylor said. "It will be hard for Weegin to accept Nugget. But he has you now, Ketheria."

"Yes, he does," she replied.

I looked at Nugget, frozen in the middle of the sorting-bay floor, and I actually felt sorry for him, even though I didn't know what Ketheria was talking about.

"Can you unfreeze him?" Ketheria asked.

"Certainly."

Theylor raised his hand again, and the startled Nugget shot off across the bay.

"Enough with the reunion—let's implant the little bugger!" Switzer cried, scanning the room for Nugget.

Switzer had hated the implanting procedure more than most, but he smiled and rubbed his hands together. I think he enjoyed watching people suffer.

"C'mon, freak," Switzer growled, moving a crate to expose the small alien shaking behind a metal container.

"Stop it!" Ketheria yelled at him.

"Please, big thing. Please," Nugget begged as Switzer closed in. Switzer reached out for the alien, but Ketheria stepped in front of him. Even though Ketheria was eight years old now, she was still only half the size of Switzer.

"Stop," she said, holding up her hand.

"Get out of my way, freak," he said while taking a cautious

step backward. Switzer never seemed comfortable around Ketheria after we found out about her mind-reading abilities.

I moved to intervene, but Theylor stepped between them.

"That will be enough, children," Theylor said. "Ketheria, could you bring Nugget to me, please?"

Ketheria knelt in front of Nugget and spoke softly to him. I could not hear what she was saying, but I knew he couldn't understand her anyway. She tickled him under the chin some more and then stood up, taking his big hand. Ketheria led Nugget over to Theylor and the R5.

"Thank you," Theylor said.

"Freak," Switzer mumbled under his breath.

"Nugget will not be hurt. As you all remember, the procedure is painless and only takes a moment to perform," Theylor said.

Theylor reached for Nugget's hand, but he wasn't having any of that, so Ketheria had to lead him over to the chairlike robot. She helped Nugget get comfortable and gently pressed his face down on the headrest.

"Please," Nugget whimpered.

"It's all right, Nugget," she comforted him and caressed his dark-purplish wings.

The robot shifted, making adjustments for Nugget's size. Nugget struggled to free himself, but the machine held him in place.

"Danger! Danger! Daaaaann . . . !"

Before Nugget could finish shouting, the R5 had implanted a small port at the back of Nugget's left ear.

"What about the codec?" I asked. The central computer interprets all of the different alien languages for us using a translation codec that is uplinked through the neural port. It even connects with your optical nerves so you can read in any language.

"This R5 is now equipped with the translation codec. Everything is done at once," Theylor said. "Nugget should now be able to understand everyone."

The R5 released Nugget, and he scrambled to the other side of the sorting bay.

"Danger! Danger! Danger!" he screamed, and found a crate to hide behind.

"Hey! Freak! Can you understand what I'm saying to you?" Switzer shouted at Nugget.

Nugget cocked his head to the side and slipped out from behind the crate.

"Yes?" Nugget said, but it was more like a question. He squinted his eyes and waited for a reply from Switzer.

"Good. Now get out of here and leave us alone." Switzer pointed to Weegin's office. That was not a good idea. Nugget puffed out his chest and stomped his oversize feet toward Switzer.

"No. Work. Work! To work now, big thing!" Nugget cried, pointing at the conveyor belts and snapping his jaw. "Work!"

"Great," Theodore said.

"Thanks, Theylor," I said. "I guess."

Nugget darted around the room corralling the other children and goading them toward the belts. Theylor smiled with his right head while his left head turned toward me. "Will you give this to your Guarantor please, Johnny?"

"Sure, Theylor," I said. "What is it?"

"You will know everything shortly," Theylor responded. I hated it when he was so vague. It usually meant something was about to change. "And Johnny?" Theylor turned before he was out the door. "Enjoy Birth Day," said both of Theylor's heads, and then he was gone.

"It's Birth Day?" Theodore asked.

"I guess it is. Happy fourteenth," I said, just as surprised as the rest.

"What's on the scroll?" Max asked me, motioning to the glowing screen scroll the Keeper left for Weegin.

Max and Theodore stood there staring at me.

"How would I know?" I asked them.

"Take a peek." Max nudged me.

"Maybe he shouldn't do that," Theodore argued.

"Oh, give me that," Max said. She grabbed the scroll and unraveled the organic screen from its metal container. She pulled the uplink from the scroll and inserted it into her neural implant. The glow from the metal casing flashed: INVALID USER.

"Told you," Theodore said.

"Here, you do it," Max said, holding it out to me. "Do the *push* thing," Max said. She knew very well I could sneak into hard drives, network arrays, light drives, anything to do with a computer.

I was about to push into the scroll when an alarm went off. I looked up and saw the field portals at the top of the outer metal dome sparkle to life and begin to fade away. *Could a cargo shipment really be arriving?* I wondered. Nothing had come through those portals in over a phase. I stood next to Theodore and watched as the robotic cranes warmed up by stretching out their huge tentacles. But before they were in position, a small metal crate was thrust through the opening. It dropped from the sky like a meteor, right toward my sister.

"Ketheria, watch out!" I yelled and leaped forward, catching my sister's arm and yanking her aside.

"You all right?" Max questioned her.

Before she could answer, Weegin burst from his office and scurried down onto the sorting-bay floor.

"This has to be it. It has to be," he said, rubbing his three-fingered hands together.

"What *has* to be it?" Switzer said, inspecting the metal projectile.

"Shut up. Get back, you imbecile. Move away from here," Weegin scolded him.

Switzer simply stepped aside, scowling, but that didn't stop me from creeping forward. *What was in the crate?* I wondered.

"I said get out of here!" Weegin snapped before I could get close. "All of you. I'm deducting one chit for not listening." He used his small body to shield the contents of the crate. Nugget scrambled next to his father, but Weegin only pushed him aside.

"How can you deduct chits? You haven't paid us for a whole phase," Switzer protested.

Weegin ignored him and attached a thick data cable into his own neural port. He glanced over the ragged nubs on his shoulders to make sure none of us could see him tap an access code into the O-dat. Satisfied with Weegin's entry, the crate hissed open and Weegin jammed both fists inside the container. Quickly, he pulled out an unmarked plastic box and clutched it to his chest. His eyes darted over each of us without looking at anyone in particular. Then he grinned and raced off toward the lift. If Weegin still had wings, I'm sure he would have flown.

"I wonder what was inside," I said, walking over to the empty carcass Weegin had left behind.

"Nobody is to disturb me!" he shouted from the second floor as the latest messenger drone slammed into the closing office door.

"Never mind the crate, JT," Max said. "What does this scroll say?"

"Oh," I said, looking at the screen scroll still in my hands. I pushed into the scroll, and the message instantly appeared in my mind's eye as if an O-dat was mounted inside my forehead. I read it aloud.

Joca Krig Weegin,

As previously arranged by Keeper decree, the labor force of human beings is to be transferred to work duty on Orbis 2. Since all business for Joca Krig Weegin has been forfeited on every ring of Orbis, you are called upon to surrender your humans for immediate relocation.

CENTER FOR IMPARTIAL JUDGMENT AND FAIR DEALING

"Weegin has to give us back," I said, glancing up at his office.

"He's not going to like that. We're the only valuable thing he has right now," Max said.

"This is not good. I feel it," Ketheria muttered.

I looked over at Theodore, who was rummaging through the discarded shipping crate. He froze, his eyes widening. "And I think it just got worse," he added.

2

"A replicator?" Max said, glancing up from the instruction screen Theodore had found in the crate.

"Where did he get it?" Theodore asked.

"Probably in some corrupted corner of the universe," I replied.

"What good is it going to do him?" he said.

"He's going to try to replicate things: yornaling crystals, chit cards, ID scans—anything of value that he can fit into the machine. A gadget like that will get him into a pile of trouble by the Center for Forbidden Off-Ring Materials," Max explained. "Citizens call the stuff FORM."

"How do you know all this?" Theodore questioned her.

"It's all in the central computer," she replied. "There's a kabillion things that are forbidden on Orbis, especially a replicator."

Switzer snatched the electronic paper from Max's hand.

"So what can it do?" Switzer asked, trying not to sound interested.

"It will make Weegin a very wealthy alien if he starts replicating crystals. That's why the machines are forbidden," Max told him, and snatched the instructions back. She wandered toward the rec room, poring over the replicator's diagrams. Theodore and I followed.

Inside the rec room, Ketheria was sitting against the glass wall that led to the fake courtyard. Nugget sat next to her.

I moved to the far side of the room, away from anyone that could hear me. "Vairocina." I whispered for my friend. She was the little girl I had found inside the central computer. No one on Orbis had believed me when I told them something was inside their computer, but together she and I saved Orbis from an attack by Madame Lee. Now she lives inside their enormous mainframe helping the Keepers protect the Rings of Orbis. My ability as a softwire lets me contact Vairocina by simply calling out her name. She usually responds in an instant if she is monitoring the same frequency the central computer uses to translate all the different alien languages.

"Yes, JT?" she said inside my head. I turned my back to the others.

"Is it hard to get a replicator on Orbis?"

"A replicator is a FORM item," she said. "Not only is it impossible; it is very illegal. Someone of your status should not be looking for such an item, JT. I am afraid the Keepers would not be very kind if they caught you with a FORM item."

"Don't worry," I told her. "I'm not looking for one."

"Who you talking to?" Theodore whispered. I hadn't seen him come up behind me.

"Good-bye, JT," she said inside my head.

"Vairocina," I told him.

"A game of Ring Defenders?" Theodore said, and plopped on a nearby foam lounger.

"Why not?" I replied as he started the game.

"What were you talking to her about?"

"Replicators," I told him.

"I've been thinking about those, too. I wonder what Weegin plans to do with his."

"Why?"

"Well, think about it. He can make anything he wants. If you had a replicator, what would you do?" he asked me, leaning in.

"I don't know, but you just lost a whole fleet with that move."

"C'mon, there must be something you want."

"I want a lot of things, just not a replicator," I said.

"Like what?"

"Well, I want to work, you know. To do something useful around here. Prove to these people that I'm worthy of Citizenship. But I want it to be something I choose; maybe use my softwire. Weegin certainly hasn't taken advantage of it.

I also want my parents' files back, but I know that will never happen. I want to know why we're here. I want *answers*," I said, a little worried that I was preaching again. "I don't think a replicator can make any of those for me, Theodore."

Theodore was staring at his feet when he said, "You know what I want?"

"What?"

"I want a Space Jumper's belt so I can jump off this ring," he whispered.

I just stared back at him. He was serious. Theodore had never spoken like that before. He always just did as he was told. He had never once talked about escaping.

"Do you think I could do that?" he asked.

"If anyone could just jump, why doesn't everyone do it then?" I said.

"I think you just need practice."

"I don't know, Theodore. They have to be illegal for more reasons than that. And besides, you know what the penalty is for trying to escape."

"If you were a Space Jumper . . ."

"I'm not, Theodore."

"But Madame Lee said your father . . ."

"She was lying," I told him.

Theodore didn't say anything else about the belt. He just looked out the window at the holographic garden. We sat in silence, and I caught Switzer staring at us. He must have listened to our entire conversation.

• • •

That night the dream-enhancement equipment of my sleeper steered me toward the crystal moons of Orbis, glowing bright purple and orange against the empty void of space. But just as I was about to touch down on Ki, I was ripped from my dream. I awoke to find Weegin standing over me, thumping his fist on the lid of my sleeper. His beady red eyes glowed brighter than the moons in my dream, and his raspy breath stunk of burnt hair.

"Weegin, what's the matter?" I asked him, trying to focus.

"It doesn't work," he growled. The crevices in his face appeared deeper than normal, and there were dark crimson circles around his eyes.

"What doesn't work?" I whispered.

"It doesn't work. Get up."

"Weegin, are you all right?"

"Get up now. You must make it work," Weegin pleaded, almost out of breath as he shoved the lid of my sleeper back into the wall.

I did as I was told and slid off my sleeper.

I followed my Guarantor through the darkened sorting bay in my plastic pajamas. The robot cranes slouched over us as I trudged behind Weegin toward his private lift. It was the same lift I'd taken with Ketheria, Max, and Theodore the night Madame Lee stole my sister and forced me into the central computer to destroy the Keepers' security devices.

"Weegin, have you slept?" I asked the alien after he stumbled into the lift. He was having trouble keeping his eyes open.

"No time. No time," he mumbled.

The door to the lift disappeared, and Weegin paused for me to exit. A trail of stench led me to his glass cubicle. We had left the *Renaissance* in complete disorder, but then *we* were kids. Weegin's office was littered with unanswered screen scrolls piled everywhere, and it looked as if Nugget had clawed or chewed every single item in the place. I was shocked at the mess and searched for the smell that was coaxing the dinner tablet from my stomach. Then, in the far corner I saw it. It was another larva that Weegin must have been nursing. Only this one was dead.

In the center of all the garbage sat the replicator. It looked simple enough: a shiny metallic cone inverted over a small, black circular base. On the base sat a glowing blue dish. The whole thing stood just taller than my knees. Weegin stumbled next to it and placed a small crystal on the dish.

"Make it work," he ordered.

"I don't know, Weegin. Maybe Max should . . ."

"Make it work!" He screamed so loud I jumped back. Weegin dropped to his knees and caressed the peculiar piece of metal.

I moved closer and knelt next to Weegin. I scanned the device for a chip or any computer device I might be able to manipulate. But there was nothing—just some simple circuits that worked the lights. Basically the inside was empty. Weegin had been scammed. He'd purchased a dud.

"Weegin, I don't . . ."

"You're all I have. You have to make it work." The alien was begging now.

"But . . ."

"I'll give you ten percent of everything I replicate. You must!"

"Weegin, it's not . . ."

"Fine then, half! Half of everything," Weegin said spitefully.

"It doesn't work, Weegin. The replicator's a fake."

Weegin just stared at me. His face shifted under his tough, wrinkled skin, and if he possessed any emotions, I mean real emotions of sorrow, he was fighting desperately to hold them back now.

"Don't you want to stay with Weegin?" he said, almost whimpering. "Don't you want to stay at Weegin's World?"

I hesitated. I shouldn't have, but I wasn't good at lying. Weegin was no telepath, but he read my mind at that very instant.

"Fine," he said, and his tone grew meaner. "There are worse out there than me." Weegin stood up. Any emotion on his face now turned to anger and mistrust.

"Weegin, I read the screen scroll from the Keepers. I'm sorry. I know you have to give us back."

"Not if you make this work."

"But I can't."

"You're worthless!" Weegin said, and kicked the replicator. It flew across the room and shattered against the wall.

"Weegin . . ."

"You owe me!" he shouted so loud it could have woken the dead larva.

"Owe you what?"

"Get everyone up. Bring every child to the recreation room," he said. His voice was firm and filled with a dark determination.

"Why?"

"Do as you are told!"

"Please, tell me what you're doing."

Weegin moved to the edge of his office and looked out over what was left of his business.

"The scroll said I had to take you back, right?" he said.

"Yes . . . ," I replied.

"But it didn't say when, did it?"

"Well, I think it said immediately."

"Fine, then. We leave tonight," Weegin said.

3

Was I really worthless? Was Weegin right? What *was* I doing on the Rings of Orbis? I was glad to be leaving Weegin's World. Surely there had to be some purpose for me on the rings. I was eager to see what the Keepers had in store for me. I mean, I had helped them avert a war against all those Neewalkers. And it was me who set them up with Vairocina. Maybe they would reward me with an important job—one that didn't lock me inside the central computer but that proved I was capable of more than sorting trash.

I was still fantasizing about my new job by the time everyone gathered in the rec room. All twenty of us huddled in different groups, chatting, as we waited for Weegin.

Max turned to me and whispered, "Theodore said the replicator was a fake."

"Just a shell," I told her.

"What's he going to do now?"

"I don't care. Anything's better than this place," Switzer said, and sprawled himself on a lounger. "I'm glad we're leaving."

Secretly, I couldn't help but agree with him.

"Trip! Time for trip!" Nugget shouted as he entered the room, followed slowly by Weegin.

Weegin's shoulders drooped as he walked toward us. His eyes were half closed, and he shuffled more than walked. He mumbled, "Is everyone here?"

"Yes," Switzer said.

"Weegin, why—" Max started to ask.

But Weegin snapped at her. "Enough with your questions. Grab your stuff and follow me."

Nugget spun on his heels shouting, "Time for aucti . . . !" But Weegin clipped him in the back of the head with his walking stick. "Shut up, you annoying little runt!"

Nugget frowned, rubbing his bald head as he retreated back toward Ketheria.

"What was he gonna say, Weegin?" I asked. "Where are we going?"

"I said move!"

"But wait . . ."

"*Wait! Wait!* You have no right to tell me to wait." Weegin was no longer slumping. "You are *still* in Weegin's World. You *still* belong to me," Weegin said, thumping his chest with his fist. "You will do anything I tell you. Now move!"

"Come on, Weegin," Switzer said, pushing his way up next to him. "I got my stuff. I'm ready to put this place behind me."

Weegin looked at Switzer. He lifted his chin slightly, but he did not get angry. He simply stood there, trembling. Then he looked around at each one of us.

"Come on, Weegin. Don't go soft on me now," Switzer said.

"Shut up," Max said.

"Weegin?" I nudged him.

"I have no choice. You have no choice. It is in the hands of the Keepers now."

Weegin slumped once again and shuffled toward the door.

"Move! Follow!" Nugget shouted.

I followed my Guarantor across the sorting-bay floor and out of Weegin's World. I admit I was very excited, even though I didn't have a clue where I was going.

The trip on the spaceway lasted long enough for me to realize just how much my feelings for Orbis had changed in one rotation. On the *Renaissance* I couldn't wait to land and start my new life. Even when I learned I would be forced to work to pay off my parents' debt, I still believed there was a better life for me on the Rings of Orbis. I clung to the fact that my parents must have known what they were doing, even if I didn't understand why. They chose to come to Orbis. No one forced them. Yes, it was a complete malfunction that I had to slave away for a bunch of ungrateful aliens, but what choice did *I* have? I couldn't escape. Switzer tried that on the *Renaissance* and failed. If I tried and failed here on Orbis, they would put me to death. I could never take that risk because I wouldn't even try to leave without Ketheria, and I would never risk Ketheria's life like that.

So I put all my focus on Orbis 2. At least I was going back to the Keepers now, and I liked the Keepers. Well, I liked Theylor anyway. Despite the fact he had wanted to stick me inside the central computer forever. It wasn't his idea, I told myself. He tried to warn me. I trusted Theylor.

"Get up!" Weegin barked at us once the shuttle docked.

"You think you're gonna miss him?" Theodore snickered.

"Like a foot in my face," I whispered.

We followed Weegin into the spaceport while Nugget ran about pushing us all together with his big snout.

Whenever I thought of the spaceport that shuttled passengers to and from the Rings of Orbis, my mind was always filled with images of exciting journeys to faraway stars. It had been a while since I'd been here, but I vividly remembered the wonder and awe I felt the first time I walked across that vast polished floor. Back then I really believed that anything could happen and I could be whoever I wanted to be on Orbis.

But this time was different.

The oversize crystals floating high above me. They seemed to cast their warm pink glow on everything but us. The sweet music that filled the air soured every third or fourth note, and the smell from the cascading flowers seemed more on par with the radiation gel back on Weegin's World. I watched the Citizens stride powerfully through the atrium, dressed in rich cloth and sparkling jewels. I looked at my friends. Max's vest was scratched and dented. Theodore's boots no longer matched, and my sister traipsed behind him dragging an old tattered shipping bag stuffed with little souvenirs. That's when it hit me. Even though I still wanted to carve out a better life for myself on Orbis, just as I had when I first arrived, things were different now. *I* was different. This time I knew my position on Orbis. All of this was built for them, not us. I was here to work for the Citizens—I was just a Knudnik—and that's all that seemed to matter to them.

I couldn't help but wonder if that would ever change.

As I walked with everyone, I saw a small creature standing beneath the gigantic windows that lined the atrium. He was not wearing a Citizen emblem, and he was clutching a tattered and soiled sack. *Definitely a knudnik,* I thought as I stopped to watch him. He stood a little taller than Ketheria, and stared out at the space barges docking on the ring. He gazed at the enormous barges with longing, almost love.

"Get out of my way," someone said, and shoved me aside. The alien, who looked like a Solinn, with one of their distinctive fleshy bubbles perched upon her head, stomped toward the little creature. Without warning she clipped the knudnik across the back of his head, knocking him to the floor.

"What did I tell you?" the Guarantor screamed, but the knudnik did not answer. Instead, he quietly gathered up the contents of his sack and scampered past me. The look of love in his eyes was gone.

The Solinn followed but stopped in front of me, focusing on my skin, the vest that told everyone I was a slave.

"Where is your Guarantor?" she demanded.

"You didn't have to do that, you know," I replied.

"What?"

"Hit him. You didn't have to hit him."

The Solinn took a step back, almost as if I had insulted her. I don't think she knew what to do at first, but finally she spoke up. "How dare you tell a Citizen what to do, you ungrateful waste of space. Security!"

"Don't bother," I said, ducking around her.

"Security!" she yelled once more, but I was already back with my sister and Theodore.

"What's her problem?" Theodore said.

"Knudniks," I said. "What else."

"Is that all?" Theodore said.

"Yeah, well, Weegin's problem isn't just knudniks— it's everyone on the ring," Max said, nodding toward our Guarantor.

I turned to see Weegin shove his way through a small line of Citizens waiting at an array of O-dats.

"Get out of my way!" he snapped at any alien who protested.

When he reached the O-dats, he began pounding his leathery fingers on all of the angled screens.

"This is outrageous!" Weegin screamed, and slammed both his fists on the nearest O-dat.

The screen sparked, and two security drones flew in and forced Weegin away from the machine. Weegin took a swing at one robot, knocking it into the other.

"Weegin, what are you doing?" I said, running up to him.

Just then, a 3-D hologram of a pudgy alien wearing an official-looking uniform appeared in front of Weegin and me.

Its green headpiece was adorned with the Orbis insignia—four rings surrounding a glowing star.

"Your account lacks sufficient chits for passage to Orbis 2," the hologram droned. "This delinquent behavior is unacceptable. You will be charged for the damage you have done according to Keeper decree number 1436711 . . ."

"The damage *I* have done!" Weegin screamed, almost lifting himself off the ground. "You fools have destroyed everything I ever owned. I charge *you* for the damage."

"If you continue with this behavior, I will be forced to confine you and your property for a hearing at the Center for Impartial Judgment and Fair Dealing," the hologram warned him.

Weegin scurried around to the back of the O-dats, but the hologram stayed close behind. Weegin grabbed one of the screens and tried to pry it from its metal base. If he got it loose, I was sure he was going to throw it at the official.

"Do something, JT," Max said.

"Me?"

"Yes. Anything."

Quickly, I searched the atrium and noticed a group of aliens waiting by another bank of O-dats on the far side of the room. I assumed that they were waiting to get tickets too, so I darted toward them. I weaved through the thick crowd, skipping around a slow-moving alien only to plow right into another.

"Hey, watch it, knudnik!" the Trefaldoor shouted as I pushed off her enormous form. I kept on running and shoved my way to the front of the line.

"I'm sorry, this is an emergency," I said to the alien protesting behind me. I pushed into the O-dat's computer chip, feeling the rush of energy pass through my mind as it slipped into the machine. I sidestepped the alphanumeric security algorithm and quickly processed twenty-two one-way tickets to Orbis 2.

I rushed back to Weegin, who was still trying to pry the O-dat loose. "Here," I said, and held out the tickets. "Compliments of the Keepers."

"Where did you get these?" he asked, abandoning the demolition of the O-dat to take the tickets from me.

I couldn't believe it. I had just lied *and* stolen—for Weegin, of all aliens.

"Do you really care?" I said.

Weegin stared at the small transparent tickets. A single yellow tear rolled down his crusty face and puddled in a crevice.

"We could have done great things, you and I," Weegin muttered. He sighed, and his shoulders drooped even farther.

Yeah, but we didn't, I thought. "Come on, let's go," I said. "I've never seen Orbis 2."

By the time we filed onto the space barge to Orbis 2 and found a section with empty seats, I was exhausted, anxious, and excited all at the same time. This was my first trip off the ring since arriving on Orbis, and the thought of being reassigned by the Keepers made it almost overwhelming. My only hope was that my new job would be something exciting. I assured myself that anything would be more interesting than the last few phases I'd spent at Weegin's.

I sat down on the soft, curved lounger that lined both sides of the ship. Ketheria sat against the window that ran the length of our compartment. She and Max shared a snack given to them by the servant drones that ran back and forth above our heads.

"This is really nice," Theodore whispered.

"I was unaware they were letting workers sit in a Citizens' cabin," said a tall, regal alien, who was tethered to the ship by a thick yellow cable attached to his neural implant.

I didn't know what to do. Did I purchase the wrong class of tickets? I glanced at Theodore, but he just shrugged.

I started to say, "I'm sorry . . ."

But the alien held up his hand and said, "Relax, I've never met a human before." His voice was warm, not authoritative at all. "I'm Captain Tapp."

"Hello," I replied. "My name is Johnny Turnbull. This is my sister Ketheria, and these are my friends Max and Theodore."

"Are you the Softwire we have heard so much about?" the captain asked.

I stared at my feet. I didn't like being recognized as the *Softwire,* especially with the other kids watching.

"Do not be ashamed. You should be proud to be different. It will come in handy someday," Captain Tapp said. I felt my face grow hot. He was only making it worse. "I'm sure it already has. In fact you can stay right where you are. My guests. Enjoy your trip."

The captain slid away to greet more of his passengers. I didn't know if I could agree with him, though. The only thing my ability seemed to do for me was to get me into trouble or cause unwanted attention. *At least we don't have to move,* I thought. I did not want to imagine where they let the knudniks sit.

∴ 4

The trip between the rings lasted a whole spoke. Weegin made everyone wait until the barge was emptied before exiting with us in tow. When I stepped into the spaceport, I immediately noticed its stark contrast to the spaceport we had just left on Orbis 1. There were no towering windows to walk under, no crystals hanging from the ceiling. Instead I saw thick, blackened support beams and dim plasma lights; the soft notes of musical instruments had been replaced by the clattering of machinery.

"What's that smell?" Max said, sniffing the air.

"It's better than the radiation gel," I reminded her.

"Anything is better than that," Theodore added.

Head down and Nugget at his side, Weegin charged forward, and I hurried to keep up.

As she rushed along, Max stepped around a grimy alien and onto an automated roadway that kept branching off in different directions. A very battered but determined cart-bot, the biggest I'd ever seen, was headed straight for her. It showed no intention of stopping.

"Watch out, Max!" I shouted.

Max saw the cart-bot and jumped off the road. "Thanks," she said.

The hulk of metal slipped past us with its load of . . . Actually, I couldn't tell what it was carrying, but it looked very heavy.

"I wonder if it would have stopped," I said to Max as we watched the bot get swallowed by the crowds.

A group of burly aliens I had seen on the barge greeted friends and shared containers filled with frothy, colored liquids. I couldn't help but notice that they shouted at each other a lot. They were larger, beefier, *stronger*-looking Citizens, built for manual labor, although they had probably never lifted a finger in their lives. They did, however, look prepared for a much tougher existence, and it made me wonder what kind of job was waiting for us here.

Weegin marched us through a collection of busy little trading chambers stacked one on top of the other. The crowds thinned as we followed him to the spaceway. We boarded, took our seats, and let the gravity cushions settle over us. As we headed out of the spaceport, Theodore asked, "JT, you visited the Keepers once, didn't you?"

"Yeah, in Magna. Well, actually underneath Magna," I said.

"But Magna is back on Orbis 1. Why did we go to Orbis 2 if Weegin has to take us back to the Keepers?"

He was right. My mind raced to the screen scroll I had

read back at Weegin's. Where did it tell Weegin to take us? I just assumed it was Orbis 2 because we were supposed to spend one rotation on each ring. But Weegin was being forced to give us up now. Did that make things different? Were we supposed to go to Magna?

"There have to be Keepers on Orbis 2," I told him. "I mean, they control all the rings, not just Orbis 1. I'm sure they have a city like Magna on Orbis 2. They have to."

"That's what I thought," Theodore said, and looked out the window at the moons.

I leaned toward Weegin. "Weegin, where *are* we going?" I whispered.

"It's not my choice," he mumbled, staring out the window also.

Max was eavesdropping. "Weegin, what do you mean it's not *your* choice?" she said.

"I have nothing left."

"It's not our fault you have nothing," Switzer interrupted. "You should let us go then!"

I shook my head over Switzer's stupid remark. Why did he always do that? Weegin looked at him and wouldn't talk to anyone anymore. He just stared out into space. There *must* be Keepers on Orbis 2, I told myself—more than once.

When the spaceway came to a stop and the gravity cushion eased off, Weegin was the first one out of his seat. We followed our Guarantor off the shuttle and into a deserted spaceway station. A row of broken plasma lights buzzed on and off, flashing long shadows against the dingy tiled walls. I noticed a sign on the wall that read CORE CITY. Then two cloaked figures broke my line of sight. I thought—actually I hoped—they were Keepers, but when I tried to make out who they were, the figures only slipped into a darker corner.

"It smells like fish," Max whispered.

"Doesn't it remind you of something?" Theodore said.

I looked at him. I knew what he meant. Were there Neewalkers at this station?

"There are no Neewalkers here," Ketheria said. Max and I both looked at her.

"This place gives me the creeps," Max said, shivering.

"Let's hope this isn't home," I said.

Ketheria said, "It's not."

I stared at my sister. "Enough already. Now you're creeping me out."

Ketheria shrugged as Nugget took her hand. The unfamiliar territory seemed to humble him. If I didn't know better, I would say he was scared. I'm sure he wasn't the only one feeling that way.

"Get in a line," Weegin ordered everyone.

"What for?" Switzer said. Weegin bared his fangs, and Switzer fell into place.

"Hold out your left hand," Weegin demanded.

The alien walked down the line handing each of us a tiny, clear-blue crystal. Max examined hers closely.

"Keep your left hand up. Keep the crystal in your hand," he barked.

Switzer begrudgingly stuck his fist out. We all stood there, holding the crystals up while Weegin shoved his gnarled fingers into his mouth.

"Ewww," a girl named Grace said.

Weegin dug another blue crystal out of his mouth, exposing his rotten, yellowed fangs again. He held the saliva-drenched stone up to admire it. Max looked at me. I just shrugged. I'd never seen Weegin store crystals in his mouth before.

"Keep quiet! Hands up!" Weegin snapped, placing the crystal on his hip. He pushed the crystal into his skin and said, "Creok!"

Immediately my palm warmed and a crackling beam of pale blue light shot through my left hand. I tried to release the crystal, but my fingers were frozen in the glow. I looked at the other kids trying to shake off the light, but the beam ran through everyone's hand, connecting all of us together. The end of the light beam roped around Weegin's waist where he had pushed the crystal into his skin, embedding it in his hip. Then Weegin turned and marched into the darkened space-way station. I felt a tug on my left arm, and I still could not release the crystal from my hand. I was forced to follow in line, linked to the next person by the mysterious glowing rope.

"Weegin, I think we can stay together on our own," Max complained. " This is not necessary."

"Did you ever think we might not want to go where he's taking us?" Switzer said.

I did, but Weegin had orders from the Keepers. No one went against an order from the Keepers; it was law.

"Where are you taking us, Weegin?" I asked.

"Do as you're told," he replied.

I looked at Ketheria.

"This is not good," she muttered, shaking her head slowly.

What was Weegin planning? I heard shuffling in the darkness ahead of us, but I could see nothing.

"Weegin, I want to know where we are going," I pleaded.

"They owe me," he said. "They owe me."

"Who owes you what?" Max said.

"They *owe* me!"

The back of the space station was clothed in darkness. Not the kind of darkness you stumble through to find the bathroom, but the kind you don't want to go near. The air tasted like rust, and the feeling that something was lurking ahead of me grew stronger. I held up my hand to see with the light from the rope, but the glow wasn't strong enough.

Weegin dragged us deeper into the shadows.

"Stop. I won't go any farther," Grace protested.

"You will," Weegin growled and yanked the light rope once more.

"I don't want to die," Grace cried.

"No one's going to die," I reassured her.

"We don't have to do this, JT," Max said. "This is not right."

"So much for your beloved Orbis," Switzer whispered to me. "Kinda wish you listened to me back on the *Renaissance*, don't you, split-screen?"

"Be quiet. You're not helping," I said.

But he was right. I had a bad feeling about this, but what could I do? Weegin was still our Guarantor.

Grace began to whimper. We huddled tightly together and shuffled deeper into the unknown. The only light was the pale blue glow of the rope that linked us together and tied us to the crazy alien.

Weegin stopped. I could see nothing, but the alien found a door and thumped on it with his fist. A red light blinked on above the door.

The light sent *things* scurrying back into the shadows.

"*Tewk, twek,*" came from behind the door.

"*Crawdon,*" Weegin said, and the door disappeared.

"What's happening, JT?" Theodore whispered.

"Why can't we understand them?" Max asked.

"What does *crawdon* mean?" I said.

No one answered. I don't think anyone could. What we saw standing in the doorway left everyone speechless. An enormous alien, draped in a thick emerald cloak with a carved metal collar, towered over Weegin. The back of his collar was attached to a metal plate that molded over the alien's head and bolted to his skull. Metal piping extended from his mouth and curved around his head, attached to crystals where his ears should have been. The creature looked down at Weegin, examining him with piercing red eyes, his brow a permanent scowl. The alien glanced at all of us.

"*Traack* want *shool* make *gleet,*" Weegin said. I could only understand every other word. It was as if my codec was not translating everything. I knew this wasn't right. I had to get help.

"Vairocina?" I whispered. But this time my friend did not reply. "Vairocina?" But still nothing. "Max, do you understand what they're saying?" I asked.

"Only pieces."

"Me too," Theodore said.

"Vairocina?" I yelled inside my head. Why was she not responding? Vairocina always responded.

The big, ugly alien let Weegin pass. I looked at Ketheria. Her eyes were closed. I tried to take her hand, but Nugget now had both of them.

"Vairocina?" I called out once more as Weegin pulled us through the door and down another corridor.

Red globes hung from the walls, illuminating the hallways. Inside each globe something moved, but I could not tell what it was.

"I don't like it," Max said.

"I'm not afraid of this," Switzer boasted.

Theodore was mumbling, "Three hundred twelve, three hundred thirteen, three hundred fourteen . . ."

He was counting his steps again. "Good idea," I whispered.

There are twenty-one of us, I thought. *If we all worked together, why couldn't we drag Weegin back the way we came? What about that guy at the door, though?* I didn't like thinking about running away. It's not what I wanted to do on Orbis. I was trying to make a life for myself here.

"Get in," Weegin snapped. He was stopped in front of three shallow rafts that fit snuggly in a narrow trough. "Get in!" He jerked on the rope, making Ketheria stumble.

"Where are we going, Weegin?" I asked.

"Get in or I'll *cheelo* into the water," Weegin said. He spoke each word slowly, as if giving time for our translation codec to work, but the codec still failed to translate completely.

"This isn't the way to Magna, Weegin. I want to know where you are taking us."

Weegin grabbed Grace and pulled her to the water's edge. The kids closest to her were forced down also. Grace screamed as Weegin wrenched her hand over the water.

"It's your choice," he said, baiting me. "*Tey* Hoolies would *chi* a snack."

Grace stared at the water, crying. The black surface rippled. Grace yanked herself back, but Weegin held tight.

"Don't, Weegin!" I shouted, stepping onto the raft. "You win."

I don't know if Weegin was lying about the Hoolies, but no one said a word as we loaded ourselves onto the narrow rafts. The metal skiffs then drifted along a river of black water that sucked up the light bleeding from red globes mounted to the walls. A heavy dampness crept over me, and the only sound was Grace's sniffling. She was attempting to compose herself after Weegin's threat, but she still flinched every time the water rippled.

"Do you smell that?" Max whispered.

A sweet aroma lingered in the air.

"What is it?" I said.

"I don't know."

The narrow channel finally emptied into a wide cavern,

maybe three floors high. My raft came to a rest at the edge of a large pool crowded with similar skiffs.

"*Treck* Core City *shool tok* edge," Weegin said, stepping onto the pool's concrete banks.

"What did he say?" Max said, and Theodore shrugged.

"I don't know. Just follow him," I told them. "Unless you have a better idea."

Weegin yanked the light rope, and one by one we stepped onto the landing. The rope shrunk as we gathered together. Then Weegin climbed a narrow stone staircase that curved up and along the damp wall and ended at a small arched tunnel.

"What is this place?" Max asked.

"It's not a good place," Ketheria said as we followed Weegin through the arch.

Farther down the tunnel, torches of purple fire lit the old stone walls. Weegin stopped in front of a large, fleshy, human-like alien draped in blue silk. I could hear the high-pitched chatter of several smaller aliens crawling all over him. They looked like bugs, yet they seemed to be talking to each other. The big alien guarded another archway glowing with a red light that reflected off the creatures as they munched on whatever they could pull off his body. He grunted something at Weegin, but I could not hear him over the shouts and other sounds coming from the red hole in the wall.

"JT, ask Vairocina where we are," Theodore said.

"She won't answer," Ketheria said.

"How do you know?" I asked. "Vairocina?" I whispered, but there was still no response. "Vairocina?"

"It's no use. She can't hear you," Ketheria said.

"Why?" Max asked.

"Because the central computer is not online here. There is no connection to the computer that runs Orbis. That's why we don't understand what everyone is saying," Ketheria said.

"How do you know?" Theodore asked.

Ketheria tapped on the device the Keepers used to control her telepathy.

"It doesn't work?" I asked her, and Ketheria shook her head. "You can read our thoughts?"

Ketheria nodded.

"Then they must be using a smaller computer to translate each other. I can understand some of the words but not all of them," Max said.

"The smaller computer can't translate fast enough," Theodore guessed.

"If the central computer is off-line, then this whole area must be outside of the control of the Keepers," I said.

I was used to being connected to computers. In a weird way it gave me comfort. *I don't like this,* I thought.

"Me either," Ketheria said.

"Don't do that," I told my sister.

When the alien finally let Weegin pass, we filed through the red-glowing door and gathered on a landing perched above a wide staircase. Nugget reached up and took my hand. He held on to Ketheria with his other. We were at the top of a huge room. Hanging on the back wall were three floors of balconies with aliens huddled around pots of seeping smoke.

The yellowish haze collected over the center of the room and stung my eyes. I watched one alien point at Ketheria's headpiece and then snatch up a pile of crystals on his table to the protest of a trio of bald creatures. There must have been a hundred aliens. Every one of them fell silent when they saw Weegin desend the stairs with us in tow.

"This can't be good," Max said.

Weegin tugged on the rope, dragging us to a thick counter that looked like it was carved from a single stone.

"*Cha* now *Paka koo*," he barked at two identical buglike aliens. The one farthest from Weegin reached under the counter, and a green spotlight cut through the smoke, exposing a small stage in the center of the ground floor.

The audience of aliens burst into cheers. A thick creature with four metal tubes protruding from a mask that covered his face reached out to Ketheria. His brown robe stunk of rot, and his gloved hands were wrapped in some sort of glistening wet weed. Weegin slapped the alien's paw away and jerked the light rope toward the center of the room.

"What are you doing, Weegin?" I asked.

"*Che* quiet," Weegin snapped.

The cheering grew louder.

"No!" I stopped and grabbed the rope. The crowd responded with more shouting. "What are we doing here?"

"I'm getting my payback. That's what I'm doing," he said slowly. "Now come here!" Weegin grabbed Nugget.

"No!" the little alien yelped.

"Leave him," Ketheria shouted.

"Not for sale," Weegin snapped, pushing his son aside.

"For sale?" Max said.

That's when I noticed more than one alien counting crystals on the tables. I saw another hurriedly waving over smaller robot drones, which then scurried back to the two aliens at the main counter.

"You can't sell us," Switzer protested.

"You're supposed to take us back to the Keepers," I reminded him.

"They have a decree," Theodore said.

"I will be *drrek* gone before anyone *eesh* aware of *tey* transaction," Weegin said.

I saw Switzer staring at me. He looked at me with a smirk, slowly shaking his head.

"Really thinking about that opportunity you gave up on the *Renaissance* aren't you, dumbwire?" he said, referring to his futile attempt to hijack our seed-ship.

I was. I could not think of any way out of this. I could not talk to Vairocina or alert the central computer. I could not break the rope Weegin used, and even if I could, I didn't think I could make it out of there. I couldn't figure out what to do. There were no options.

The large alien in the smelly brown robe was now next to me. He put his hand on my head and shouted, "They're diseased!"

Weegin whipped around and pulled me away from him. The crowd was on its feet. Max tried to say something, but all I could see were her lips moving in the racket.

"He lies! He's crazy!" Weegin shouted to the crowd. "They are healthy. Perfect condition. Soon they will be of breeding age."

"Weegin, please. Stop this. You can't do this to us," I begged.

"I am doing it," he growled at me.

"*Dreekt* ten *foort* crystals. For the *semel* female!" yelled one alien, standing on his stool.

"*Ne, ne, ne!*" Weegin yelled back, quickly waving his hands above his head. He stepped onto the stage and pulled us up with him. "*Ne Dreekt.* You must take *trell!*" he shouted.

The alien who bid made a hissing sound at Weegin. One of the small aliens, with a narrow forehead and big eyes, pushed the large, cloaked alien aside and stepped onto the stage with Weegin.

"We have to do something," Max whispered.

"I don't know what to do," I said.

"Who would expect anything else? That dumbwire isn't worth the brain it's stuck in," Switzer sneered.

"What? If you're so smart, then you do something," I told him.

"I will."

The bug-eyed alien began to speak. Its voice resonated throughout the entire arena, and everyone grew silent. The alien spoke slowly so every word was translated.

"Joca Krig Weegin . . . is offering . . . these twenty . . . human children . . . for trade," the alien shouted.

"This can't be happening," Max said.

"Trading begins . . . at forty thousand yornaling crystals," he added.

More than one alien laughed at the price. Others sat back down at their smoking pots, shaking their heads.

One alien yelled out, "Not for the whole ring."

"One child is a telepath. The other is . . . a Softwire," the buglike alien announced.

There was a brief moment of complete silence before the entire crowd erupted into a fierce bidding war. A tall slender alien whose spine and ribs appeared to be outside its body stepped forward and bid forty-one thousand yornaling crystals. Another bid forty-two thousand, then forty-five. Then a large, burly alien with long teeth and thick, gray skin shouted out ninety thousand. I couldn't keep track, things were happening so fast.

"JT?" Max whispered. There was panic in her voice.

If there had been some kind of computer translating the alien languages, then maybe I could have used that to link back to the central computer. Didn't *they* have to do that, I wondered, for air control or waste management or the zillion other things the central computer controlled on the rings? I didn't know, but it was my only shot.

The pace of the bidding increased, and I scanned the area around me for any sort of computer terminal. All I found was a small blinking key plate on the wall behind the stage. *It's a start,* I thought, and slunk toward it as far as the rope would allow. I pushed into the device and immediately sensed something was wrong. My ears burned hot, and the inside of whatever computer I had just pushed into was dense with a thick, green fog of static electricity. Normally, a cool rush of current surges across my skin and the colors inside the computer brighten with an enhanced sense of clarity. But not this time. Security devices were mounted on top of more security devices, and everything looked as if it was patched together, piece by piece.

I pushed in farther and turned down a corridor, looking for anything familiar. The dataway opened into a long, thin hallway that was at least a thousand times taller than any computer I've ever been inside. Way up, through the thick, crackling soup of data, I saw something floating above me. The hallway darkened as someone bellowed, "Who is in my computer?"

I thought my head was going to crack open, literally. I yanked myself out of the computer and staggered back, bumping into Max with my hands clamped around my skull.

"JT, what's wrong?" she asked as an alien with pitch-black eyes and cracked copper skin stood up from the top railing.

"One million yornaling crystals for the Softwire," he announced, flinging back his cape and motioning with his gloved hand to one of his entourage. The alien placed his hands on his hips and stared at everyone below, as if challenging them to outbid him. But no one else in the room bid again. My head was still pounding. The stage was spinning underneath my feet. *What was happening?*

"The generous SenniUg has offered one million yornaling crystals for the Softwire. A moment please," the buglike alien shouted to the crowd, then leaned in toward Weegin. He whispered frantically, occasionally glancing over his shoulder at me.

"JT, snap out of it," Max said. "We have to get the light rope off Weegin's belt."

But Weegin took care of that. He removed the blue crystal from his hip and chomped down on it. When the crystal was crushed between Weegin's teeth, the light rope released each of us from its grip.

"Deal!" Weegin shouted up at the black-eyed alien, and stepped toward me, grabbing me by the shoulder.

"No!" Ketheria cried, but Weegin pushed her away.

"If you have any ideas, Switzer, I would really like to hear them right now," Max said, but Switzer didn't move. He looked to the other kids, but they were waiting for him.

The aliens shouted and chanted. One alien bounced up and down on his chair while another howled at the ceiling. Why all the commotion? What did it matter that this alien had just purchased me? Who was he?

"He is a very bad person," Ketheria said.

SenniUg strode across the balconies on the third floor toward the stairs. I looked at the doorway, but the stage was surrounded by at least thirty aliens, maybe more. Two aliens who had been seated with SenniUg earlier stomped toward the stage. One, sporting a scar that circled his knobby, bald head, handed Weegin a metal case. Weegin smiled and grabbed at the case. It secreted a blue gel that molded around Weegin's fist.

"JT, what are we going to do?" Theodore said.

"You are going to do nothing," Weegin snapped.

I leaned toward Max. "The computer here is no help to us. I tried. We have to make a run for it. You grab a person and—"

"Who is in my computer!"

I fell to my knees and squeezed my skull to keep my brain from spilling out of my ears. *Who was saying that?*

"JT!" my sister screamed.

What happened next was such a blur that it's hard to describe. The building shook with the tremor of an explosion. The far concrete wall cracked under the pressure, and the explosion was followed by another brain-melting scream. I pulled my head to my knees, trying to hide from the voice tearing at my brain.

"Do you hear that?" I shouted.

"Who doesn't? This place is gonna blow up," Theodore panicked.

"Not that," I said. "The voice."

"What voice?" Max said.

The arena rumbled again. In the middle of all of this I heard the words: *Who dare enters my computer?*

I looked around, but no one else seemed to notice the strange voice.

Show yourself, intruder.

The walls of the cavern shook once more. This time the stone behind the stage cracked. Water sprayed through the opening.

"The tank has been breached," the insectlike alien screamed, and bolted for the stage. When the water hit the alien, he screamed as if it was burning his skin.

Another blow. I didn't think the room could take much more.

"Move," Theodore screamed when the wall behind us came crashing down. Water gushed toward every corner. The aliens tried to scramble to higher ground, but once the water caught hold of them, it seemed to suck the life from their bodies.

I jumped to the other side of the stage, but Weegin was not as lucky. A piece of the stone wall struck him, pinning him to the ground. He screamed out in pain as the water rose around the stage.

"The tank. The tank will flood Core City!" someone shouted.

"This way!" another shouted.

SenniUg, the alien who had tried to buy me, was now on the lower level. He maneuvered through the water toward us.

"Hurry," I shouted. "Head for the stairs."

"Don't touch the water!" Max yelled.

"Nugget!" Ketheria screamed, searching the stage for her friend.

The little guy was kneeling next to his unconscious father, too frightened to move. He whimpered and stroked Weegin's forehead with his big hand.

"Choo, choo," he said as Ketheria knelt next to him.

"We have to help Weegin," Ketheria begged.

"No, we don't," Switzer replied.

"Nugget, come with us," Ketheria urged the alien.

The little runt looked up at my sister. He would not leave his father. Even though the vile creature had never showed him a single tender moment, he would not go. Instead Nugget tried to pull Weegin from under the rubble. Ketheria began to help him.

"We can't," I said. "Weegin's fate on Orbis 1 would be far worse than the fate he will suffer here. Trust me."

Two of SenniUg's goons reached the stage, and one grabbed me by the shoulder. Max wheeled around with both fists clenched, catching one alien across the chin and knocking him back into the other one. They both fell into the rising water.

"Thanks," I told her, then turned to my sister. "C'mon, Ketheria. Now is our only chance!" I said. More and more aliens rushed the stairs, and fewer of them seemed to care about us anymore.

My sister stood up as Switzer disabled the last alien with the remnants of a chair. Nugget knelt down next to his father again. He looked up at Ketheria.

"I find you," he mumbled. "Nugget . . . stay."

Ketheria swallowed hard, but she could not hold back her tears. Her eyes welled up as she scratched Nugget under the chin.

"Now, Ketheria!" I shouted, grabbing my sister.

We pushed our way to the stairs as the room shook once more and a wave of water and debris washed away SenniUg and the others.

5

After SenniUg and his trolls disappeared, little effort was made to stop us. I think everyone was too busy trying to save their own lives at that point. Max stormed through the debris, screaming at anyone who stepped in her way. The large, fleshy humanoid that guarded the door sat slumped in the corner, unconscious and bleeding from his head. A thick chunk of stone lay at his feet, and his alien parasites were gone.

Ketheria kept looking back and crying out for Nugget.

"You have to take her, JT," Theodore said, and I hoisted her up into my arms. This only made her cry louder.

"Don't, Ketheria," I told her. "You're making it harder. You're too heavy."

We had never been separated before our arrival on Orbis. All two hundred of us lived together on that seed-ship before the Trading Council divided us up. Until then we had never experienced the pain we felt when they took the other kids away. But things were different now. Ketheria *knew*, and I think she feared never seeing Nugget again.

I stayed close to Max as she navigated through every shortcut, every twist and turn, and found the only dry way out of there. Theodore adjusted our direction a couple of times. His counting had come in handy. *But what do we do now?* I looked back and wondered if I would have left this way with SenniUg. If something hadn't started destroying the building, would I be leaving without my friends? And who was that screaming back there, anyway? Or rather *what* was that? It was like no computer I had ever entered before.

Once outside, Theodore said, "I think you should contact Vairocina, JT."

Switzer snorted, but he looked too tired to make fun of me.

"Let's get a little farther away first," I said.

"But I'm tired," Grace complained.

There was a lot of commotion in Core City. People were running, and an alarm wailed in the distance. It wasn't Magna, that's for sure. Core City was a small, crude metropolis bursting with activity. Trams loaded with aliens or the same battered crates I had seen at the spaceport raced from building to building. I walked past dingy trading chambers, but there were no toonbas for sale, no glowglobes, not a single place that looked like the Earth News Café. Instead, the shops were packed with tools and contraptions and things that could only have been used as weapons.

I was forced to squeeze against the wall as a transport shuttle floated down the street and then up and over a building. It carried more of those battered crates. An alien was yelling at me, but all the beeping, shouting, and roaring engines made it impossible for me to hear him.

"What's he saying?" Max shouted.

Across a tram channel cut into the ground, I saw a concrete platform. It was dark, and no one was around it.

"Over there," I said, pointing toward it.

We scurried across the channel and huddled under the shelter.

"Vairocina?"

"Are you kidding me?" Switzer scoffed. "We need to keep moving. Are you gonna believe this freak after he talks to some *malf* voice in his head?"

"Keep quiet," Max scolded him.

For the longest time, the Trading Council and the Keepers hadn't believed that Vairocina was real either. They argued fiercely over her existence, pointing fingers (or whatever they had) and accusing each other of sabotaging the central computer.

"Vairocina?" I said.

"Yes, Johnny Turnbull." Vairocina's voice echoed in my head.

"How are you?"

"I am exactly the same as I was last time we spoke," replied the little girl. For an eternity she had isolated herself inside some sort of computer, so it was going to take a while for her to get used to communicating with other people again.

"Does anyone believe this dumbwire?" Switzer said,

raising his arms in the air. "You're just talking to yourself." Switzer mocked me like he had on the *Renaissance* when he wouldn't believe I could speak to Mother, the ship's computer.

"Ignore him, Vairocina. He's as dumb as he looks," I said.

"Dumber," Max added. Theodore snickered. Switzer took a step toward Theodore.

"Do you find something funny, split-screen?" he said to Theodore, who got very quiet. I rolled my eyes. It was getting old. Sometimes I wished Theodore would stand up to the bully.

"Maybe this will help," Vairocina offered.

In front of me, the air bent and distorted, pulling colors from everything around us. A form began to take shape.

"How's this?" Vairocina asked, now floating in the air in front me, no more than twenty centimeters tall. She was a six-year-old girl who looked a little like Ketheria, with her long brown hair, only Vairocina's was lighter and did not move the same way. If you looked very close, you could even see little streams of computer code running under Varocina's skin.

Everyone circled her.

"Wow!"

"Amazing!"

"See?" Max said, scrunching her face at Switzer.

"How did you do that?" I asked Vairocina.

"It is simple, really. I used the same program that the Trading Council members use to project their images as 3-D holograms," Vairocina said.

Max poked Vairocina, but her finger went right through her image.

"I cannot manipulate solid objects as they can since I have no real physical form anymore," Vairocina added.

"But this works," I told her. "I like it."

Everyone stared. They all knew about the computer virus that had wreaked havoc on Orbis, but they had never *seen* her before. Only I saw Vairocina when I pushed into the central computer.

"That's it? That's what was causing all those problems?" Switzer said mockingly.

"I was not the cause of all . . ." she started to argue.

"Vairocina, don't bother. Listen to me. We're in trouble. I need your help."

"Certainly, I'll contact the Keepers."

"Don't call the Keepers!" Switzer demanded.

"Yeah, not the Keepers," Switzer's sidekick, Dalton, said.

"Then who should I contact?" she asked.

"We need to tell the Keepers," I said. "The rules . . ."

"Enough with the rules, JT," one of the kids said.

"Was Weegin following the rules when he tried to sell us?" Switzer snapped. "Freakocina, or whatever your name is, do not tell the Keepers where we are. I have plans of my own."

"No Keepers," someone else murmured.

"I'm afraid you will not survive on Orbis on your own," Vairocina protested.

"Contact Charlie," Ketheria said.

"OK. Charlie would be good. He helped me before," I agreed.

"I now have a code address for him, but I have no way of telling him your location. Do you know where you are?"

I looked around. "We're near Core City," I said. "That's all I know."

"I don't think we are too far from the spaceway," Max added.

"There are many spaceway stations, and Core City covers over twenty-four square kilometers," Vairocina said. "Give me a moment. I will make a digital representation of where you are and download that to the terminal where Charlie purchases his passage to Orbis 2."

"What if you get the wrong terminal?" Theodore asked.

"I won't. I'll monitor for his chit scan and present it then." Her image distorted, sending shapes and colors back into the air. Then Vairocina was gone.

"That's incredible," Max said.

"She does look like me a little," Ketheria said. "I like her."

"Stupid computer tricks," Switzer scoffed.

"Why do you always have to be so negative, Switzer?" Max asked.

"Why do you always have to defend your boyfriend, Maxine? He wanted to call the Keepers."

"He's not . . . oh, forget it."

Before the argument was over, Vairocina was back. Ketheria stepped toward her.

"Hi, I'm Ketheria," my sister said.

"*Hi, I'm Ketheria,*" Switzer mimicked.

"It's a pleasure to meet you, Ketheria," Vairocina said, holding her hands together in a formal fashion. "Charlie Norton has been contacted. It will be the better part of a spoke before he can arrive. Is there anything else I can do?"

"Can you tell us what happened on Orbis 2, in Core City?" I asked.

"Everyone is going nuts around here," Max said.

"And I'm not sticking around to find out," Switzer said, "C'mon Dalton, let's leave these malfs here. Anyone else want to join us?"

I remembered when Switzer tried to rally his friends to take over the *Renaissance,* and lots had joined him. But this time only one other kid besides Dalton joined his side: a small boy who always looked up to him.

"That's it? Then you're all malfs. Good riddance," Switzer said, and stepped out from under the concrete shelter.

"Where you going to go?" Max asked him.

"Anywhere but here," he said, and left with Dalton and the small boy.

"They'll be back," Ketheria said, but I wondered. Was this the last time I would see Switzer?

"He will not get far. The Samiran has breached his crystal-cooling tank," Vairocina said.

"What's a Samiran?" Max asked.

"Samirans are amphibious mammals from the planet Samira, a water planet ravaged by poachers. Samirans are massive. If my calculations are correct, one Samiran would not be able to fit inside your rec room at Weegin's World."

"That's huge!" Theodore exclaimed.

"What do they look like?" Max asked Vairocina.

"On Earth, they could be considered similar to an elephant or a whale but much larger."

"We've never been to Earth. We don't know what an elephant or a whale looks like," Ketheria reminded her.

"Samirans are extremely powerful and very dangerous. The only known Samirans in captivity are on Orbis 2."

"Why did he break the tank?" I asked.

"I do not know," she replied. "But I'm sure it doesn't concern you."

I wasn't too sure about that. Something told me that what I saw inside that strange computer had something to do with the Samiran breaching its tank. I just couldn't figure out what.

"I'm tired," Ketheria said.

"Yeah, and I'm hungry," Grace added.

I looked around for something Ketheria could sit on. Some plastic piping ran along one of the building's walls, and four metallic cylinders sat by themselves as if waiting for someone. I made a space behind them.

"We'll wait here, Ketheria—until Charlie arrives. C'mon, you can lean against me."

I plopped on the ground, and the other kids followed after Ketheria sat down. It wasn't cold, but everyone huddled close anyway.

"I will monitor Charlie's progress," Vairocina said.

"Thank you," I said as the particles of light dispersed, taking Vairocina with them.

The larger of Orbis's two crystal moons pushed a dark blue shadow across the ring and over Core City. I leaned against the cylinder and wondered about Weegin. Was he dead? Did I care? I felt I should, but he tried to *sell* us. How many other knudniks were sold like that? Maybe I should have gone with Switzer. What was I expecting from Charlie? For that matter, what was I expecting from Orbis 2? I followed the curve of the ring up and over my head. The Rings of Orbis 2 looked different to me somehow. I felt different. I didn't like it.

"Wake up, split-screen," I heard Switzer say, but when I opened my eyes I saw Charlie.

"Well, don't you bunch look like a bucket of fish outta water," Charlie said.

"Thanks for coming, Charlie," I mumbled, rubbing my eyes.

"Don't thank me. Thank these guys," he said, grabbing Dalton and Switzer by their vests and holding them up for inspection. "I found them trying to sneak on a starship in the spaceport. But they decided they would rather show me where their friends were stranded. At first I thought they might be trying to escape, but I'd like to believe they're smarter than that." Charlie glared at Switzer.

"Traitor," Switzer mumbled at Charlie.

"Just be thankful some *Citizen* didn't find you and have you both put down for farts and giggles," Charlie said.

Ketheria laughed, and the little boy who had left with Switzer and Dalton quietly snuck back in with the rest us.

"What should we do now, Charlie?" I asked.

"Yeah, Weegin tried to sell us," Theodore said.

"And now we think he's dead," Max added.

"Well, let's go then. Gather up your things. Theylor is waiting," he said.

"Theylor!" Switzer scoffed. "And you call yourself a human?"

That made Charlie frown.

"Why did you contact the Keepers, Charlie?" I asked.

"Look," he said. "You didn't belong to Weegin any more than you belong to me. As far as they're concerned, you belong to Orbis. Who looks after you is merely a formality. Workers are traded between Citizens all the time on the rings."

"Some of those aliens we saw weren't Citizens," Max told him.

"Understand that you have to do it their way, and it might make it a little easier. You don't have that long before your first review."

"Three rotations!" Dalton complained.

"There is no choice, guys," Charlie said while looking directly at Switzer and Dalton. "You may think there is, but if they catch you, I promise you they will kill you just as easy as they would squash a bug. There are a zillion others who would eagerly take your place."

"Pfft," Switzer scoffed. "Let them have my place."

"Is that what you did?" I said. "Just looked the other way? Did you just wait it out?"

"Not exactly."

"What do you mean?"

"That's not important. What's important is that the Keepers

have requested the presence of young Mr. Turnbull here," Charlie said to everyone. "Don't get too excited, but I smell a very important job in your future, JT. C'mon, we have to hurry. I wasted too much time dragging these bolt-heads back here."

"I told you to just leave us," Switzer said.

"Shhh. What important job, Charlie?" I asked. "Where are you taking us?"

"To the Samiran Caretaker," he said.

Charlie led us to a couple of trams and piled us in. Without a word, the driver sped along a shallow channel carved through rows and rows of buildings. Tiny lights glimmered through the grimy exteriors and blended in with the stars on the sloped horizon.

I was anxious to put Core City and the events of the last cycle behind me. I was also very curious about this Samiran Caretaker and the job Charlie mentioned. I sat behind Charlie with Ketheria. I was glad I had called him now and had not listened to Switzer. *What was the job?* I wondered as the blackened buildings blurred against the ring. And why me? Would I get to use my softwire abilities? How important was it? Charlie turned and looked at me.

"What?" I said.

He looked down at my foot and smiled. I guess I was hitting the back of the chair a little too hard.

"Relax, we're almost there," he said.

After only about a kilometer, the vehicles slowed and stopped in an open stone court. I got out and stood in front of a building so massive that it blacked out the stars. It must have been at least ten times the size of Weegin's World. Six different spacecrafts scoured the building with blinding white searchlights. The ground under my feet pulsed red while smoke from sparking construction drones drifted through the searchlights.

"Stay together!" Charlie shouted over the crackling din.

Water trickled down the soaked steps as we climbed up them to the Caretaker's. "Do you smell that?" I asked.

"I do. It smells like those creepy tunnels where Weegin took us," Max answered.

We followed Charlie up the wide steps and through an enormous stone archway. The corners of the building were rounded from age and the whole thing felt old to me, really old, like Magna, the city where the Keepers lived on Orbis 1. Yellowish plantlike material sprouted from the cracks that ran along the walls, and everything looked wet. Charlie inserted a crystal ID disc into a metallic device next to a doorway so tall I couldn't see the top of it. A thin, red beam of light sprang from the doorway and scanned Charlie and then all of us. When the light beam seemed satisfied, the two incredible doors drew apart as if they were floating in space.

Standing on the other side was Theylor. "Welcome," he said.

"Hi, Theylor," I said.

"Are we glad to see you," Max said.

"Speak for yourself, malf," Switzer whispered under his breath.

"Hello, children," Theylor said, awkwardly opening his arms to imitate the Earth gesture of a hug. Max and Ketheria rushed the tall, two-headed alien and hugged him. Theylor smiled — both of his faces.

"Theylor?" said another familiar voice. Drapling stepped out from behind Theylor. Although he, too, was a Keeper, Drapling was not one of my favorite aliens. He always seemed to look at me with contempt. "Quite the homecoming, is it not?" he said with his left head.

"Not really," I replied. "What . . ."

The ground shuddered violently beneath our feet, and the cavernous building echoed with thunder.

". . . was *that*?" Max said, finishing my sentence.

"That was the Samiran," Drapling said. "May we proceed?" He looked at Charlie and said, "You're late."

Drapling turned, and we all followed him under another archway. I tugged on Theylor's purple robe.

"What are we doing here, Theylor?" I whispered.

"It appears you may be quite helpful to us once again, Johnny Turnbull, but we will have to see. Follow me, and please stay close together. Do not wander off, for I am afraid it may not be safe."

6

We all followed Theylor deeper into the moist labyrinth. Its dampness wrapped around me like a thick, wet blanket that was impossible to get out from under. A silky sort of light rained down upon us and gathered in puddles of blue and silver on the floor. After every ninth or tenth step, the stone foundation would tremble beneath our feet.

"That one was quicker," Theodore mumbled.

"Quit counting, malf," Switzer said.

I glanced up and began to make out large cracks where the support columns met the arched, ribbed ceiling. It looked like they were new cracks, too, where the yellow slime had not yet grown.

"We will wait here," Drapling said, raising his hand.

Everyone filed around Theylor.

"Will we live here now?" Max asked.

"This has yet to be determined," the Keeper replied.

"I don't like it here," Grace said.

"Quiet," Drapling ordered.

A form shifted in the shadows just beyond Drapling. Then a small bowl-shaped craft emerged from the darkness. At first I thought I was seeing things. The device hovered less than a meter above the ground, floating under its cargo—a glass cylinder with dark metallic trim, filled with a murky yellow fluid. There was someone floating in the liquid.

"Yuck," Max said, staring wide-eyed as the alien drifted toward us.

The creature's head poked above the foul liquid, and its long arms reached out the sides of the container straight through the glass that then sealed tight around his arms. The creature's skin was colorless and wrinkled. Not wrinkled from being old, but wrinkled from being in the water too long. There was a marking on his right temple—some sort of circular symbol, much darker than his ghastly skin. At times, the alien appeared to struggle to keep his head above the liquid, sinking into the container up to his bloodshot eyes. On the top of his bald head, the skin was gathered together and tethered to a cable that connected to the top of the glass enclosure. The whole contraption, alien included, was just taller than Drapling.

I was speechless. Theodore was speechless. Even Switzer was speechless.

"Again, yuck!" was all Max could say.

Drapling said, "Children, this is Odran, the Samiran Caretaker. If all goes as planned, he will act as your temporary Guarantor."

"How temporary is temporary?" Max said.

"That will be up to you, Johnny Turnbull," Theylor replied.

"Me? Why me?"

Odran hovered closer, and we all took a step back. "I told the Council this is unnecessary. I can handle the Samiran myself," he gurgled in a deep voice.

"Your efforts have been fruitless," Drapling said, and Odran spat against the wall of his tank. Drapling seemed to quiver. I could tell he did not like Odran.

Theylor started to say, "The children—"

"Children? How precious," Odran interrupted. His sarcasm was obvious.

"Mind your tone, Centillian!" Drapling barked at him. "You will do this!"

Odran's contraption slid silently back and forth as he examined each one of us.

"Does my appearance frighten you?" he asked us. "Good. I require constant moisture, and this support glider is the most suitable means for me to continue my very important work with the Samirans."

"Enough with this," Drapling said. "Can we get on with the test?"

"What test?" I asked.

"There is no way this will work. I know the beast like no other," Odran said.

"What test? I deserve an answer," I demanded a little too strongly.

Odran's support glider moved toward me, quicker than I

imagined it could. "You deserve nothing. You are worthless. You will remain quiet and do as you are told," he snarled. "All of you."

"Why?" Switzer questioned him. He moved next to me and folded his arms. He was actually backing me up. I looked him in the eye, but he just stared at Odran. All the children moved and stood behind us. I guess they hated being called worthless just as much as I did.

"This is unnecessary," Theylor said. "The arrangement for your work rule, made prior to arrival, has been interrupted due to Joca Krig Weegin's misfortune. Despite what Odran has told the Trading Council, he *will* test the young Softwire because it is vital to the well-being of the Rings of Orbis and the many planets that rely on the crystals harvested from our moons. Since the Harvest of the Crystal of Life falls in this rotation, your assistance will be invaluable," he finished, turning to me.

"But what does he have to do?" Max said.

"We want to see if young Johnny Turnbull can communicate with the Samirans," Theylor replied.

"What?" I said.

Charlie nudged me and brought his fingers to his lips. "Shhh."

"The Samiran language is far too complicated to be translated through the simple codec implanted through our neural port. The codec needed is too large to uplink into anyone's cortex. We have tried many different techniques, but nothing has worked," he informed us.

"How does he talk to him?" I said, pointing at Odran.

Odran slowly dipped his entire head into the snotty liquid within his container. He resurfaced, blinking his bloodshot eyes before he answered.

"I don't," he replied. "They have accepted the codec, and they understand my language. I have been with the creatures for so long that I've found other ways to understand them."

"Then what do you need me for?" I asked.

"I don't. You are unnecessary."

A thunderous boom rattled the building. The Keepers looked over their shoulders into the darkness.

"Despite Odran's efforts, they have grown restless," Theylor said.

"And we *must* know why," Drapling added, casting an accusing glance toward Odran.

"Isn't there anyone who can understand the Samirans?" I asked Theylor.

"I am afraid not. Since the Space Jumpers have been banished, there has been no one who can understand the crystal-pullers' language," he replied.

"So no one has understood what they've had to say for a thousand rotations?"

"Exactly," he said.

"Why can't the central computer simply listen to them and print out a translation or something?" Max asked.

"It doesn't work that way," Theylor replied. "The central computer requires a living brain to assist with the codec. The language is extremely complicated."

Odran smiled; it was almost evil. "Why don't we simply

remove his brain and be done with it?" he said, but Theylor did not reply to his remark.

They can't do that, can they? I wondered.

"How old are they?" Max asked Theylor.

"Samirans have been known to reach the age of three hundred thousand Earth years."

"Enough! These questions are ridiculous. This will not work, Keeper. *He* is not a Space Jumper," Odran spat.

"But he *is* a Softwire," Theylor's left head said to Odran. His right turned and spoke to me. "And we were hoping you might be able to communicate with the Samirans and discover what is wrong. You and your friends would live here and help Odran with his simple duties in exchange for your work rule." Theylor put his hand on my shoulder and pulled me slightly away from the crowd. He bent over a little and continued. "The Harvest of the Crystal of Life is extremely important, Johnny. This is a great opportunity for you to do another wonderful service for Orbis. It comes with great honor, and only you are capable of performing this task. You should take pride in that."

I was excited by what Theylor was telling me. It made me feel important. *Could it be true?* I hoped so. This is what I wanted.

"I only need the Softwire," Odran gurgled, the sludge thick in his throat.

"You take them all. That will be the arrangement," Drapling said. "Do not argue this."

Odran hovered back and spat against the glass again. "First we'll see if he will even be able to do the job," he said.

"He will," Charlie assured him.

"We'll see about that," Odran replied, and spun the support glider about, slipping back into the shadows.

Theylor motioned us to follow, and the ground trembled once more as if calling us to come deeper into the Samiran's domain. Charlie looked down at me, and smiled, with one thumb up, whatever that meant.

"Don't be scared," he said. "This will be good for you."

"I'm not scared," I said.

By now my eyes had adjusted to the darkness, and I could see that the walls and ceilings were covered with carvings of aliens and strange symbols. Aliens grasping ropes harnessed to stars stood amid swirling circular symbols and smaller carvings of more aliens. I think they were supposed to be working or digging, but they were so high up I really couldn't tell.

As I followed Theylor deeper into the building, the air thickened and the sweet pungent scent, almost like overripe fruit, grew stronger. When I passed under the last archway, I stepped into a vast open space. Keepers and Trading Council members scampered about shouting orders to construction drones flying over my head. The entire room was bathed in foggy green light. The iridescent glow oozed from an enormous sheet of glass that ran the length of the chamber and curved away farther than I could see. Behind the glass was a wall of water—it was a gigantic water tank, four, maybe five, times as long as Weegin's entire sorting bay and just as high. Drawn to the huge structure, I walked away from the others and toward the glass until I could brush my fingers over the stones that ran along its base. The blocks were as tall as me and adorned with the same exquisite carvings as the ceiling in the entry. The stone base curved along the glass and met a very wide staircase that climbed to the top of the mammoth reservoir.

"What's that for?" Max asked, staring at the tank.

"That is the crystal-cooling tank. It is used to solidify some of the elements we harvest from Ki and Ta," Theylor said.

"The most important harvest being the Crystal of Life, which happens every seventy rotations," Drapling added.

"The Harvest is extremely important to the well-being of Orbis," Theylor said. "That is why we brought you here."

"It is a waste of my time," Odran scoffed.

Drapling turned to Odran with both heads scowling. "Your time *is* my time. *Your* time belongs to Orbis. The Harvest of the Crystal of Life comes only once every seventy rotations. I needn't remind you that your lack of success with the crystals is the very reason we have chosen such an unorthodox experiment with the Softwire."

"And I think we should proceed with the experiment," Theylor urged.

I looked up at the top of the tank and saw that the waterline was far below it. I guessed about a fifth of the water was gone from the tank. Three drones clung to the outer glass, repairing a crack above the waterline. Theylor saw me looking.

"Toll is quite angry," Theylor said.

"He's really done some damage," Charlie said.

"Who?" Theodore asked.

"The freak causing all that damage. Aren't you paying attention?" Switzer said.

Charlie stopped and turned to Switzer. "That's enough," he said, and waited for Switzer's reply. There was none.

"The Samiran's name is Toll?" I asked. And that's when it hit me. I don't know why it took so long. I looked at the tank and pointed. "He lives in there?"

"Yes, and I have never seen him like this," Theylor said. "We will have to use the ocean to refill the tank."

"Ocean?" Max said.

"Orbis 2 has beautiful oceans," Theylor told her.

Drapling sneered and broke away from Theylor. "Follow me, Softwire," he ordered.

"The Samiran will be around again," Odran said. "We'll meet him on the top. Take the chute at the top of the stairs, and I'll meet you on the platform. Do it quickly."

Odran pointed to a light chute at the top of the stairs, and I quickly began my ascent behind Drapling. As I climbed, I tried to peer into the tank, but I could see nothing. At the top I let Drapling go up the chute first. I had used them before at the Center for Impartial Judgment and Fair Dealing. I stepped into the pale purple light beam and was instantly transported to the platform atop the humungous tank. I looked down at my friends, dwarfed by the size of the reservoir. I saw Odran rising up to my left inside his container. He did not use the lift.

I turned and looked across the tank. The only thing I had ever seen bigger than the cooling tank was space itself.

"Samirans are incredible beings," Drapling said as Odran landed on the platform. "Besides being unbelievably strong, they are faithful and determined."

"I expect humans to share the same qualities," Odran said. "If you can do what they say."

I can do it, I said to myself, and looked at Drapling. "Does Toll always bang on the tank?" I asked.

"It started a few rotations ago. Only Toll does it, not the other," he replied.

"There is another Samiran?"

"Yes. The crystal can never stop. It must be in constant motion until it is cooled. Otherwise it will sink to the bottom of the tank and fuse with the foundation. The crystal will be contaminated and worthless."

"How long has Toll been doing this?"

Odran turned and looked at me. "Almost two thousand rotations."

"He's been dragging crystals around for two thousand years?"

"Toll and the other Samiran," Drapling reminded me.

"No wonder he's upset. Switzer has only worked for Weegin for one rotation, and he's ready to jump the ring."

I shouldn't have said that. Odran spun his bucket of sludge toward me and pinned me against the thin railing.

"You wish to escape? To abandon your duty?" he said. "Keeper, you've given me a creature who thinks such dishonor?"

"That's not what I meant . . ." I said.

"The penalty is death. I will not hesitate to—"

"I know. I know. No one wants to escape. Forget what I said. It was wrong of me."

"Odran," Drapling said. "You know the young human's history. You are aware of his efforts with the central computer."

Odran fixed his bloodshot eyes on me, searching for some sign of weakness. "That's what worries me the most," he mumbled, dunking into the yellow muck. When he surfaced, he was still staring at me, studying me. Sizing me up. He scared me.

"I don't like you," he said, his voice thick as if there was still fluid in his mouth. "I don't care what you've done in the past."

"I'm telling the truth," I protested.

Odran turned to the Keeper. "If we must do this, then lower him into the tank quickly," he said. I saw him glance toward the others at the base of the tank. "I have more important things to do than this foolish test."

Lower me into the tank? The waterline was at least five meters below me. Was he crazy?

Even Drapling looked at him, "I have never heard of that," he said. "Is this safe? I understand the water can . . ."

"Safe? Since when is the safety of a knudnik so important, especially at such a crucial time as this? You yourself pointed this out." Odran then turned and looked at me. "Don't feel special; no one's safety is of concern to me right now."

Drapling spoke quietly but sternly. "Life is always the first concern of a Keeper. It is the gift of Source. Your comments are an affront to that symbol you've marked on your face."

Odran dipped into his sludge and came up blinking but not speaking. He stared at the Keeper, his chin still in the slime. Drapling waited.

"The Samirans are hard of hearing. They will never hear the child from this far up," Odran spoke softly. "But even then I doubt the child will understand."

"We must try," Drapling said. "Get what you need to lower the child in."

Odran showed me a small circular platform that hovered just above where we stood.

"Step onto this. A small energy shield will protect you from any spray. Just try not to fall off."

I stepped onto the metal platform, and it jostled under my weight. It felt very unsteady, so I knelt down. A greenish-blue energy shield sprang up about one meter high around me. I looked at Drapling.

"Do your best," he whispered.

"For your own sake," Odran added.

"I will," I said. "I want this to work, too." I looked at Odran. "Aren't you going to signal the Samiran to come?" I asked him.

Odran looked at his metal staff leaning against the railing. "I already have," he said to me.

The small craft lifted and moved out over the rim of the tank. I was floating above the tank now and high above the floor below. I saw Max and Theodore watching as I disappeared below the tank's edge.

The smell from the water grew sickly sweet, and I breathed through my mouth to avoid it. My hovercraft came to a stop a little less than a meter above the water. I knelt there waiting, but nothing happened. I looked out across the green water. There was no sign of the Samiran.

"Toll?" I shouted, but nothing. "Hello? Toll!"

If he couldn't hear me from the platform, how was he going to hear me shouting across the water?

But near the horizon, I saw the water ripple. It was too far away to judge the size of the waves, but they quickly grew closer. If Toll was making those waves, he was moving fast. At first he circled wide, the water cresting much higher than the device I was on. I knew not to touch the water, but that wave was going to drown me.

"Get me out of here!" I shouted up to Drapling, but my craft did not move. "Drapling! Get me out of here. Now!"

I thought I could see something moving in the water. The wave grew closer, and the water thundered against the glass walls of the tank to my right. Now I could see the shape of Toll under the water. To say there was a beast inside the tank seemed to trivialize the creature. What swam toward me was a monster. The enormous alien barreled straight toward me.

"Toll! I am Johnny Turnbull. Please stop!" I shouted over the crashing waves. The water was so high now I could not see the edge of the tank. And then I heard him. My skull felt like it was going to crack as the alien bellowed out, "I am Toll the Samiran. Where is the Softwire?"

And then the wave hit me.

I have never felt so much water in all my life. It was like being weightless in space but far more invading. The water was in my eyes, in my ears, in my mouth. It was everywhere, and I was tumbling through the waves, sinking into the tank.

At first the water felt warm, but a prickly sensation crept along my skin and then I began to feel the cold. A deep cold. Not as if the temperature changed, not as if I needed to bundle up, but rather a feeling that started in my veins and worked its way to my heart. Something was sucking the heat from inside my body, pulling it out of me, and devouring me. I could do nothing. I tried to swim but I didn't know how.

I opened my eyes, searching for help, only to see the monster's murky shadow bear down on me. Its thick, tapered tail thrust the green liquid. Two broad front flippers that ended with clawed fingers rested over its huge belly.

I sensed the world slipping away. I remembered when Madame Lee's evil programs ripped my essence from my body, leaving me to die inside the central computer. *You're dying now,* I thought. Could it be happening again?

Instead of hitting the ground, I landed on the tough, crusty skin of Toll. It was hard as concrete and rougher than anything I knew. The force of the water pinned me against Toll's forehead, and the Samiran rushed to break the surface.

The silence of underwater gave way to shrieks and screaming as Toll tossed me onto the platform. Hands grabbed at me, pulling at my arms and legs. I was so cold. I tried to suck oxygen into my lungs, but my throat froze shut.

"You imbecile!" I heard someone shout. I think it was Charlie.

"How could I know humans were so weak," I heard Odran say.

"Johnny! JT!" I heard my friends somewhere in the frozen darkness as I felt my body being bundled up and hoisted off the ground. The cold finally reached my brain and shut the lights out.

"Do you have any idea the risk you have taken?" someone said, right next to me but a mile away in my head.

"What are you implying?" someone else said—someone who sounded nervous.

"I refuse to do this dance. Tell him."

Was that Charlie?

"May I remind you whom you are speaking to?"

"May I remind *you* whom you will deal with if this boy dies?"

"He is nothing more than a child. A human child who is here to work," a new voice said.

"You could have the Scion right under your noses and you wouldn't even know it."

"Scion! Now I know you are foolish." *Who said that?*

"I will not stand here and debate the prophecy of the Ancients with *him*."

Another voice spoke up and then another. I was cold. Very, very cold.

"The Trust will receive my report at the next gathering."

"We have done nothing against the Trust. The central computer will provide evidence of this."

"You better pray to whatever it is you pray to and hope that boy lives."

Darkness came as the cold took me once more.

8

"You're starting to make a habit of this," Max said.

I sat up and rubbed my eyes. My fingers were wrapped in a yellowed plastic that stunk of decay.

"Where are we?" I asked.

"Our new rec room," she replied.

"You're awake! Welcome back," Theodore said, leaning next to Max. "Not bad, huh?"

Theodore turned his palm up to the tall, slender windows that started at the floor and curved up and over my head. I could see the stars in the sky and even the other side of the ring when I looked out. The brilliant moon, Ki, floated across the windows. It felt like I was on the observation deck of the *Renaissance.* All the windows in the oval room converged on a massive pink crystal that hung down from the center of the ceiling and illuminated the entire room.

Theodore saw me staring down the row of sleepers that lined the windows. "Twenty brand new ones," he said. I lay in the one second from the end.

"Compliments of the Keepers," Max said.

"Yeah, Odran wanted us to share a couple of blankets and a pot," Theodore said.

"Theylor made him order the sleepers. He wasn't too happy about it," Max added. "I'm at the other end with Grace and Ketheria."

"Where is Ketheria?" I asked.

"She's saying good-bye to Charlie," Theodore said. "He sat with you every cycle, but he had to leave. He said he had things to do."

"He'll be back, though," Max added.

"Has anyone heard anything about Weegin?" I said.

"Nothing," Theodore said.

I looked around my new home. "How long have I been like this?"

"Over a phase," Max said.

"A phase?"

"You almost died, JT," Theodore whispered.

"Again," Max said teasingly.

"How?"

"That's the best part," Max said, sitting up.

"The bio-bots tried to suck the life out of you," Theodore said, interrupting Max.

"May I?" Max said to Theodore.

"Sorry."

"You know Toll, the Samiran?" she said. There was an eagerness to her voice.

"Uh . . . yeah."

"Well, the water is treated with bio-bots. Really, really tiny things that help keep the Samirans cool. They're just so big and with the crystals, well, it just creates too much heat for them. So the bio-bots consume the heat and then . . . you know . . . they make that sweet smell."

"They fart," Theodore said.

"Do you have to say that?" Max frowned. "They're engineering marvels. Engineering marvels don't fart."

"Well, that's where the smell comes from. Ask Charlie," Theodore argued.

"Why don't they just use those bio-bots to cool the crystals?" I asked.

"They only work with life-forms. That's why they went after you, but you're so small . . ." Max stopped. "Well, not small. I mean small compared to Toll. That's why you almost died. It was very easy for them to drain the heat from your body."

"You almost froze to death," Theodore said.

"But Toll saved you," Max added.

"He did?"

"Yeah. He jumped right up onto the edge," Theodore exclaimed, his eyes widening. "He has hands, like ours, on the end of his . . . the end of . . ."

"Fins. I think they are called fins," Max informed Theodore.

"I guess I should thank him then," I said.

"You'll have plenty of opportunity," Max said.

"Why?"

"We live here now," Theodore said.

"With Odran?"

"Yep, all of us now belong to the Samiran Caretaker," Max said.

I was awake but hardly ready to begin exploring my new home. My toes and fingers, even my joints, hurt if I put the slightest pressure on them. I laid on my sleeper remembering the things I had heard while I was recovering—little pieces of conversations, unfamiliar voices, and I think I even heard Toll. But I couldn't tell what was real and what was a dream. There seemed to be a lot of upset people running around, and I didn't know why. What did it have to do with me? Nothing, I told myself. I was a knudnik.

I woke up one spoke finally feeling rested. Almost over-rested, in fact. It was time to find out what was going on. I swung my feet around and sat on the edge of my sleeper. The room seemed to spin a little as I adjusted to being up for the first time in a long time. While I stared across the room, waiting for it to settle in one place, I compared it to Weegin's World. My new home may have looked different, but I still felt the same way about it. Like an outsider. Like I was just looking in. What would my mom and dad tell me right now if I told them how I felt? Would they be sitting next to me telling me not to worry, that everything was going to be all right? I saw that in an entertainment file once. I wondered what that felt like.

"Feeling better?" Max asked as she entered the room with

a cup of water and a bowl with some sort of burnt-looking mud in it.

"Pretty good, I think," I said. "What's that?"

"Breakfast," she replied, wrinkling her nose. "You'll get used to it."

I stuck my finger in and tasted it. "That'll take a while. What is it? It looks like the snotty liquid in Odran's tank."

"Odran wants us on a high-protein, high-vitamin diet. He wants to keep his new *stock* in top working form," she said, trying to mimic Odran's gurgling voice.

"It tastes like paper."

"Some of the kids stole some sweetener from Odran, and they use that to kill the taste."

"They stole it?"

Max just shrugged.

"So we're stealing now," I said.

Max sat down next to me. "We have no choice. I don't think Odran likes the idea of having us around, anyway."

"I got that impression already."

"He hardly ever talks to us, and if he does, he only asks if you're awake."

"They fix the tank?"

"Almost. They brought in a lot of equipment to do it. A lot of computers, too."

I thought of Madame Lee and all the computers she had used to mess with the central computer. "Why would he need computers? The central computer can handle everything. That doesn't make sense."

"Nothing makes sense anymore," she said.

I looked at Max. "What am I doing here?" I whispered. "What does the Universe have planned for us?"

"Do you want to know what I think?"

"Sure."

"I don't think I'm supposed to be here," she said. "I mean I don't think any of us are supposed to be here."

I chuckled.

"Are you going to laugh? Because if you are . . ."

"No, I'm sorry. I really want to hear."

"Well, sometimes I feel like Mother got things mixed up and we landed at the wrong place."

"There's only one Orbis, Max," I said.

"I know. But think about it. We know the *Renaissance* was attacked before we were even born. Madame Lee admitted to that. Who says your father . . ."

I frowned when Max mentioned my father. She knew I didn't believe Madame Lee.

"OK, who says *she* didn't mess things up or change something so we wound up on Orbis instead of where we were supposed to go? I know it's wishful thinking, but I just don't understand why my parents would leave Earth to be a slave. Did they not think we would be forced to do the same?"

I didn't say anything. I just sat listening. I'd asked myself these questions many times.

"It makes me cry at night sometimes, you know, thinking about all of this," Max continued. "Hoping that it's just some bad dream. But then I think about Ketheria and I think about

Theodore and Charlie . . . and you. If we were someplace else, we may not all be together, and you know what? That makes me even sadder. So if I have to do some dumb chores for a few rotations, so what? We're smarter than them, JT. Let's just do what they want and be gone. All right?"

I smiled at Max.

"Besides, look at you now," she said. You have an important job, JT. Charlie says it's really golden that you're going to be able help the Keepers. Odran has had too much control for too long. They never had to worry when Space Jumpers were working with the Samirans. You should be happy."

"Somehow I just pictured it differently," I said, and looked down at the brown glop. "Max, you ever heard of the Samirans having bad hearing?"

"I never heard of Samirans until a phase ago."

"Have you ever heard or uplinked anything about something called a *Scion*—something to do with the Ancients?"

She shook her head. "Never. Why?"

"Nothing. I was just dreaming. Forget it," I said, and set the bowl aside. The food *was* awful. I needed to get some of that sweetener from the other kids.

By the next cycle, I was able to stand on my own, and I set out to explore my new home. Construction robots still zipped about as I scaled the mountainous stone steps to the top of the tank. The tank had been refilled, but there was no sign of Toll. I sat near the edge, where the aroma was strong, and looked out over the water. The sugary smell didn't seem as sweet now that I knew those little bio-bots were farting up a storm in there.

I have to admit that I was a little excited to have my own job on Orbis. Did I get a title? The *Samiran Caretaker's Assistant* didn't have a very good ring to it. But wasn't *I* the Caretaker now? I mean if I could talk to Toll, then why did they need Odran? Maybe that was why Odran didn't want me around. Max was right, though—just three more rotations and then I could apply for Citizenship. Both Theylor and Charlie mentioned how important this job was. I had to do well. This was my chance to prove myself. Looking out over the tank, I decided to do the best job possible, no matter what Odran thought of me.

Without warning, something surfaced right before my eyes. No more than two meters away was a Samiran. It wasn't Toll. This one was smaller and a little lighter in color—more of a gray-blue. It lifted its head out of the water just far enough so it could speak.

"Are you Johnny Turnbull?" it said in long, drawn-out vowels. My head throbbed with each word the Samiran spoke, and I stood up.

"I am. Who are you?" I said, hoping I was speaking loud enough.

"I am Smool. Mate of Toll," she said.

"Nice to meet you!" I shouted.

"No, it is far nicer to meet you," she said. "It has been a very long time since we have communicated with anyone on Orbis. You should be very proud. Your name will be added to a list of very honorable people."

I squeezed my temples with the palm of my hands.

"You'll get used to that," Smool said. "Your small brain will adjust over time."

"Is that why Toll is so mad? Because he can't talk with anyone here?"

"That is for him to communicate. But would you permit me to ask you a question?"

"Of course!"

"Why are you shouting?"

"So you can hear me," I said, lowering my voice. "I was told Samirans could not hear very well."

"A Samiran can hear the purr of Linkian two hundred kilometers away. I am afraid you were misguided," she informed me.

A long, deep vibration rippled through the water. It did not translate. I held my hands to my ears.

"I must leave," the Samiran said. "Toll would enjoy a conversation with you at the start of this spoke, next cycle."

"That's my job now," I said.

"Are you the Caretaker now?"

"Well . . . no, I don't think so. I mean Odran's still here. I guess I'm like a helper—but an important helper," I said.

Smool sank back into the water, swirling hundreds and hundreds of liters of murky green water in her wake. *Important helper? I'm such a malf.*

I watched Smool swim to the horizon. *Why did Odran tell me they couldn't hear very well?* Smool could hear perfectly. *Did he want me to go in the water? Did he want me to freeze to death?*

I turned toward the light chute and ran smack into Odran's tank.

"You are to inform me every time you speak with the Samirans," he said. Odran glared at me as if he was searching for something.

"Of course," I replied.

"What did the female want?"

"She said Toll wants to talk with me this spoke, next cycle."

"Don't be impressed. I will alert the Council. It is them he wants to speak to," he said, and turned his glider away.

"Odran, why did you tell me they couldn't hear—the Samirans, I mean?"

Odran turned back. "I never said that."

"Yes, you did. When—"

It happened very fast. Odran hit me with some sort of prod: a metal device that sent a shock wave through my body, knocking me to my knees. I clamped my hands around my jaw, not to keep from screaming but to prevent my teeth from falling out of my head.

"Think twice before you call me a liar, knudnik," was all he said.

9

By the next cycle, six members of the Trading Council had arrived at Odran's along with Drapling and Theylor.

"Pretty impressive," Max whispered.

"What is?" I said.

"They're all here because of you," she replied.

"Yeah, you're gonna be pretty important around here," Theodore added.

I was more worried about my teeth than what was going on around the tank. Ever since my incident with Odran, I'd been convinced my back molars were loose. I kept checking and rechecking to see if they were staying put.

"What are you doing?" Max said, catching me with my fingers in my mouth.

"Nothing."

Another group of aliens shuffled about in long red-and-white silk robes, following the Keepers. They crept along with their feet bound together and their arms extended out from their sides as they entered the tank area.

"Nagools," Ketheria said, pointing to the aliens.

We sat and watched from a room off the top of the great stairway.

"Nagools?" Theodore asked.

"They study OIO. We saw them before on Orbis 1, in the Trading Hall," Max said.

"OIO?" I said.

"The art and science of cosmic energy," Ketheria said matter-of-factly.

"Oh." I looked at Theodore and raised my eyebrows. Theodore shrugged.

"Didn't you see the markings?" Max said, and pointed to the circular shapes painted on the ashen face of one Nagool.

"Odran has the same one on his temple," Ketheria said.

"I can't look at that guy for long without feeling weird," Theodore said.

"He's a believer," Ketheria said as she continued watching the procession of aliens.

Meanwhile, the Trading Council members had grown restless, walking in circles and only stopping to shout at each other. Two council members had sent their holograms, which floated above a portable seating area attached to the platform. They, too, bickered, but the Nagools ignored all of it. I could see the water rumbling on the horizon, so I stood up and said goodbye to my friends. Toll would be at the platform soon.

"Where is the Softwire?" Drapling called out. "It is time."

"I'm here," I replied.

I stepped onto the platform. Everyone in attendance was staring at me, but I didn't mind. They needed me, and that felt kind of good. I looked at the group; there was no sign of Charlie.

"Very well then," Drapling said. He turned and addressed the others, his voice filled with authority. "We are eager to gain a better understanding of the male Samiran's heightened anxiety, especially since the Harvest of the Crystal of Life is once again upon us. Orbis and its Citizens, as well as a multitude of worlds, greatly depend on this particular harvest from the crystal moons. The Samiran's work here is of great value. We must understand what is disturbing him." Drapling's right head said the last sentence directly to me.

I was suddenly struck with the overwhelming feeling that I would not be able to understand Toll. *But you spoke to Smool,* I tried to tell myself. *Yeah, so what?* I really wanted everything to go perfectly. I wanted to show these Citizens that I could do this. I wanted to show them that I was important, too.

Max attempted to move Theodore and Ketheria toward the platform, but a Trading Council member, dressed in glimmering silk robes, pushed them back. Citizens only, I supposed.

I stood at the edge and waited for Toll. My vest itched from the Citizens staring at my back. I wanted to scratch it. I wanted to turn around and tell them to stop staring, but I didn't. I focused on the water and shut them out of my mind. *Concentrate. Make this work.*

I followed a row of cool-blue crystals that lined the inner edge of the tank. They spread out as far as I could see, and in the distance they looked as small as the stars in the sky. The waves were closer now, and Toll slowed as he approached. The green water bubbled in front of me and the hard shell of his back broke the surface of the water, then his massive head. Toll's eyes were half the size of my whole body, maybe even bigger. A huge flap of leathery skin with two giant nostrils partially covered his mouth. He looked straight at me, and I instantly saw sadness in his enormous green eyes. At least that's what I felt. I'm sure he saw only fear in mine. Toll made a snorting sound with his nostrils. Odran motioned me to move forward. The protective clear skin over Toll's huge eyeballs peeled backed as he lifted his head far enough out of the water to speak.

"I am glad to see you are here," he said in long tones that only tickled my skull this time. The pain inflicted by his voice was lessening, just as Smool had predicted.

"Thank you for saving me when I fell in, Toll."

"I apologize for that," he said. "I never imagined they would be foolish enough to put someone in the tank."

"Odran said it was the only way you could hear me," I whispered to him.

"Odran's motives can be obvious sometimes."

"Please proceed with our needs, Softwire," Drapling urged.

"Sorry," I said. "Toll, they want to know why you're so upset, why you keep thumping on the tank. They want to know what's the matter. Is something wrong?"

"Many things on Orbis are wrong, my friend . . ." Toll stopped. "I'm sorry. I do not wish to be bold. I do not mean to burden you with the obligation of friendship," he said.

I didn't quite understand Toll's meaning. The central computer stumbled sometimes when it came to cultural translations "That's all right, Toll," I said. "We can be friends, if that's what you mean."

Toll's eyes widened and his mouth cracked opened slightly. I think it was a smile.

"This is good," he said. "It is a privilege to have a Citizen as a friend."

"I am not a Citizen, Toll," I informed him. "I am here to work. Just like you."

"You do not look like a Space Jumper."

"No, I'm a Softwire," I said. "A human Softwire."

"This is very unusual."

"I'm contracted to work here and help out, find out what's wrong."

But Toll didn't seem to be listening. He wasn't looking at me anymore. He was looking past me. What was he thinking? I hope I didn't say something stupid. I did not want anything to go wrong.

"Then you are here under the same Keeper decree as myself and Smool," he said.

"That's right."

"And you must do as they say. You are forbidden to leave. You have no status on Orbis," he said. The water stirred. Toll dragged his front fins through the water.

"So I understand how you feel. I can understand what you are going through. Tell me what's wrong," I said, and glanced over my shoulder.

It happened very fast. Toll thrust forward and exploded onto the edge of the tank. His big hands gripped the edge, crushing the crystal light as he held up his colossal frame. The group shrieked and shrank away. Water splattered everywhere. I felt droplets land on me, but they only managed to freeze my skin slightly.

"I am Toll. For nearly two thousand rotations I have done your bidding and cooled your crystals." My skull felt like it was cracking again as the giant bellowed. "And now you send me a child—a slave like myself—when we are in need."

I held my hands over my ears. This wasn't making a good impression. I was sure of it.

"Toll, what do you mean? What needs? Let me help you!" I shouted up at him.

Toll twisted his huge head around and looked down at me. "My friend, I have no anger with you, but those you serve are guided by other hands. I know. I have seen it with my own eyes. Be wary of whom you trust. Tell them . . ." Toll lifted his right fin, and the monster teetered on his left hand. He pointed at the Trading Council. "Tell them it is time to release us!"

Toll shoved off and twisted his body in the air high above the tank.

"Move away!" someone shouted, and Theylor flung his robe around me. I was covered in darkness. I heard a huge splash as Toll hit the water. More screams.

"That didn't go too well," I said to Theylor as I pushed the robe away.

The water, thick with bio-bots, didn't hit anyone, and the council members sidestepped the puddles on the platform. Everyone moved quickly.

"What did he say?" Odran demanded to know.

"He said you must release him. His time is up," I replied.

My announcement sent the Trading Council members scrambling. A few circled around Odran, shouting at him, their arms flinging about and pointing at the tank.

"This has gotten out of hand," I heard one say.

"He is still a knudnik," said another.

"I know what is wrong with Toll," Ketheria said, sneaking up to us amid all the commotion.

Theylor touched her head just above the device she wore to control her telepathy.

"You do?" Theylor said.

"It is Smool, his mate. She is with child," Ketheria informed them.

Everyone in attendance turned to Ketheria.

"How does the human know this?" someone asked.

"Are the child's abilities not contained?" I heard another whisper.

Drapling strode over to my sister. "How *do* you know this?"

"I just do," she said.

"Ketheria, go back with Max, OK?" I told her.

Ketheria returned to Max, who was now as close as she could get in order to hear as much as possible. Theodore kept tugging on Max's skin, but that did not stop her from inching closer.

"It is impossible for the child to know this," Drapling said.

"My sister's not lying. Why would she?" I said. "What difference does it make if Smool is going to have a child?"

No one answered. The council members huddled near Odran's tank. He watched them closely, almost nervously. When Odran tried to move closer, one of the council members turned his back to him.

"This is none of your concern, Caretaker," the alien said.

The Trading Council members huddled tighter, whispering and occasionally glancing at the Keepers. Odran stayed close to them, as if he were part of their conversation, but they did not include him. Occasionally he would nod as if a council member were talking to him, but they were clearly ignoring him.

The Nagools were now on the stairs with Drapling.

"What's wrong?" I asked Theylor.

"Nothing's wrong . . . right now," he said. "Will you confirm this news with Toll?"

"Sure," I said. "But how will I contact you?"

"I will return shortly," he said, and followed Drapling down the stairs.

Max and Theodore ran over to me when the last of the council members had drifted down the stairs.

"Did you see the size of that thing?" Theodore exclaimed.

"His name is Toll," Max reminded him.

"I know but—wow, huge!" Theodore said, standing near the edge of the tank and looking out.

"What's wrong, JT?" Max said.

"I don't know, but something doesn't feel right," I told her.

"What do you mean?"

"Things just aren't adding up."

"It's not our business," Theodore said.

"I think it is," I replied.

Theodore and Max counted eleven different aliens that visited Odran over the next three cycles. Even a Nagool came. Most of the kids hid in the shadows and watched the strange creature shuffle by, looking almost as if he were floating. The Nagool wore the same symbols embroidered on his thick robes as Odran had tattooed on his right temple.

"Can you hear what they're saying?" Max whispered.

Theodore shook his head. "It can only be about the Samiran."

"The Nagool is worried about the baby," Ketheria said. Max and I looked at my sister.

"The baby?" I asked.

"The Trading Council did not know about the Samirans' baby," she said.

"I'm tired of these three—and that one," Switzer said, pointing at Ketheria. "This is boring."

"Yeah," Dalton said, for no apparent reason except to agree with Switzer.

He stood up and pointed to me. "Acting like you own this place. I don't care what you can do for them. You're all a bunch of split-screens to me."

"Ignore him," Max said.

"Come on, Dalton, let's see what other freaks live in this place," he said.

Dalton jumped up. "Where we goin'?"

"Anywhere. Anywhere else."

We watched them leave before I asked my sister, "How do you know this, you know, about the baby? Can you still read their minds?"

"I just know," she said.

"Why haven't the Citizens let the Samirans go yet?" Theodore asked.

Ketheria shrugged and left, too.

I wanted to talk to Ketheria. She was making everyone feel uneasy with these mysterious tidbits of knowledge she kept blurting out. It only isolated her from everyone, and she didn't have many friends to begin with now that Nugget was gone.

I left Theodore with Max and went searching for my sister. At the bottom of the stairs, I turned right and walked away from the glow of the tank. *Why did Toll have to tell the council to release him?* I wondered. Doesn't that happen automatically? I reached a thick, wooden door and had to turn the knob to open it (unusual for Orbis where most doors were automated). I entered a longer, narrower room.

I weaved my way through rows of stone columns supporting the veined, arched ceiling, wondering if I would have to demand the Council to release me one cycle. A pale blue light splashed onto the floor from small lamps circling the tops of each pillar.

"Ketheria!" I called out.

"I'm over here," I heard her say.

Ketheria was plopped against a pillar in a dark corner of the long hallway. A small shaft of blue light twinkled off her headpiece.

"What are you doing?"

"Thinking."

"About what?"

"Lots of things," she said.

"Like what?" I asked.

"The *Renaissance*," she said. "I miss it."

"I thought it was Nugget."

Ketheria looked up at me. "Oh, I miss him too, but in another way. When I think about the *Renaissance,* I mostly miss the silence."

"Silence? With two hundred kids running around?"

"Not silence here," she said, pointing at her ears. "Silence here." Ketheria touched her fingertips to her chest. "There's so much pain on Orbis. It makes so much noise."

My sister sat with her shoulders slumped. She stared at her hands while she played with her fingers. She looked sad.

"Ketheria . . . the things you say . . . I mean how do you . . . *know,* like the thing about Smool?"

"I don't know how. I just do. It's like I know you're my brother. It just is."

"Oh," I said, but I really didn't get it.

"Can you . . ." I pointed at the ornate band of metal the Keepers had attached to Ketheria's head.

"This? It works a little—not that much, though. I have to concentrate, but I don't read people's thoughts anymore. I know people don't like that."

I looked at my sister. She was eight years old, but I felt like I was talking to an adult. Even the older kids giggled and ran about the corridors playing with anything they could find, but not Ketheria. Those things didn't interest her. Sometimes I felt that nothing really interested her.

"Are you OK?" I asked. "Do you miss our parents?"

"How could I miss our parents? I never met them," she said, and I felt a little foolish about the question.

"You would tell me if anything was wrong, wouldn't you? If someone was bothering you or, you know, anything."

Ketheria looked up and smiled. "My brother, you have so many other things to worry about right now. A large burden is about to be placed on your shoulders once again and not by your choice. Do not worry about me. You will have far more serious issues to deal with."

"You can see the future now?"

She shook her head and smiled. "It's your destiny. I can feel it."

I stared at my little sister.

"You know you're only eight."

"Almost nine," she said.

10

"That must be the ocean," Max said. "See, the far side of it over there, between those two buildings."

Max was pointing out one of the windows that lined the room behind our sleepers. I squinted, but the lights from Core City made it impossible to tell the ocean from the buildings.

"Get over here," I heard Odran say, and turned to see him drifting into our room. We moved quickly toward his glass-and-metal support. "If I'm forced to feed you and board you, then I intend to get my money's worth."

Odran handed me a metallic screen scroll.

"What's this?" I asked.

"I'm making you the controller. You are in charge."

"Me?"

Max gave me a little nudge and smiled. *I was going to be in charge of everyone?* I looked around for Switzer, but he wasn't in the room.

"I don't know what your aptitude is for handling others, but I'm sure we'll find out. You are responsible for each person's actions and ensuring the work gets completed. If it doesn't, I will hold you personally responsible. Do you understand?"

"I can handle it," I said. "The work will get done."

"I hope so, for your sake."

"What about social study classes?" Grace asked.

"I have no intention of paying for your education. Take that up with the Keepers."

A couple of the kids smiled. They didn't like taking the classes. Neither did I. *But I do like the idea of being in charge,* I thought. Maybe they were beginning to see that I could do good things on Orbis, that I was more than a second-class citizen. I was a Softwire. Didn't that count for something? I cradled the screen scroll in my hands. I wanted to poke inside and see what the work was.

Odran was counting all of the kids. "Two of you are missing. Where are they?" he demanded. Most of the kids shuffled around, staring at their feet. Switzer was not the most popular person, but no one dared give him up.

"Right behind you, alien sir," Switzer said. I could see beads of sweat on his brow. He had just finished running from somewhere.

Switzer tried to slip around Odran, but the alien turned his tank and grabbed Switzer by the skin.

"Hey, let go of me!" Switzer protested.

"Where were you?" Odran asked.

"Uh . . . we were watching the big fish," Dalton said.

Odran twisted Switzer around and pushed him toward me. "Is this the one you told me wanted to escape?"

What? "I never told you that. I mean, I know . . ."

"Figures," Switzer mumbled under his breath.

"Any knudnik caught trying to escape can and *will* be killed. There is not a Keeper on these rings that can stop me," Odran said to everyone.

"I wasn't trying to escape," Switzer protested, glaring at me.

"And a liar, too?" Odran said. "Controller, come here."

What did I have to do with this? I moved toward Odran.

"Controller?" Switzer scoffed. "Him?"

Odran handed me the same device he had electrocuted me with and said, "Administer the punishment."

I looked at the prod and I looked at Switzer. I couldn't do this, even to Switzer.

"No," I said.

"How can you expect to be in charge if you're not willing to punish those who disobey?" Odran demanded.

Suddenly I didn't want to be the controller anymore.

"I can't," I said. "I won't."

"Pathetic creatures," Odran spat. "Fine. Then I will administer the punishment to each one of you as a lesson." He turned to me. "You have a sibling here, do you not? We can start with her. Bring her to me."

"No! Stop!" I shouted, putting my hand against Odran's floating tank. It was warm under my skin, like I was touching a warm-blooded person. "You can't do that. He's the only one that should be punished."

Odran grinned and handed me the prod. "It's your choice."

I stood between Switzer and the other kids with the black metal stick at my side. Everyone's expression was the same: *What's he going to do?* I already knew what I was going to do. It wasn't a choice for me. I knew what a zap from that thing felt like. There was no way on Orbis I was going to let Odran touch Ketheria.

I thrust the metal prod at Switzer, striking him in the chest. Switzer cried out in anguish and dropped to his knees. Someone else screamed, too. I looked at Odran. He was smiling—I think he enjoyed it. But I couldn't look at the other kids. I had attacked a human at the orders of a Citizen. I hated myself at that moment more than I hated Odran.

I stared at Switzer shaking on the ground. His eyes were filled with tears, but he fought to prevent a single tear from hitting the floor. Letting the others see him cry was a worse punishment than getting zapped by the prod, I figured. I wondered which Switzer would make me pay more for—the zapping or making him cry in front of everyone.

"Make sure all of the work is completed on time. This is the rotation of the Harvest, and you have no time to waste," Odran said, and turned away. "I'll leave the *enabler* with you in case you need it again, Softwire."

I looked down at the device, then let it slip from my hand. It clinked against the stone floor. *Enabler.* What an ironic name, I thought.

• • •

After Odran left our room, Dalton tried to help Switzer to his feet.

"Leave me alone," Switzer told him.

"I don't care what's on that scroll. I'm not doing anything for that bucket of sewer water," Dalton said.

"Yes, you are," Switzer replied, and pushed himself off the floor, sitting up slowly.

Another kid, one who always avoided Switzer at all costs, asked, "You all right?"

Switzer nodded and tried to stand, but his knees wobbled. Dalton grabbed his arm.

"You're hurt," Grace said as she helped steady Switzer. "Why don't you sit on my sleeper?"

Several of the kids moved aside, making room for Switzer. Where were the insults, the threats? I waited for some forewarning of the damage he was going to inflict on me, but none came. Then Max walked over to Switzer and said, "No, use my sleeper; it's closer."

I think I hated that the most.

"What's on the list?" Switzer finally said to me.

"Don't worry about the work, Switzer. We'll do it," Max said, and looked at me.

I focused on the screen scroll Odran had left, and the instructions appeared in front of me. I was to assign some of the kids to feed the Samirans, while the others were to prepare Odran's quarters for guests. It seemed Odran was having some sort of dinner party. I didn't see what any of these chores had to do with the Harvest, though. Odran was just using us.

Max, Theodore, and Ketheria offered to feed the Samirans while some of the others went to tend to Odran's party. Grace and a couple of others followed Max, and I let Switzer do what he wanted. We did not speak to each other.

At the bottom of the list were my instructions: wait near the tank until the Samirans wish to speak with you. That was it. *So be it,* I thought. I didn't want to be around anyone right now, and I didn't think anyone wanted to be around me.

I hiked the steps of the cooling tank and took the light chute to the top. I sat on the platform and stared across the water. The results of my new responsibilities had a very familiar feeling. I had felt this way many times on the *Renaissance:* alone, isolated, always looking in from a distance. It's not what I wished for, but then what did I want? Validation? Praise? Gratitude? *Like I was going to get any of that here,* I told myself as I squinted across the ocean of pale green water. I thought I could see lights flickering just below the horizon. *Is that where Toll and Smool live?* I wondered. *Did they build some sort of dwelling down there for themselves?*

The scroll told me to wait, but how long? I glanced down the steps, wondering if the others were finished with their chores. I didn't want to go back just yet, though. I moved toward a small O-dat located on the far side of the platform. While I waited, I decided to dig out some information on the Samirans by pushing into the central computer. When I slipped inside the computer, though, a mesh of yellow light beams crisscrossed in front of me and obscured my vision.

The beads of light seemed to follow me wherever I looked, blocking my access. They appeared harmless enough, so I tried pushing through them.

Everything flashed white as if an alarm went off, and my brain curdled from a bolt of electrical shock. It was just like being zapped by the enabler.

I pulled out of the computer. "Vairocina?" I said out loud.

"Yes, Johnny Turnbull," she answered, but did not appear. Her voice echoed inside my head the same way the ship's AI did on the *Renaissance*.

"Something in the central computer just tried to fry my brain," I said.

"Let me examine your location," she said.

"You know exactly where I am?"

"Of course."

I widened my jaw, making my ears crackle. *What was that?*

"Someone has used a quantum encryption device to restrict access to any computer in your building."

"Can you break it?"

"You need their secret key. Even with unlimited computing power, I could not generate such a key; the laws of physics prevent it. The data travels as a stream of photons. Anyone who attempts to interact with the photons will cause an irreversible change in the particles. Earth's very own Heisenberg uncertainty principle—"

"Whoa, whoa, whoa. What are you saying?"

"I'm afraid you're really, really locked out," she said.

"Oh."

"Someone has gone to great lengths to keep their information private."

"Or to prevent a Softwire from entering," I said.

"What were you trying to find?" Vairocina asked.

"I want to know where the Samirans live."

"In the cooling tank," she said.

"I know that, but where in the tank?"

There was a long pause.

"Vairocina?"

"I cannot find any information that answers your question. Shall I keep looking?"

"No, forget it," I told her.

"More creatures than Toll and Smool live inside the crystal-cooling tank. An entire ecosystem thrives inside there."

"I never thought of that."

"A new crystal is arriving from Ta," she said.

"How do you know?"

"I am always monitoring activities where you are."

"Why?"

"Because you are my friend," she said. "You are my only friend."

It must be lonely for Vairocina, too, I realized. I knew about her before anyone else on the Rings of Orbis. No one believed me when I told them a little girl was inside their precious central computer.

"I'm glad you're my friend," I said. "When is the crystal arriving?"

"Now."

High above the tank, deep in the black ceiling, a circle of twenty or more ruby-red lights pulsed in unison. This was followed by the distinct sound of metal chimes. I stood and looked around, but no one came. There were no workers, no sign of Odran, no fanfare of any sort.

The lights stopped blinking and remained bright red, and the area inside the circle crackled with electricity and then disappeared. It was an energy field like the field portals at Weegin's World. Across the horizon the water rippled. One of the Samirans was on the move.

A purple ball of fire descended through the opening in the ceiling. It hissed and sparked as the color of the glowing crystal shifted between purple and blue. I could see a long metallic bar, curved and polished, hanging from the crystal by thick ropes that disappeared into the glowing ball. The crystal itself was hanging from the same type of greenish-gray ropes that attached to a spacecraft, which was now visible hovering in the ceiling's opening. The craft was tiny—a slick, white flier, marked up from many trips between here and the crystal moons was my assumption.

The craft descended until the metallic device hanging from the crystal kissed the water. I could see one of the Samirans coming closer. It slowed and then broke the surface.

It was Toll.

He opened his huge mouth and clamped down on the metal. It fit perfectly, sliding back to the corners of his mouth.

The Samiran began to swim slowly as the purple crystal

was lowered into the water. By the time the purple firestone was submerged, Toll was swimming at full speed and the ropes released the crystal. The entire procedure was performed flawlessly, the result of two thousand rotations of practice, I thought.

The craft continued to hover within the open ceiling portal as Toll swam away. The empty ropes hung motionless a couple of meters above the water, as if waiting for something. Was there another crystal? I watched for some time as Toll came about and returned to the same spot.

Once again I watched Toll break the surface of the water. Crouched on the top of his head was a creature dressed completely in a slick, black material. Even its face was covered. When Toll passed under the cable again, the slender thing sprang up to grab the cable.

It missed.

Toll did not slow down, and the alien landed off balance on Toll's back, almost tumbling into the water. He steadied and quickly jumped once more, catching the cable with his right hand. Now he was only centimeters above the tank and his feet kicked at the water. Toll kept swimming forward, and the burning crystal rushed toward the creature. *What would happen if he couldn't climb the rope?* I wanted to shout out, to tell him to get moving.

Now!

With one huge lunge the alien twisted his body, swung his left arm around, and grabbed the cable. With two hands securely on the rope, he began the long ascent to the waiting flier.

Who was that? What was that? Where is he going?

I caught a glimpse of Toll's huge green eyes before he dove into the water and headed for the horizon. Did he see me? I stood there and watched the alien reach the flier. Once he was inside, the lights in the ceiling blinked off, and the hatch sparkled shut.

I found Theodore in the open dormitory. "You wouldn't believe what I saw," I told him. I sat on his sleeper. "Hey, where is everybody?"

"Some of the others got sick."

"Sick? Why?"

"You ever fed a Samiran? Our new chore is quite the adventure."

"What's that smell?" Something was off. I moved closer to Theodore. "Something really stinks, and I think it's you."

"That would be left over from the *gruel*. I tried to wash it off, but it just won't go away."

"The food tablets? For the Samirans?"

"Some tablet," another girl said, walking past Theodore's sleeper. "I'll never be able to eat again."

"It's awful, JT. We have to pack these creatures into tubes after we cover them with some sort of slop—vitamins or something. It's like they know where they are going. They're gonna eat them, live. I almost threw up."

"What are you talking about? Who is?" I said.

"Toll. The Samirans. It's really disgusting. I don't think I can do this, JT."

"Where's Max?"

"The food fought back. The little aliens figured out we were sending them through to be eaten. One of them nailed Max pretty bad, knocked her out. She's with Odran."

"Ketheria, too?"

Theodore nodded.

I turned and bolted for the door. "Where are you going?" Theodore shouted.

"To find Ketheria."

"Wait, Odran does not want to be disturbed," Theodore yelled after me.

"Too bad," I said, and Theodore followed me out the door.

Odran's room was not far from ours. I burst through the doors and stopped. Crystal sculptures, alien silks, and art taller than I was hung in every nook and corner. Warm light washed the maze of tiny tiles on the floor, and the spicy smells I remembered from the trading chambers on Orbis 1 replaced the sweet smell of the bio-bots. Either Odran was paid extremely well for his services or he found another source of income.

"Johnny!" Ketheria said. She sat on a small stool made from . . . bones, I think. Thick, yellowed bones. I could not imagine what sort of alien died for that piece of furniture. Ketheria played with a shiny, coiled wire that dangled a purple crystal.

"Are you all right? Where's Max?" I said.

"Odran's with her. She'll be fine."

"What happened?"

"Some of the food started to fight back," she said.

"I heard? How can food fight back?"

"You would be surprised," Theodore said, shaking his head.

"It was sad," Ketheria added. "They knew their fate. They knew they were going to be eaten, and they decided they didn't want that to happen."

I watched my sister as she thought about her own words. She stared past me but then quickly shrugged and shook her head.

Twirling the wire in her fingers, she said, "Let me check your nodes."

"I'd rather see Max. Where is she?

"This way." She got up but stopped. "Wait. Odran is not in his tank. Don't get upset when you see him."

Theodore and I looked at each other. *Not in his tank?* I didn't know he ever came out of it. This was going to be interesting.

Ketheria led us through several rooms filled with the same kind of art and rich furniture until we reached Odran. *Interesting* was not the word I would use to describe the site of Odran out of his tank. *Frightening* would be good. *Horrifying* maybe even better, but *interesting* just didn't describe it.

Odran was suspended by cables as he hovered over a stone slab.

"Max!" I shouted, when I saw my friend unconscious on the table.

Odran jerked around at the sound of my voice. The lower part of his body, a fleshy mess of tentacles, was scooped together in a metal bucket that hung from the wires. Cables and tubes ran from the bottom of the bucket and tapered off into the shadows. His skin was a sickly pale pink color, severely wrinkled from the solution he spent most of his time in. More tubes ran from his nose, and a whole set of small cable sensors bore into his skull. His skin was swollen and red where they penetrated his flesh.

"What are you doing here?" he snapped. "If you have nothing to do, then go and help the others prepare for my guests. Those are my orders. You are not to be wandering around."

Theodore stood there staring at Odran, not saying a word.

"You're ugly to me, too, you know," Odran said.

"What did you do to Max?" I said.

"I did nothing. She was injured while she was working. A simple infection, but you pathetic humans are so fragile. Get back to your room."

I ignored Odran and walked up to the stone slab. Max lay there, her vest removed. She smelled worse than Theodore's old socks, and her hair was covered in a gray slime. A large purple bruise covered her swollen left eye, and a deep scratch ran down her neck. Part of it was covered with a plastic patch sprouting little sensors that Odran monitored with a handheld device.

I looked around the room. Odran was *working* on other things, too. There was a cart-bot dismantled on another stone and some wetwire device blinking in the corner, its flesh and wire pieces strewn about the floor. Max was just another of Odran's broken possessions.

"I don't think the other kids should do this work anymore," I told Odran. "It's too dangerous."

"You don't *think*," Odran said, almost chuckling. "You have no right to think. The well-being of Orbis is my goal, not the health of you or your friends. Now get out of my way before I punish you for your rudeness."

Ketheria tugged at my vest, but I was too angry seeing Max lying there. I felt responsible. She was only here because I could talk to the Samirans.

"This isn't what we're here to do," I said to Odran. "This isn't right. You're only doing this because you don't like me for some reason. What did I do to you?"

Odran wrenched his metal bucket forward, forcing the supporting chains and wires to slide along the ceiling. He was next to me in an instant.

"I will not tolerate this attitude, you worthless mass of carbon. You are under my roof and you will do exactly as I say, whether you like it or not," he seethed, his teeth clenched. "No rations for you. You can starve for all I care. Now prepare my meal!"

"Johnny?" Ketheria begged. I just stared at Odran. What he was doing was not right. Ketheria tugged on my vest once more. "Leave it," she whispered. "Come."

"Odran, you can't—" I started to say, but he cut me off.

"So you still want to argue? Fine. Then nothing to eat for any of you. How do you like that? Shall we continue with this stupid conversation? I can let your pathetic little friend die, right here. It's your choice. I love a good debate," Odran said. "Or you can stand with the others and watch me eat."

"Johnny, stop!" Theodore pleaded. "Fix Max, Odran. Now, please."

Ketheria took my hand and dragged me out. Theodore followed us. My feet were heavy. I wanted to stay and fight Odran. I hated him. With everything inside of me I hated him for what he was doing to my friends.

"Do you think that was smart?" Theodore asked as we walked through the building. "You don't need Odran as an enemy."

"I don't care."

"We'll you should, JT. You're starting to sound like . . ." Theodore stopped. His words stung.

"Switzer?" I said.

Theodore did not answer.

"Look at you. Look at Max," I said. "What if Ketheria gets hurt next time, or worse, one of you gets killed?" It was a possibility. How could he argue? "Maybe that knudnik is right."

"Who is?" he said.

"Switzer. Maybe we should find a way and get off this ring."

"No, we shouldn't, " Ketheria said.

We walked in silence toward the dining hall that Odran used to entertain his guests. We reached the round room as several aliens were arriving. I counted four. Some of the other kids were lined against the wall waiting, including Switzer. He stared at me as I entered and took my place. Suddenly, I wanted to tell him I was sorry. He had to realize I didn't want to hurt him. But I knew an apology wasn't going to happen. There was too much friction between Switzer and me. I don't think he would have accepted it anyway.

The aliens seemed familiar with Odran's dining hall as they tapped little pieces of yellowed glass on the floor with their feet. Small individual tables grew out of the floor and clustered together in the center. It seemed as if each alien was waiting for the others to sit first. They paraded about the room, admiring the art but never making eye contact with any of us.

Odran entered the room as another alien came rushing in.

"I hope I'm not too late," the tall alien said, and tapped the floor, taking his seat immediately. The others still lingered, each wanting to be the last Citizen to sit down, I supposed. "You understand," the late guest added. "Council business."

"Yes, Hach. Do share with us. Something exciting, I imagine," Odran gushed in an overly pleasant tone I'd never heard him use before.

"Odran, you know better than that," Hach replied. "Just because you covet a position on the Trading Council doesn't mean I'm allowed to share details with you." His tone was teasing but diplomatic.

Odran concentrated on the small O-dat mounted on his table.

"Sorry, Hach, I didn't hear you. The kitchen needed my attention."

Hach smiled. This seemed like a game to him. The alien removed his thick brown jacket and handed it to one of the kids. He wore a belt that looked like it was made of stones or maybe glass. I couldn't tell. The Orbis emblem decorated the clasp.

"I was just asking you how it was going with the Samirans. I understand there was a bit of trouble," he said.

Another alien, a female covered completely in black except where her pale white face poked through, spoke up. "I really don't understand what all the trouble is. They are still knudniks, aren't they? Or has something changed that I am not aware of?"

Grace and another child entered the hall balancing small bowls of something burnt and brown. Grace placed a bowl on the table of the pale alien, who nibbled at the greasy appetizer as she spoke. "And please, do not preach to me about the importance of their work. I do not need to be reminded again that this is the rotation of the Harvest. Can't they simply be punished and we be done with this nonsense?"

The alien tossed the carcass of what she was eating on the floor. Odran motioned for Theodore to pick it up, which he did.

"What do I do with it now?" Theodore whispered.

"I don't know," I replied. "Odran needs some of Weegin's scavenger-bots."

"I think that's what we're here for."

Hach responded to the pale alien's comments by saying, "Punish them, Pheitt? How do you propose that we punish a Samiran?"

Pheitt only sniffed the air. "Those are details beyond my concern," she said.

"Well, maybe a solution to the problem would be a little more helpful to the Rings of Orbis," Hach replied. Pheitt sniffed again and dug into the bowl, throwing the smallest pieces to the floor. I think Hach rolled his eyes, but it was a little hard to tell since he didn't have pupils.

"What sort of solution have you come up with, Odran?" said another alien with thin shoulders and a very broad nose. Grace re-entered the room with more plates of food and placed them on the tables.

"Well, you do know that it was I who summoned the Softwire. The Keepers were against it, but I insisted."

What a liar, I thought.

"You will find no one on the rings more concerned about the well-being of Orbis than myself," he continued.

"Yes," Hach replied. "You have reminded us many times."

"The Samirans know that their work rule is ending. They're simply holding us hostage," Odran said. He did not mention Ketheria's discovery of the unborn Samiran.

"But certainly you've devised an alternative manner in which to cool the crystals? With all the glory of Orbis at your fingertips, you should have come up with something by now," Hach said, his tone slightly accusatory.

"I've been working on it for a very long time," Odran said slowly, dipping into his tank's solution. "It is not that simple. I do not possess the boundless resources of your mining businesses."

"What else have you been working on?" Hach asked Odran, almost as if he were baiting him.

"With the Harvest approaching so rapidly, I've had time for nothing else."

"I think we should simply extend their work rule," said another alien, seemingly unaware of the tension between Hach and Odran. "I mean look at the damage Toll caused in his last outburst. Who will pay for that?"

Without thinking, I interrupted. "You can't do that," I said. "They've worked here for almost two thousand rotations. It's not fair."

The room fell silent. Pheitt looked at Odran, who glared at me.

"Knudniks should be seen and not heard," he said. The edge in his voice cut straight through the slime in his tank.

"Such an outburst," Pheitt mumbled to the alien on her right.

The alien with the thin shoulders shook his head and said, "I feel for you, Odran. I gave my knudnik an Ebolo to play with, and the thing ate it. The knudnik couldn't work for two phases! Apparently he was allergic to it. How are we supposed to know these things?"

"It really is a nuisance sometimes," said Odran, looking at me.

Did they not know we were standing right behind them? Maybe they just didn't care. This only made me want to prove them wrong even more.

"One knudnik had the nerve to refuse the skin I ordered for her. She claimed it was against her religion. And under my own roof. I don't know why we put up with it sometimes,"

Pheitt said, and shuddered. "I avoid the very ground they walk on."

Hach took his plate and dumped it at Pheitt's feet, splashing a little gristle on her black gown. "Pheitt, will you get that for me?" he asked.

"Excuse me?" she replied.

"Pick that up for me and throw it in the garbage, will you?"

"Touch the trash? Have you lost your mind, Council Member?"

"No, but apparently the Citizens of the Rings of Orbis have lost the ability to clean up after themselves. You made these creatures what they are," he said, pointing at us. "I doubt they stood around waiting for your crap to hit the floor on their home planet."

Hach stood up, grabbed his jacket, and flung it over his shoulders.

"Odran, thank you for your hospitality, but I must leave. I have a knudnik to beat," he said.

Odran moved away from his table. "But I was hoping we could discuss—"

But Hach cut him off. "I am well aware of your desire to sit on the Trading Council, Odran. But as much as you try to avoid them, there are procedures that must be followed. I'm sorry, but it is really out of my hands."

Odran glanced at the other guests. I don't think he wanted Hach to be so public about his intentions.

"I like that guy," I whispered to Theodore as Hach left.

"Clean up his mess," Odran ordered.

11

Two cycles after the dinner party, almost every one of the kids displayed some sort of cut or bruise from their chores, and Max was still not back. Odran's screen scrolls arrived and I rounded everyone up to announce the cycle's work.

"We have to face those creatures again?" Grace said.

"It says here every other cycle," I informed her after reading the scroll. "But maybe I can finish early and come by to help." I quickly scanned the list of chores Odran had ready for me. It was a lot of work.

"Don't bother," Switzer snapped, snatching the screen scroll from me. "You've done enough already. Thanks to you, I'm starving now. Go play with the fish." It was the first thing he had said to me since our incident.

"Really, Switzer, I want to help," I said, but I could see something behind Switzer's eyes, something different, like he just didn't care anymore.

"I said don't bother."

I stood there and watched them file out.

"Be careful, Ketheria," I said, and my sister just smiled. Someway, somehow, she simply accepted it. I wished I knew how she did it.

After they left, I scanned my scroll again to look at my work. There was a map to the location of a supply room and an illustrated list of tools I needed. This was followed by a step-by-step diagram of some first-aid procedure.

"Uplink," I whispered to myself, and the contents of the scroll came rushing toward me. Now that every single detail was stored in my brain, I set off to find the tools I needed.

The building that housed Odran and the Samirans was truly immense. Besides the enormous cooling tank, there seemed to be room after room of nothing. I called up the map in my mind's eye and followed it to the storage room, passing through many empty rooms. The Ancients had built the building, but whatever they had used it for was beyond me.

With my work list tucked neatly inside my cortex, I entered the storage room and scanned the rows of glass-doored shelves. With each step, the floor and ceiling between the rows of items glowed pale blue. Behind one door I saw a small glass container of what looked like tiny fingers. I tried to open the door, but it was locked.

The room reeked of medicines. I located the items on my list, and each time the door opened easily. *Must be my skin,* I thought. *But who programmed that?* There were too many items for me to carry, so I ordered one of the cart-bots to transport the items back to the cooling tank. The little robot, loaded with all of my supplies, followed obediently. I looked over my shoulder as it hovered behind me.

"We have a lot in common, you know," I said, but the metal machine did not respond. It was too busy doing *its* work. *Is that how the Citizens look at us?* I wondered. I wanted to prove them wrong, that we were worth more than that, but I just couldn't figure out how. Did they even appreciate a job well done, or was that simply expected from us?

I reached the cooling tank and waited for my cart-bot to use a utility chute to reach the top. *How am I going to contact Toll?* I wondered. Then I remembered the information I had uplinked earlier. I was to strike the edge of the tank with one long tap and two short ones. That was the strange thing about uploading information before reading it. I often answered my own questions.

Nestled into a notch in the railing was the metal rod Odran used to contact Toll. On the edge of the tank was a small depression in the metal rim just above the crystal lights. I knelt down and felt it. It was more of a button.

I stood up and grasped the metal staff in my right hand and struck the button. Where was Toll and how did he receive the signal? Maybe it created a vibration through the water that only Toll could understand. I looked out over the huge body of water for some sign of the Samiran. While I waited, I unloaded the supplies off the cart-bot—four ten-liter pails, a rubber jacket with some sort of metal harness, and several large application brushes. The brushes stood taller than me.

"Hello, Johnny Turnbull."

I spun around and saw Toll floating at the edge of the tank. He must have finished pulling the purple crystal that had arrived the other cycle.

I immediately noticed a long red gash near the corner of Toll's huge mouth.

"You're hurt," I said. The cut must have been as deep as my fist and three times as long as my arm.

"The ropes are too close to the edge of the bit sometimes. It is a hazard I endure."

"What's that?" I said, pointing at two dark-purple platforms on each side of Toll's body.

"These are for you. Put that jacket on. The magnetic straps connect to my harness ropes. They use a small charge to move with you. I will hold very still while you get on," he said.

"Get on? You mean I'm going to climb onto those things?"

"Were you not instructed on the procedure?"

"Yeah," I said as I accessed the illustrated instructions I had uplinked earlier. I *was* getting on that thing, and I was taking the pails and the brushes with me. Then I was going to apply the salve in those buckets onto that nasty gash. I could hardly believe my own thoughts.

"Put the buckets on first. Use the locks provided for them on the platform."

"All this technology here and this is how they help you?" I grabbed one of the heavy ten-liter buckets.

As the instructions said, I put the jacket on last. Toll positioned himself close to the edge, and I reached out to grab the harness.

"Are you sure this is safe?" I asked Toll. I did *not* want to touch the tank water.

"Purrfeckly," Toll said from under the water.

"What if I fall in?"

Toll lifted a little out of the water. "You won't," he said.

And I didn't. Once on the platform, I attached the safety strap to the harness and secured the buckets.

"Hold on," Toll said, and with a great heave he lifted himself to the edge of the tank. His hands grasped the edge of the tank, lifting me at least four meters above the water line. The platform I stood on automatically leveled off.

"You may begin," Toll said.

I cracked the computerized seal on the first bucket, and the lid disappeared. Inside was a pale blue cream, thick and smooth. I dunked the brush into the ointment and moved toward Toll's wound.

"Wow. Does it hurt?" I asked.

"Yes."

I'd seen Toll's skin before, but never up close like this. It looked like a wet rock, bumpy and crevassed, but where the rope cut in was soft pink tissue just like a human. The deep crack ran from Toll's mouth, where the bit sat, and extended back for about two meters. The crack was wide enough to stick my head in, and it was bleeding and infected. I took the brush and stuck it in the wound. Toll shook.

"Sorry," I said, and proceeded to go more slowly. I sat on the platform with my knees against Toll and painted his wound with the brush. *I will have to use all four pails,* I thought.

"Why do you pull the crystals if it causes you so much pain?" I asked.

"I have no choice. The survival of my species depends on it," he said. "The planet of Samira is a water planet. At one time we swam our world at the top of the food chain. We built great cities underwater, and our population reached the billions. Then the Arelions came. They hunted us for food, building huge colonies above the water and using technologies we could not hide from. For centuries they ruthlessly pillaged our planet."

"Why didn't you fight back?"

"It was not our way. We had no capacity to fight. We never needed one. We attacked their structures, but they just built more. We tried to hide, but they found us. There was nothing we could do. We were heading toward extinction."

"What *did* you do?" I asked. My problems suddenly seemed to pale in comparison to Toll's.

"The Arelions captured several Samirans alive, which they displayed on their home planet. A Softwire, like yourself, saw them and encoded them with an implant. After some work, my fellow Samiran told him everything."

"A Softwire? You mean a Space Jumper?" I asked.

"Yes. The Space Jumpers were aware of the damage the Arelions were causing on our planet. He offered us a deal."

"A deal? To be a slave on Orbis?"

"The Space Jumper said they would take two Samirans from the planet and bring them to the oceans on Orbis. In exchange we would work for two thousand rotations on the ring."

"Two thousand rotations!"

"Samirans can live for hundreds of thousand of rotations. It was a small price to pay for such a great gift," Toll said. I felt his huge body shiver as I went too deep with the brush.

"Sorry."

"We did not have the technology to leave our planet. The Arelions would have slaughtered every last one of us. Our great race would have disappeared."

"So you agreed?"

"The Space Jumpers battled ruthlessly with the Arelions to get myself and Smool off the planet. They did not want to give up even two Samirans. It was brutal, but the Space Jumpers were successful."

"And now you are here."

"For a thousand rotations we worked in this tank with the Space Jumpers before they were banished. That is how I met your father," Toll said

My father?

Toll said it as if it was no big deal, as if it was common knowledge.

I put the brush down and just sat there. The words repeated in my head. *My father.*

How? It's impossible, my mind told me.

"There is no way you could have known my father," I said, and suddenly I felt anger. "Why would you say that, Toll? Why would you say you knew my father?"

"I'm surprised this angers you," Toll replied. "I will not talk about it any further."

I applied the ointment, but I did not speak to Toll. Why was I so angry? *Was Toll playing a trick on me?* It was not the first time, however, that someone from Orbis had mentioned my father. Madame Lee made similar remarks, but I could only assume that she was lying. That's what she did.

There was a chain ladder that ran across the top of Toll's head and down to the platform on the other side. As I finished with one wound, I crawled across to the other, dragging the bucket with me. I made another trip for the brush.

My father died on the *Renaissance.* My father was human. I had told this to myself many times after Madame Lee *claimed* to know my father, too. She also said he was a Space Jumper. I didn't believe her either. *But what if she was right?* Space Jumpers were ruthless enforcers that guarded the Keepers. I had seen one before. How could my father be a Space Jumper? There are no human Space Jumpers. Space Jumpers are aliens.

I sat in the harness and continued my chore.

"Your father sat there once doing the exact same thing you're doing," Toll said, breaking the silence.

"You're talking about it again."

"Do you not wish to learn of this?" Toll asked.

"My father was a human that died on the space flight here. There is no way he could have been on Orbis a thousand rotations ago," I told him.

"Your father and I made a deal. He spoke of a very important mission to a strange new planet. A planet called Earth, where he would return with a special offspring from the human race. I now realize that was you. Your abilities are needed on Orbis now that Space Jumpers are no longer on the rings.

"Many rotations after the Space Jumpers were banished, your father jumped to Earth in slow time, and then on your flight back, time dilated. It stretched. Time is different for Jumpers. The Earth that exists now is not the Earth you left. Time is a very strange thing. Orbis aged, too, as you manipulated the speed of light, so it *is* possible that he was here a thousand rotations ago *and* died on that space flight. The Keepers have only ever sent one Space Jumper to Earth, and that was your father. You have a great purpose here, Johnny Turnbull."

I was no longer applying the ointment. I just sat there staring over the water. *Purpose?* I wasn't too fond of the "purposes" they handed out on the Rings of Orbis. What if I wanted to choose my own purpose?

"Can I show you something?" Toll asked.

"I don't know if I can take any more, Toll."

"The seat you are on—open it and remove the garment. Then put it on," he said.

I stood up, almost in a daze. Inside the seat was a slick, purple-black suit.

"Toll, I saw—"

"Put the suit on."

I did as Toll instructed. The material was soft and pliable. It stretched and contracted to fit me perfectly, as if the material possessed a mind of its own or as if someone had manufactured it just for me. I don't know which thought scared me more. The last piece I put on was the hood. It completely covered my face and formed a perfect seal around my neck.

"Toss the brush and empty buckets on the deck," he said.

"I'm going to get wet, aren't I?" I said.

"The suit will protect you. Can you see?"

"Perfectly," I said. Despite the black material over my face, I could see right through.

"Now climb to the top of the harness and get ready."

"Ready for what?" I scrambled up the rope and sat on top of Toll's head. I could have sat all my friends up here with room to spare.

"Hold on!"

Toll pushed off the edge of the tank with his gigantic fins and twisted in midair, pummeling the pale green water with a huge splash. With one forceful pump of his mighty tail we set out across the fake ocean. Toll swam just above the water so I could see everything. The speed, the air, and the rushing water—it was amazing. I was free!

Toll swam so fast that when I looked at the water, it was nothing more than a blur. We sped toward the horizon, and the tank's platform shrank behind me. Soon I could see nothing but water. *If only Max and Theodore could see me now,* I thought.

Toll moved up and down, leaning from left to right as I clung to the harness on top of his head. He dipped into the water splashing it all over me, but I didn't feel a thing. The suit protected me completely.

Toll began to slow.

I looked down and saw the water sparkling with lights, illuminated from deep inside the tank. Silver, blue, and gold flickered in the waves as Toll circled the mysterious glow.

"It's beautiful, Toll. What is it?"

"Another question for another time," he said, and resumed his frantic pace back across the water. I gripped the harness while Toll tore through the waves. The ride ignited my insides. I never felt anything like this before. I was *happy*.

Toll finally reached the platform and grabbed the edge. A million more questions raced through my mind as I returned the water suit to the container on the harness.

"That was incredible, Toll. I can't wait to tell my friends," I said.

"But you must not tell them about the lights," he said.

"Why?"

"I took a great risk to show you that. A risk to myself as well as others."

"Oh."

I think Toll could tell I was disappointed. It was the kind of "oh" that said "What good was it if I can't tell anyone?"

"I want you to trust me the way I trust you," he said. " I am not lying to you when I speak of your father. He was a great person—strong, honorable, and trustworthy. I see the same in you, Johnny Turnbull."

I looked at my feet. I felt bad for thinking of myself, but I didn't know where to put Toll's words. My mother and father were scientists—from Earth—and they were dead.

"I'm sorry, Toll. I need more proof," I said, looking at him.

"It will come, my friend. It will come."

Toll sank into the water. I watched as he swam back toward the secret lights. What was out there? *Who* was out there?

Orbis was a strange and curious place.

12

"Who do you think it was?" Max asked.

She was back from Odran's workshop but still healing, confined to the dormitory for one more cycle. I was glad to have her back, and of course she acted as if nothing had happened. I sat on her sleeper with Theodore, recapping the story of the alien climbing the cable to the flier. I said nothing of Toll's claims about my father or the lights in the tank, but it was difficult to keep them from my thoughts. I wanted to know more.

"I don't know," I told her. "The central computer wouldn't let me in."

"How come the bio-bots in the water didn't kill the alien?" she asked.

"It must have been the suit," I said. I wanted to know how he got in the tank. Did his presence in the tank have anything to do with the lights? I couldn't make things add up.

"Did you ask Toll about the alien when he took you for the ride?" Max said, cautiously scratching her bruised eye.

"He avoided it." *But he did let me see the lights,* I thought.

"Do you think I could take a ride on Toll?" Theodore said.

"What were you doing when this was happening?" Max asked. "When the alien was *escaping.*" She whispered the last word and looked quickly around the dormitory.

"You don't know he was escaping," I said.

"Did Toll see you?" Theodore asked.

"I . . . don't . . . know," I repeated as Switzer entered the room behind Dalton.

"What else is new?" Dalton said. "You're right, Switzer. He doesn't know anything. He just admitted it."

I watched Switzer follow Dalton to his sleeper, where he grabbed a small, soiled bag from under the sheet. Max saw it, too.

"What's that?" she said, pointing to the bag Dalton cradled as if it were some precious treasure.

Switzer looked at the bag and then back to Max. "That? That's nothing," he said, and glared at Dalton. "Are you an idiot?" he said with his teeth clenched.

Now I was curious. "What is it?" I asked.

But before I got my answer, Odran entered the room in his support glider. "There are two unopened food crates in the delivery area. What are they doing there?" he asked me.

"You're asking me?" I said.

"You are the controller; find out. Or is the simple task of feeding the Samirans too much for a human to handle?"

"No, it's not," I replied.

"Then what are the crates doing there?"

I didn't have an answer. I looked at Theodore, who simply shrugged. The other kids acted as if it was none of their business.

"I'll take care of it myself," I told him.

"Or else someone will have to be punished," Odran threatened. "You, the telepath," he said, pointing to my sister on her sleeper, "what is your name?"

"Ketheria," she said.

"Follow me, Ketheria."

Odran turned to leave the room. Ketheria did as she was told and followed the alien. It felt wrong.

"Wait!" I yelled. "I'm going to take care of the crates. Leave her alone; she didn't do anything."

Odran turned slowly.

"Unless I ask, I see no need for you to speak, Softwire," he said.

I didn't know what to do. I didn't want him to take Ketheria away. I had to stall him. "But what am I to do while the Samiran is pulling the crystal?"

"Wait."

"Is there anything more than that?" I asked. Now I was pushing it.

"I will forgive you for your actions this once," he growled. "I can see through your foolish games. Your sibling will not be punished. She is not your responsibility.

"The core crystal will be arriving within this rotation, and with it, the Festival of the Harvest. It is an extremely important crystal, and the Samirans are allowed a rest period prior to its arrival. You will have plenty of time to talk to them and make your reports to the Keepers. Their wounds from the pull ropes will need more tending to, and our situation will be explained to them during this period."

"What situation?" I asked.

"Their release," he said, and turned away.

"Is something wrong with their release?" I shouted, but Odran did not respond. I watched him leave with Ketheria.

"Better go check on those crates," Switzer said. He was smiling and whispering to Dalton.

Another girl said with a snicker, "Yeah, and I don't think that's going to be the last time either."

"What do you mean?" I said.

"I'm not going near those creatures again. I'd rather get zapped by the enabler."

"But don't you see? That's what they want—to prove that we can't do anything right. They want to keep us as second-class citizens. We're never going to finish our work rule if we don't do a good job."

"That's your battle, not mine," Switzer said. "I could care less what these malfs think about me. C'mon, Dalton."

"Where are you going?" Max asked.

"None of your business," Switzer spat and dragged Dalton, clutching the soiled sack, from the dorm.

"That scares me," Max whispered.

"Me too," I said. "Switzer usually brags about anything he finds."

"I wonder what they have," Theodore said.

"I think we should find out," Max said. Her eyes widened as she smirked, nodding slowly.

Theodore's tone changed when he saw her doing this. "I don't know about that," he said. He always became hesitant when Max had that look.

"What do you want to do? Take the bag?" I asked.

"No, I want to follow them," she said.

When I turned around, Max was up and getting dressed.

"Where are you going?" I asked her.

"To follow."

"Odran?"

"No, silly. Switzer and Dalton."

Was I the only one who cared about what the Citizens wanted us to do? I started to think that maybe I was. Yes, the other kids complained, some even joked, but none of them seemed concerned about the threats the Citizens made if we didn't do the work assigned to us as knudniks.

"I have to check on the crates that were left out," I said rather loudly so everyone heard me.

One of the boys said, "Enjoy yourself, Mr. Controller."

"We'll come with you," Max offered.

Max took the lead, and we left the rest of the kids in the dormitory.

"I appreciate you showing the other kids we have to get this work done," I told her.

"Oh, we're not going to check on those stupid crates," she told me. "I've already had my beating this phase."

"Where are we going, then?" Theodore asked.

Max turned and grinned, wiggling her eyebrows a little.

"No, Max," I said. With everything going on around me, chasing after Switzer was the last thing I wanted to do, but she was already scouring the hallways, sniffing out Switzer's trail.

"Max, I can't use that enabler again. If no one is going to do the work, then I have to do it. I thought you understood that."

"But what if Switzer *is* up to something? You don't want him and Dalton getting in trouble while you're the controller now, do you?"

I looked at Theodore. He just shrugged. She made a good a point. "Where *do* you think he's going, then?" I asked her.

"Wait," Max whispered. She tucked behind one of the carved stone columns, dragging Theodore with her.

"Again?" I heard Dalton say.

"Shut up," Switzer said. "We have to get as much as we can now."

Max peeked around the corner.

"Come on. They're heading this way," she said.

We hid in the shadows as Switzer and Dalton marched past.

"What are they doing?" Theodore whispered.

"Shhh, we'll know soon enough."

But I couldn't help thinking about Ketheria. What was Odran doing? Why did he single her out? Should I have forced the issue with Odran? Maybe I could have gone with her. Max motioned to me, and I snuck under another archway into a room I'd never seen before. The three of us hid near the entrance to the vast and empty room until Switzer cleared the other side.

"Keep up," Max whispered.

"Sorry," I said.

It was hard to focus on Max's adventure. If I wasn't worrying about my sister, I was thinking about my father. Questions actually, just more questions. What if Toll was right, for instance? For that matter, let's say Madame Lee was telling the truth as well. What did it mean to me? *He's still dead,* a voice inside my head reminded me. And I was still just a knudnik on the ring. At best, the information only gave me a possible explanation for my softwire abilities. Nothing more.

"JT!"

Max and Theodore were halfway across the room.

"C'mon," Max said, and waved at me.

I raced after them to the other side. Max opened a door that led to an unlit narrow flight of stairs.

"They went down there," she said, pointing. "There's no other place to go."

I couldn't see a thing. "But they don't have a light."

"We're not supposed to do this, guys," Theodore reminded us. "We should go back."

"Come on!" Max begged. "If we get caught, just tell Odran that you saw them wander off and you took the responsibility to chase after them."

"That's weak," I told her.

"It's good enough," she said, and headed down the stairs.

I looked at Theodore and shrugged. "We shouldn't let her go alone," I said, and I nudged him toward Max.

"Hey," he protested.

"Don't worry—I'm right behind you."

Each step began to glow as Max stepped on it.

"They'll see the light and know we're following them," Theodore said.

"If I can't see Switzer, how's he going to see the lights?" she said, and continued her descent.

When I reached the bottom, I tapped Theodore on the shoulder and asked, "How many?"

"Fifty-two," he replied. "We descended fifty-two steps."

The staircase opened into a small atrium, from which three round tunnels, each about three meters tall, branched off into different directions.

"That's convenient," Max mumbled.

"I'm not splitting up," Theodore said, sounding panicked.

"How are we going to find them, then?" she asked.

"We'll pick one," I offered. "Which one would they pick?"

All three of us headed for the middle tunnel.

"Easy enough," Max said.

The tunnel widened and curved upward. The thoughts of my father and my sister were now replaced with a genuine curiosity about what Switzer was up to. How did he find this place, and better yet, why?

A neon-blue light sliced the sides of the passageway, illuminating the tiled walls as we ventured farther into the tunnel. The ground was covered with debris. Rotten stuff that looked old. Moss grew in the cracked tiles, and many broken tiles littered the ground. Everything smelled stale, as if it was just about to start rotting. I turned back to see how far we had traveled, but there was only darkness.

"What is this place?" Theodore said.

"I don't have a clue," I replied

"I don't think anyone uses it anymore," Max said, and stopped. "Did you hear that?"

"No," Theodore and I both said.

"Come on. I heard them. They're down here," she whispered, picking up her pace.

Max was quick.

The intricate stone carvings I had seen on the ceiling of Odran's were nowhere to be found here. Instead, rows and rows of patchy, dirty tiles spread out in front of us with the odd rusted grate poking out every few meters.

"Wait!" Max stopped and threw her hands up.

Max stood at the very edge of a large hole. It was at least four meters in diameter.

"That was too close," I said.

Our tunnel ended, and the lights that followed us now circled the top of the hole. I stood at the edge and looked down, and then I looked up. The hole was really another tunnel slicing off the one we had come down. Thick metal chains with heavy-looking rings placed about every two meters hung down the tunnel. Where these chains started though was anyone's guess.

"Look," Theodore exclaimed. One of the chains wiggled slightly, twisting in the open void.

"Someone's on that chain," I said.

"It has to be them," Max said.

"Are they crazy?" Theodore protested.

"Listen." Max got on her belly and hung her head over the hole. "I can hear them."

"Are you sure it's them?" I questioned her.

"Listen yourself," she said.

I laid on my belly, too, and listened very hard.

"More . . . try . . . Dalton . . ." I heard these words come up the tunnel.

"It's them all right," I said.

"They *are* crazy," Theodore said.

"They used that rope to lean out and grab the chains," Max theorized. She pointed to a metal grate in the wall on her right. Someone had tied a rope to it.

I asked her, "How do you know?"

"Because that's what I would do," she said.

"What are we gonna do now?" Theodore asked Max.

"We're getting our own rope," she said, jumping up and running back the way we came.

"What? Max, wait," Theodore yelled, running after her.

I lay there listening for more. What were they doing? Were they trying to escape? Would Switzer really do that? He knew the punishment if he got caught. Even I didn't think Switzer was that dumb.

"Almost..."

I jumped up and chased after my friends.

The lights along the tunnel kept pace with us as we retraced our steps back to Odran's. When we got there, Ketheria was pacing in the doorway of the dormitory.

"Hurry, they're waiting for you at the tank," she said to me anxiously.

"Who?"

"Odran and some of the Trading Council," she said.

"Where were you?"

"Don't worry. I'm fine. Odran is angry. You need to go. I'll tell you later."

Max and Theodore followed me to the tank. Odran hovered near the edge as four members of the Trading Council posed behind him. I recognized one of them immediately—it was Pheitt, one of Odran's dinner guests. Each council member was quietly shifting in front of the other, never making eye contact with anyone. Occasionally one would glance down at me from the corner of their big eyes. Odran whirled around as I came up the stairs.

"Where have you been? It is forbidden to wander off. You have been told of this," Odran scolded me. His voice was harsh but restrained.

One council member turned its back to us and slinked away as if our presence was offensive.

"Your controller told us you needed the garbage from the

new shipments discarded," Theodore said. Max and I both turned when we heard his fib.

Max added, "We were looking for a place for the garbage."

"Convenient," Pheitt scoffed. "Can we proceed? Punish them later, Odran."

I moved toward Odran. "What's this about?"

"We need information from the Samiran," he said.

I looked at everyone in attendance. "Shouldn't a Keeper be present?" I asked.

One alien looked at Odran and frowned. Another, an alien with wet-looking skin, stated, "This is none of their business."

"Council member Burash is stating the obvious," Pheitt said. "Do we need to be explaining this, Odran? To a knudnik?"

Odran sank into his tank and came up spitting, "How dare you question me, child?" he growled. His bloodshot eyes shifted quickly from the Trading Council members to me. "I do not need the authority of the Keepers. I am the Samiran Caretaker. You will do as you are told, or you will be punished severely!"

"It is incredible what we must endure from these ungrateful creatures," a council member said.

"I assure you this was not my idea," Odran countered. "These creatures are worthless, in my opinion. If it were not for this one's softwire abilities, I would have fed them to the Samirans long ago."

Odran struck the button on the floor twice with the tall, thin staff and turned back to me. "You are to confirm the rumors that the female is with child," he said.

I wasn't going to debate Toll's eating habits with Odran.

Nothing good could come from embarrassing Odran in front of the Council anymore. I wanted to keep my job, and I didn't want him taking it out on any of my friends. But Odran seemed nervous to me, fidgeting with something in his tank and constantly looking at the council members out of the corner of his eye. He even glanced at the light chute several times, and his anger felt like an act put on only for these aliens. The council members were now huddled together, whispering to each other. Odran struck the button again, anxiously. *He is doing something wrong here, and the Trading Council is participating. I just know it.*

"There is more, Odran," the last member said. The alien's pasty face was covered with a yellowish dye in an attempt to cover its sickly skin. *Bad choice.* "Tell the Softwire."

"Yes," Odran replied. "The Samirans' work rule, very similar to yours, is due to expire before the Harvest of the Crystal of Life. We need to be assured that the Samirans will extend their work rule to cover this period."

"Do they have a choice?" I asked.

I could see Odran clenching his jaw. The support glider jerked in front of me, blocking my view of the council members.

"*You* don't," he growled.

The Citizens had had two thousand rotations to get ready for the Samirans' release. That's a long time. Couldn't they have figured out another way to cool the crystals? Was this going to happen to us? Was our contract going to be voluntarily *extended* for the convenience of Orbis? I stared at Odran.

"This is very important," a council member said.

I bet it is, but for whom? I said to myself.

The Samiran surfaced, and I moved to the edge of the tank.

"Hello, Toll," I said.

His big green eyes blinked as he said, "It is a pleasure to see you again."

The sound of his voice no longer hurt my head. My brain was used to it now.

Toll continued, "The Keepers have asked you to speak with me?"

"No, Odran and some of the members from the Council," I said. "They want to know if Smool is going to have a baby."

Toll's eyes widened. He stared at the aliens on the platform. Then Toll pushed back, and his tail broke the surface of the water, splashing in the tank behind him.

"Who has spoken of this to you?" Toll bellowed. There was anger in his voice now.

"My sister guessed it."

Toll shifted about in the water. He slipped into the water, then came up quickly. The council members cautiously stepped back.

"There's more," I said.

"There always is," he replied.

"Your work rule ends before the Harvest of the Crystal of Life. They need you to finish the job before you leave."

Toll smacked his tail on the water in frustration. I looked back at Odran and the council as they waited, looking confident. Almost too confident, I thought. That's when I realized that I was being used. Just like a laser drill or any other tool they owned, the Citizens of Orbis were using me to get more out of the Samirans. What was I doing? I felt dirty, as if I was tricked into doing something bad.

"You and I have many things in common," Toll said. "We have both traded a portion of our lives to work for the creatures that control these rings, and we both have families sharing this same burden."

"That's true," I replied.

"If I am correct, I also believe that we both want more for our families. Is this also true?"

Of course it was. I nodded.

"Does that mean yes?" he asked. "The up and down movement of your head. I assume that means I am right."

"You are."

"And I also believe there is one small difference between us."

"What's that?" I asked, looking back at Odran, who was watching intently.

"I know where I come from and why I'm here, but you have many questions. Questions about these rings you live on, questions about why you are here . . . and questions about your past and the lives of your parents."

The last sentence resonated in my brain, bouncing around inside my skull.

I knelt down to the edge of the tank and whispered, "We talked about this, Toll. I need more proof."

"First we must come to an understanding. First you and I must make an agreement," he said.

"What?"

"If you are to translate what I say for the Trading Council or anyone else, you must promise me to tell them only what I say to tell them. I must trust that my secrets are safe with you."

"Why me?"

"Your father and I made this same agreement."

What secrets? What was Toll offering me? How could he know the answers to my questions? How could he possibly know anything about my parents? I looked back at Odran. I wished Theylor was here, but I couldn't deceive Theylor either, could I? If Theylor asked for the truth, could I lie to him? I glanced over at Max and Theodore—I wanted to ask them what I should do, but I knew it was too risky. Odran saw me and turned to my friends.

"Go back to your room, humans," he said. But they didn't move. I think they understood that I needed them.

"Now!" Odran shouted, and they were forced to turn away.

"Your knudniks are disgracefully disobedient, Odran," Pheitt spat. "You should let me have them for a few phases. I would show them their place."

"Do we have an agreement?" Toll said as I watched my friends shuffle down the stairs.

I looked up at Odran, who glared at me. There was fire in his eyes. Odran was up to something, and I knew he was using me. But then he wasn't the only person on the Rings of Orbis to try to use me. I thought of Drapling and how he connived to put me inside the central computer. I thought of Madame Lee and how she used me to try to start a war. Then there was Weegin—he tried to sell me!

I turned back to Toll and nodded. "Yes," I whispered.

"Good," he replied. "Tell the Trading Council that it is true; Smool is with child, and the child should arrive near the Harvest. I will pull the Crystal of Life Harvest Crystal while she rests. I will need only a few things for the birth of the child, but we shall be fine once the three of us are released from our work rule immediately following the Harvest."

"What is he saying?" Odran asked me.

"Are the rumors true?" another said.

"Yes, they are," I replied.

I stood up and told them exactly what Toll wanted. The aliens huddled together, whispering. I could only hope I had done the right thing. Odran turned to me with a forced sense of superiority.

"Agreed. Although the Samiran has no right to bargain, we will grant his request in return for his work. He will be released after the Crystal of Life has cooled," he announced.

I turned and nodded to Toll.

"Remember, your softwire ability gives you a great advantage over your oppressors," Toll said.

I knelt at the edge of the tank and whispered, "Yeah, but it doesn't seem to work around here. Every time I try to enter the computer, I keep getting zapped or something."

"At times, the best place to hide something is right out in the open," Toll said. "On the next occasion we meet, I will give you your proof, Softwire." Then Toll slipped under the water.

I turned back to Odran and the Council. What did Toll mean: *the best place to hide something is right out in the open*?

Two of the council members turned, talking rapidly as they moved to the light chute.

"Odran," Burash said as he headed down the steps. It was more of an order.

"I have many things to do," he protested, but the council member would not take no for an answer.

"In your quarters now, please," he said firmly to Odran.

"What did you make me do, Odran?" I asked him.

"Nothing that concerns you," he spat. "Go back to your room until I need you again."

I looked at Odran. I should have felt betrayed at how easily he had just lied to me, but I was used to it by then. I knew there was more going on than what Odran was telling me. I felt it. I just couldn't figure it out yet.

"What deal did you make with the Samiran?" he whispered, before moving toward the council member.

"Deal?" I said. "I didn't make a deal."

"Beware of what friends you make on the Rings of Orbis, Softwire." Odran spoke softly, almost as if he was confiding in me, but I knew better. Then he disappeared over the edge to the awaiting council member.

13

"What do you mean?" Max said to Ketheria. She and Theodore flanked my sister, her back against an old, torn lounger that looked out of place in the stone room. It was now more than a cycle after my discussion with Toll, and Ketheria had returned from Odran's unharmed, but I admit I was too preoccupied with Toll and his *agreement* to be much of a brother to her. Max and Theodore were asking her about what happened with Odran while some of the other kids napped.

"He's a believer," Ketheria told them.

"Believer of what?" Theodore said. He looked thoroughly confused. His mouth was slightly open and his forehead all scrunched up.

Max tried to explain to him, "OIO. It's—"

"The art and science of cosmic energy," Ketheria said.

"Remember the Nagools?" I added, trying to sound interested.

"I don't get any of it," Theodore said.

"It has to do with the way cosmic energy flows through the universe—" Max started to explain, but Ketheria interrupted her.

"*This* universe," she said.

"There's only one universe, Ketheria," Theodore agrued.

"No, she's right. Most aliens on Orbis believe there are an infinite number of universes," Max said, "but OIO has to do with the way cosmic energies affect our lives."

"In its simplest terms," Ketheria said.

"And Odran believes in this stuff?" I said.

"He claims to, but I think he uses it more to manipulate other people than to actually live by its teachings," Ketheria replied. "Otherwise he would never treat us like this."

"It's fascinating," Max gushed, her eyes widening. "According to the philosophy of OIO, we are all made up of this stuff called Source, and Odran performed these tests on Ketheria in his quarters—"

"Tests?" I said, interrupting.

"Nothing really," Ketheria said. "Odran simply observed my nodes to measure their spin. It was very interesting, but I think I made him nervous somehow."

"Ketheria, what kind of tests? Are you all right? Did he hurt you?"

"It was nothing. I think he was trying to read my nodes," she said.

"Yeah, there are fourteen of them in and around your body that spin or vibrate depending—"

Theodore cut her off. "Nodes? Spin? *What?* I don't get any of it."

It was like another alien language to me also. Toll quickly slipped to the back of my mind. "Are you sure, Ketheria?"

"Don't worry. It's alien mysticism. It was fun. I'm hungry," Ketheria said. Then she got up off the lounger and left the three of us standing there.

I watched her go through a crate and pick out her favorite food tablets from the supply Charlie had left for us.

"She acts older than most of the other kids here," Theodore whispered.

"She does, doesn't she?" Max murmured. "She's golden."

Ketheria was in her own little world, and if Odran did hurt her, she certainly wasn't showing it. *She is fine,* I said to myself, and then proceeded to tell Max and Theodore about what happened with me and Toll, the deal I made, and how odd the council members acted. I knew Toll wouldn't mind if I shared with my friends, but I still made them promise not to tell anyone. I did not tell them, however, about what Toll said about my father and the deal Toll made with him. What if it was a lie, a trick? I kept that part of the agreement to myself.

"There should have been a Keeper present. I feel like I did something wrong," I said.

"Something must be wrong with the Harvest, and Odran doesn't want anyone to find out," Theodore said.

"Odran is the one who should be nervous," Max said. "I can't believe he hasn't figured out a way to float those crystals. With all that stuff in his quarters—I bet you I could figure something out."

Switzer and Dalton entered the room.

"Figure what out?" Switzer asked.

"Where you keep sneaking off to," she replied.

"You're crazy," he replied. Dalton was clutching the same dirty sack from the other cycle. He slipped in behind Switzer and over to his sleeper. Max watched him the entire time. I knew Max was dying to find out what they were doing. She probably assumed that Switzer had stumbled upon some alien technology or something Max hadn't seen yet. It had to be driving her crazy, but I was more worried about what Odran would do if he caught them sneaking around.

Odran entered our room on his support glider. Behind him stood two sturdy aliens with thick necks and low-swinging, muscular arms. They looked nearly identical with large blue eyes and hairless, round heads.

"Where is the controller?" he demanded, his voice gurgling.

"Here," I replied, and stood up.

"Good," said our Guarantor. "This is a list of work I need done. I am doubling the work shifts. There is no advantage to having you sit around when time is running out for the Harvest preparations." Odran handed me one of two screen scrolls. "This is for them. Make sure it is done completely this time, or I will use the enabler myself."

I cracked my scroll, and the information sprung onto the transparent screen in front of me.

"Everyone, over here," I said. "Besides feeding the Samirans, all of these items are to be hauled to the following places . . ."

"Before you begin, I have brought two Gleenons to train you on proper procedures to feed the Samirans. I cannot have you injured every time you do this menial work," Odran said. The two Gleenons bowed their round, shiny heads.

"Maybe you should have had them show us what to do first," Max complained.

"Yeah, like a dozen phases ago," someone else added.

"Robots do not require training. You must agree with me then that robots are smarter than humans," Odran replied.

Whenever Max got angry, she pursed her lips together and bit down hard on her back teeth. She was doing that now.

"Don't, Max," Theodore whispered. "He's just baiting us."

"Do you have a problem, girl?" Odran said, teasing her. "Or does your inferior mind fail to understand my instructions? I'm going to assume that is the problem, because even an animal has the basic instinct to avoid pain."

Max turned to me, took the screen scroll, and asked, "You comin'?"

"Leave the Softwire to his duties," Odran ordered, handing me the other scroll.

"Different orders," I said to Max. "Be careful."

"They won't get me twice," she said, joining Theodore.

I turned away as Switzer and the others followed the two Gleenons out of the dorm room. No one liked to do Odran's work. I felt bad that I wasn't helping them.

• • •

After I collected my supplies from the storage room, I dragged them to the top of the tank and waited for Toll. The water was calm, and the mysterious lights twinkled in the deep, distant water. *What are those lights?* I wondered. And how could Toll have possibly known my father?

I was clueless to so much that was happening around me that I was tired of it now. It's not that I wanted to give up, but the anger I held was tiring. Why was everything such a secret? The Keepers kept secrets from me, Odran did too, even Charlie. *Just tell me the truth!* I wanted to shout at everyone.

I saw the O-dat at the edge of the platform. I had found answers in the central computer before. I pushed inside, hoping that maybe the quantum encryption device I had encountered previously was gone, but it wasn't. I pulled out before disturbing the beams of light and pushed one of the buckets toward the edge of the tank. *Just do the work.* I laid the brushes on top. I figured that if I did the job quickly, I could get back and help the others. It made me nervous leaving them alone, knowing that Switzer was wandering off whenever he pleased.

I saw Odran's staff leaning against the railing and reached for it. I located the smooth depression in the metal on the edge of the tank. I picked up the staff to hit the button, but I stopped.

At times, the best place to hide something is right out in the open.

Could it be? I almost didn't want to try. I put the staff back and knelt down, running my hands over the cool metal button.

I pushed inside.

There were no beams of yellow light, no quantum barrier

to keep me out, just a deep, dark tunnel crackling with static electricity. The tunnel gave way to a thick soup of green fog, but I pushed through that, too. Before me laid the landscape of a computer just like the one I had slipped into when Weegin tried to sell us in Core City. The same patchwork of security devices clung to each other, and the neat, organized grid of the central computer was replaced by a twisting jungle of data.

A shadow darkened my path.

"Hello, Johnny Turnbull," he said, his voice full with long, smooth tones. I knew who it was. I pulled out of the computer to find Toll waiting at the edge of the tank.

"It was you," I said, stumbling over the bucket and landing on my butt. "What's in there? Whose computer is that?"

"Do not let that trouble you," he said, and moved closer to the edge of the tank. The crystals lining the edge of the tank illuminated his enormous face.

"This whole place is troubling me," I said. "No one tells the truth. Not the Keepers, not Odran, not even you. It's just a big game to everyone. I don't want to play anymore."

"It's the choice we've made."

"It's not *my* choice," I argued. "It was my parents' choice. They wanted to come here, and I still don't understand why. I don't even know who my parents are anymore thanks to you."

Toll didn't speak. I shouldn't have said that. I was angry with Odran, and I had unloaded on Toll out of convenience.

"I'm sorry. I just want it to be different, Toll. Tell me what's going on. What is that computer I found?"

Toll finally spoke. "Let's go for a ride," he said.

"I'm not in the mood this spoke, Toll."

"Please," he insisted. "There's something I want to show you."

"What is it? Can't you just tell me?"

"You have to see it for yourself."

I stared at the Samiran. I was telling my troubles to a gigantic swimming elephant. Could my life get any weirder? I pulled on the purple-black suit, and Toll moved so I could step onto the harness.

"I want some answers, Toll," I mumbled.

Toll pushed off and sped straight toward the horizon, straight to the spot with the strange lights he had taken me to the other cycle.

"That outfit you're wearing is a unique material. It's a living being. It will help you breathe," Toll told me.

"What do you mean?"

"Hold tight."

"But I can't swim!"

"Then don't let go," he said.

Toll dove downward, headfirst into the water. It was only a moment before the ocean swallowed me up. My first reaction was panic. I gripped the metallic harness tighter and held my breath. I braced for the cold I experienced the first time I fell in the tank, but it didn't come. I opened my eyes. I could see! The black material that covered my face was almost as clear as glass. But I could not hold my breath much more. *Toll must know this,* I thought. *How much longer is he going to keep me underwater?*

My eyeballs began to tingle as if someone was scratching them on the insides. I swallowed, searching for some last bit of oxygen. Instinctively, I gasped, expecting my lungs to be filled with water, but to my surprise, I could breathe! *That's impossible,* I thought. The air was thin, like that outside on the ring, but the material or alien or whatever was wrapped around my body seemed to adjust for my needs. Soon, I was breathing normally.

Toll swam deeper and raced along the floor of the tank. Creatures of all sorts inhabited the bottom. Long snakelike aliens covered with bristles kicked up the sand; round, bony creatures picked through the muck using long, thin tentacles and eating anything they could find. Milky-white aliens, each one just a big eye and a tapered tail, darted out of our way while still huddled together in a large group. I'd had no idea there was a whole other world at the bottom of the cooling tank.

Huge rocks, as big as mountains, loomed in front of us. Through the deep crevices in the boulders, I could see the mysterious lights I had seen from the surface. With one forceful stroke of his tail, Toll pushed up and over the underwater mountain. I could see enormous domed sheets of glass between the crevices and aliens moving inside.

It was a small city.

Toll dove under a large sheet of thick stone. Everything went dark for a moment, but when we came back up, we were in a pool in an open-air cavern.

"Amazing! Just amazing. Toll, what is this place?"

"Some people call it Toll Town," he said proudly.

Toll moved toward a smooth stone ledge. Standing there was an alien about my height. He was thin and pale with a fleshy, round face and long arms. He waved with both hands as he saw Toll and me.

"Who's that?" I said.

"That is Tang. He will be your guide during your visit to Toll Town."

Then six more aliens approached and took seats on tall chairs around the pool of water. They carried none of the snobbery of the Trading Council or the pageantry of the Keepers. In fact they were dressed more like knudniks. Tang was even wearing a vest like mine, but it was scratched and tattered.

"I have some business to deal with, and then I will take you back," Toll said to me.

"But I thought . . ."

"Tang will answer all of your questions," he said as I slipped off the harness.

"Hello," said Tang, stepping forward. "You must be Johnny Turnbull?"

"I am, but everyone calls me JT."

"You can call me Tang," he said, and bowed slightly. "Will you follow me?"

I looked back and nodded to Toll as I left with the alien. I asked Tang, "Is this place linked to the central computer? How do we understand each other?"

"Toll Town is not linked to the central computer. We have our own."

"Is that the computer I pushed into outside the tank?"

"I was informed of your softwire abilities. You are very lucky. Yes, I believe you were inside our computer. Many people who have come through Toll Town over the rotations have done quite well in other planetary systems. They have repaid their gratitude with generous gifts that let us maintain such a powerful computer as well as our extraordinary living arrangements."

Tang wasn't kidding about generous gifts. We left the water portal where Toll and I had surfaced and passed through a small stone archway that opened into a common area. Narrow streets twisted through enormous rocks, each carved with images depicting aliens on some sort of adventure. Some rocks were completely covered as if they were trying to tell entire stories. The same crystals that hung in the important buildings on Orbis 1 illuminated the street vendors handing out food as Tang led me through the slender laneways. It was obvious that Toll had some very wealthy friends if they paid for all of this.

"Would you like some?" Tang asked, holding out a pouch of toonbas he had taken from a street vendor.

"My sister loves these," I told him.

"Tasty, aren't they?"

"But I don't have any money to pay for them," I said.

"They are free. Everyone does what they can here while they wait," Tang said.

"Wait for what?"

Tang paused on an amber crystal bench next to a water sculpture that changed form, starting as a small Samiran and then breaking apart into a planetary system I couldn't recognize.

"Toll Town is a haven. A safe place for those like you and me who no longer want to stay in the corrupted work system on the Rings of Orbis but do not want to die at the hands of their Guarantors either."

I understood the reference all too well. It was spoken of many times, even before we arrived on Orbis. Disobeying the work rule or trying to escape from your Guarantor meant only one thing—death. Theylor had warned us of this, as had Drapling and Madame Lee. Everyone we met had, for that matter. We had no say in it. Once a work deal was made, there was only one way out of it.

"You were a knudnik?" I asked.

Tang winced when I said that word but nodded.

"So everyone here has left their Guarantors? They've escaped?"

"Not completely," Tang said. "They're waiting here for passage—safe passage—off the ring. It is very difficult to do this. The central computer knows everything that happens on the Rings of Orbis, and we must prepare extensively for each departure. Some people have lived here a whole rotation before they were able to sneak away."

Max was right! The alien I'd seen on Toll's back—he must have been trying to escape on the crystal flier. Did Varocina know about that?

"I saw someone," I said. "He escaped when they delivered the last crystal."

Tang's shoulders drooped, and he looked away.

"He didn't make it, did he?" I asked.

"I am afraid not. The Trading Council does not like to lose. They are aware that many of their possessions try to escape, and they are very vigilant. Someone betrayed that alien that you are referring to. We do not know who, but we are worried. That is why it is very important that you never speak of this place, even to your friends."

Did Toll show me this place because he was offering me the chance to escape?

"If you cannot make this promise, I cannot let you go back," Tang said. He was dead serious. His eyes stared straight into my brain as if he were trying to burn the image into my mind.

"You mean I would have to stay down here?"

"Toll took a great risk to show you this. He must have his reasons, but I cannot let you risk the well-being of so many others."

"Listen, Tang," I said. "I promise you I won't tell anyone. In fact, I would like to help you."

Tang smiled and his eyes widened. "That is excellent news. We have been waiting for someone of your abilities. It has put such a strain on our resources to communicate with the Samirans and even then we are not always accurate. This is a great cycle," Tang exclaimed, jumping up. "Come, I've picked out a wonderful place for you to stay."

"Stay?" I stopped him. "Tang, I can't stay. You misunderstand me."

There was that look again.

"What if I brought everyone?" I said. "If I could bring all of my friends and the other human children, we could escape together."

"That is too many at once, I'm afraid. And after the first group went missing, the others would surely be quarantined," he argued.

"Tang, you don't know how badly I want out of my situation, but I came here this cycle just to get some answers. When I saw that person climbing to the flier, I thought he might be trying to escape. It made me jealous. I wanted to be that brave and change what others did to me. But I have a sister who needs me. My friends are still on this ring. I can't abandon them. I'm sorry."

"Let me show you something," he said. "Come this way."

I followed Tang between buildings carved from the thick, reddish rock and glanced above me. Glass spanned the crevices between the rocks, creating a crystal dome. The pale green water from the cooling tank flowed on the other side of the glass, covering us in a turquoise blanket.

Tang entered a slender building made of plain stone and metal. The inside of the structure looked like the nursery on the seed-ship, with hundreds of sleepers sprawled out on the floor. I saw about forty aliens and their families sitting on the lids of their sleepers with their meager belongings scattered about them. Some sat on the floor, scratching symbols and circles into the metal floor and even on the plastic dividers that separated some of the sleepers. Most of the others, however, seemed to be doing the same thing—waiting.

"We place everyone here when they first arrive. They must wait while we process them and find a more stable environment for them inside Toll Town," Tang informed me.

"Process?"

"We work very hard to remove every record of them inside the central computer. This makes it harder for their Guarantors to catch them," Tang answered.

"What do their Guarantors do?"

"Different methods are used. Some Citizens send their runaway a screen scroll. They then scan for the location of the discarded message and send a search party to that location. They drag the person back only to enforce the severest penalty entitled to the Guarantors."

I looked around me at the aliens waiting here. I'd seen these faces before, many times throughout Orbis. They were the faces working in the trading chambers, the faces loaded down with packages following Trading Council members—the faces of my friends slaving away at Odran's.

I noticed one small creature with a bio-wrap around his damaged arm, or tentacle—I couldn't tell which. Both of his legs were encased in a glass and metal machine that looked very similar to Odran's tank. The alien's mother seemed to be crying uncontrollably.

"Why is she crying like that?"

"Her oldest child was stained by their Guarantor. We could not allow her to bring him. The staining makes it very easy for the Citizens to track their laborers. She was forced to leave her child behind."

"What happened to the young one?" I asked.

"His skin is very valuable to some of the Citizens."

"They cut his skin off?"

Tang raised his hands motioning me to be quieter. "Medical attention is a big part of the process," he whispered. "Some Guarantors treat these people worse than machines, especially the ones they get for free."

"Free? But we're repaying our parents' debt."

"Yes, but some Citizens get workers in a trade, or a Citizen may pass into the cosmic stream and leave their possessions—including their workers—to their children."

"You mean when a Guarantor dies?"

"Yes," Tang replied.

"Don't the Keepers stop this?"

"They don't know most of what goes on anymore. There are simply too many Citizens and too many of us."

I couldn't take my eyes off the young alien. "My Guarantor lives inside a similar device," I said.

"Odran suffered the exact same fate. Did you not know?"

"Odran was a knudnik?"

"Yes, but he has grown corrupted. Worse than most Citizens you can find on Orbis. I thought Odran's plight would have softened him to our cause, but I'm afraid his heart is as thick as this stone that holds back the cooling-tank water."

"Thicker," I mumbled. "Just be glad Odran doesn't know you are here."

"We have no fear of Odran," Tang replied.

I could not imagine Odran and this alien sharing anything

in common. In fact I couldn't imagine Odran having a single thing in common with *anyone* in this room. I looked across the sea of sleepers and tried to imagine these aliens in a happier time, before they decided that life would be better on Orbis. How could all these people be so blind to the real Orbis? How could my parents be so blind? I wished they were here at this very moment so I could ask them why—why am I here?

"There doesn't seem to be a word for . . . for *what* we are," I said. "What we are to *them*, I mean. Everyone uses the word *knudnik*, but I know that's a slang word. What do the Citizens really call us?"

Tang said a word that did not translate.

"I don't understand," I said.

"Different cultures have different expressions for the labor arrangement that exists on Orbis. Some cultures, like yours, try to use the word *slave*, although that is not completely accurate. Initially, work on Orbis is a voluntary process. People want to come here. They sacrifice willingly. In other cultures the 'sale' or 'trade' of one's freedom for the pursuit of money is simply unthinkable. The idea is so alien to them that there isn't even a word for it."

"I wish I could live there," I said.

"But in some cultures, like here on the Rings of Orbis, it's perfectly normal," Tang continued. "To them you are merely an object to possess, for whatever reason. In their minds, you belong to them until your work rule is complete. What they call you is of little importance. Most Citizens call their workers by the task they perform, as they would any common utility device. If you don't like this, they really don't care."

I walked through rows and rows of sleepers and saw many aliens anxiously waiting to run away. Some even looked happy to me. The deep sadness I often saw in the trading chambers seemed to be replaced here with hope.

"For some it may only get worse," Tang warned. "They are not equipped to be on their own, and I am afraid there exists far more dangerous threats to their well-being than the Trading Council."

I couldn't imagine what those threats were, but I had learned long ago to never doubt anything on the rings.

"I want to help, Tang, but I have to do it out there," I said, and pointed up. "I never want my sister or my friends to end up broken like this. I can't imagine that my parents would have brought us here if there was even the chance this might happen."

"I'm afraid there is not much you can do from out there, but in time I will understand," Tang replied. "Come. Toll is waiting."

More food vendors lined the street that led back to the water portal. We stopped when one alien asked Tang for a moment of his time. A nearby vendor was graciously offering up sacks of toonbas, and I thought of my sister.

"Would you mind if I took some for my sister, Tang?" I asked, but he was busy in conversation.

He won't mind, I thought, and accepted a pouch of the treats from the vendor. I tucked them inside my vest. I knew Ketheria would love them.

Toll was waiting for us at the water portal. Tang looked at the Samiran, and then hung his head. They must have spoken of this arrangement before. They were simply waiting for the right time. It made me feel uncomfortable knowing that they had planned this meeting. Was everything an elaborate scheme? Showing me the lights, telling me how to bypass the security? Even the story about my father?

"There is one more thing," Tang said, and reached into his pocket. He pulled out a small, transparent digi. He tapped the silicon sheet and a picture blinked on the screen. I recognized Toll. The man sitting on top of him looked familiar, too.

It couldn't be.

I looked at Toll and then at Tang. He closed his eyes. "Yes, it is," he said.

My father?

I stared at the picture again. The man sat on top of Toll the same way I did. He was a big man, bigger even than Charlie, with thick, dark hair and massive shoulders. He looked human, very human, even with the Space Jumper's belt around his waist and the helmet resting on his lap. I couldn't help but stare at the photo.

"Is this really him? Is this my dad?"

There was a photo of my father in the files on the *Renaissance,* but it was only a headshot—a rank-and-file photo file for the ship's records, nothing more. Even though this digi was small, it showed what my father must have been like. I stared at his eyes and the slight grin on his face. My father looked strong and fearless to me.

"I'm afraid that digi must stay here," Toll said.

"You will not be able to explain where you got it," Tang added.

I looked at both of them. *But what about Ketheria?* She deserved to see this, too. "I want to show my sister," I protested.

"I'm sorry," Tang said knowingly.

"We must go now," Toll said. "The others will begin to worry."

My fingers would not release the digi. I concentrated on it. I wanted to burn the image into my brain. I looked at my father sitting atop Toll as if they were friends, good friends. Odran was wrong. I was right to trust Toll. I handed the photo back to Tang.

"Thank you," I told him. "But now I have a million more questions."

"Good," Tang said. "Then I know I will see you again, my new friend."

"You will."

I climbed back onto Toll in a daze. I finished pulling on the protective suit, and Toll slipped into the water. Before I went under, I got one more look at the city.

14

I sprinted down the stairs of the cooling tank. I knew I couldn't tell a soul about Toll Town—I couldn't even tell Ketheria about the digi I'd seen of our father—but the excitement of knowing what I'd seen kept my feet moving all the way back to the dormitory.

No one noticed me enter. Most were huddled in groups with their backs to me.

I saw Theodore. "What's going on?" I asked.

"I told them they shouldn't do it," he replied.

"Do what?"

"Play with the food."

"Don't let him get away!" another kid shouted as a small alien sprang up and tore across the dormitory floor. It was pink with at least eight arms or legs, but no eyes. Two long tentacles sprouted from one end of the thing and were flickering about in the air.

"What is that?" I asked.

"That's what we feed to the Samirans," Theodore said.

"Not anymore," someone else replied.

"But that was on the work order," I said. "If Odran finds out . . ."

"Switzer said that as long you can talk to that big fish, we don't have to do our chores," another kid said.

"Well, Switzer's not in charge," I snapped, reaching down for the alien as it scrambled past. It wriggled from my grasp, ran up my arm, and socked me in the chin. "Ow!"

"That's nothing," Theodore said.

"We have to put them back," I said. "Come on—help me get them back to wherever they're supposed to go."

The other kids were laughing at me as I tried to round up the creatures. They were fast! I was never going to catch them by myself. I looked around for Max's help, but she wasn't there. Neither was Ketheria.

"Where's Ketheria?"

"She's with Max," he said. "Switzer and Dalton gave out a bunch more orders and then they left. Max waited a bit before she took off after them."

"She didn't take a rope with her, did she?"

"Yes, how did you know?"

"Theodore!"

He jumped off his sleeper and then straightened out his sheet—twice. Then he mumbled "You don't think she would have—"

"And by herself," I yelled. "Why didn't you go with her?"

"I had chores to do," he argued, looking around at all the mess.

"You didn't want to go down that hole again," I said, and Theodore stared at his feet.

"What about Ketheria?" I asked.

"I think Max needed some help with the—"

"Come on!" I said, and grabbed Theodore by the vest. I pointed at one of the boys. "Round those things up and put them back where they came from."

"No," he said.

I had no reply. I wasn't going to beg. I heard another kid snicker.

"What are you going to do? Zap me with the enabler, too?" he taunted me.

Still I had no reply. I stood there staring at the kid. *Is this how it starts?* I wondered. First we refuse to work, then the Citizens start to punish us—we grow resentful and then end up in Toll Town?

"No, I'm not," I said. "But Odran will."

I dragged Theodore out of the room and through the building faster than a light drive. It took me a little time to get my bearings, but I finally found the stairs that led down to the tunnels.

"Maybe they didn't go there this time," Theodore said, but I knew he was only trying to get out of going down to the tunnels.

"Just stay close," I told him.

I charged down the stairs, each step lighting up as I went. I chose the center tunnel, still running. I couldn't believe Max would take Ketheria. Was she crazy? What did she think Switzer had found down there? Max's curiosity really got the best of her sometimes, I thought. I only hoped Switzer wasn't trying to escape. Not with my sister.

"Ketheria!"

When I found them, my sister and Max were tying the rope to a metal grate over the open tunnel. There was no sign of Switzer or Dalton.

"What are you doing, Max?" I snapped.

"Hey guys, good timing," she said.

"Good timing? Are you crazy, taking Ketheria down there?" I said.

The girls looked at each other.

"Why are you acting so weird?" Max said.

"Me?" I wasn't acting weird.

"Yeah. What's wrong?" Ketheria said.

"It's dangerous; that's what's wrong. Theodore's right this time, guys," I argued.

"Then help us," my sister said.

Both of the girls just looked at me.

"No one's gonna get hurt," Max tried to assure me. "Besides, this is the most interesting thing I've done since we've been here. You get to work with the Samirans, but we're basically waiting around doing nothing except getting beaten up by Toll's dinner."

I looked at Max. I wanted to tell them about Toll Town, about the alien with the skin and how the families were broken apart. I wanted to warn them somehow so they wouldn't do this, not this way.

But I didn't.

"All right," I said. "But I go first."

"No, you don't," Max protested. "After me."

"Then me," Ketheria chimed in.

"I'll wait up here," Theodore said. "And keep the light on."

I stood next to Max. "Whew! You guys reek."

"You don't know the half of it," Max said as she held up a portable light. "Here, hold this. Ketheria got it from Odran's room."

I looked at my sister. "Now *you're* stealing?"

"It's not stealing if you bring it back," she replied.

"Ready?" Max said.

"What do we do?" I asked.

"Tie onto the grate with the rope, leaving enough rope in case you slip. Then lean out and grab the chain," Max told us.

"In case you slip? You're nuts," Theodore exclaimed. Ketheria was already tying up.

"I want to know what those two found," Max said.

We did what Max said, but she couldn't reach the chain. Max stretched out as far as she could, but it was no use.

So Max jumped.

"Max!" I screamed.

As her feet left the edge of the hole, my mind flashed to the escaping alien jumping for the cable under the crystal flier. He missed the first time and so did Max. She caught the chain but could not hold tight. She slipped down the chain and the darkness swallowed her up.

"Max!" Theodore yelled.

The chain jerked and then held still.

"I'm all right," she yelled back.

Ketheria shone the light on her. Max had managed to jam her foot in one of the rings that ran the length of each chain. She clung to the chain just below our feet.

"Be careful," she warned us. "It's a little slippery."

"I can see that," I said.

"You're insane," Theodore told her. "I'm staying right here."

"Suit yourself. Here, catch." Max grabbed another chain, gave it a yank, and flung it toward Ketheria. She caught it on the first try.

"How are you going to get off the chain now?" Theodore said. I think he was hoping Max hadn't thought of that.

"Easy," Max replied, and she tied the rope from the metal grate to her chain. She used it to pull herself back to the edge.

"Oh," Theodore muttered.

Once we were on the chains, we looked at Theodore, still standing at the edge of the tunnel.

"We'll be back in a bit," I told him.

"Maybe longer," Max added, and took the light from Ketheria.

"What's longer than a bit?" Theodore said. "Wait—I'm coming, too." And he tied off.

Once all four of us were secure, I carefully lowered myself down the tunnel. As we moved deeper, the crystal light cut into the grimy, tiled walls, following us from the main tunnel. Chunks of garbage were stuck in grates that punctured the walls, and there was a thin coat of slime on everything.

The air grew increasingly damp the deeper we went. We moved down the chain through a layer of mist just like the thin clouds that were at the center of Orbis 2. There was no bottom in sight.

"Let's go back," Theodore complained. "There's nothing down here."

"No, look," Max said, and shone the light on another, larger, opening in the tunnel right below her.

Ketheria clambered back up her chain.

"There's nothing. Don't be scared," Max yelled after her.

"No, wait," Ketheria said. "Do you hear that?"

We hung motionless in the air, but no one heard anything.

"There. Shine the light there," Ketheria said, pointing to a hole in the tunnel that was once covered by a grate. The grate now dangled from a single bolt.

Max shone the light into the hole. There *was* something there. I could see it squirming under the garbage and debris.

"Nugget!" Ketheria screamed. "I knew you were here."

It happened very quickly. When Nugget heard Ketheria's voice, he lifted his head from under the trash and shielded the light with his big, clumsy hands. Once he saw Ketheria, Nugget sprang toward her and launched himself from within the hole. There was no doubt that he would make it; I was only concerned that Ketheria wouldn't be able to hold on once Nugget grabbed her.

"Hold tight, Ketheria!" I shouted.

Grunting under the impact of the heavy load, she beamed and yelled, "I've got him."

My sister wrestled one arm through the metal ring in the chain and used the other to hold on to Nugget. He was as big as she was now but far more muscular.

"Kechera, Kechera, Kechera!" Nugget repeated over and over.

"He remembers me," she said, glowing.

"What do we do now?" Theodore said, staring at the alien.

"We keep going," Max replied, and pushed deeper down the tunnel.

"Ketheria can't carry him," I told her.

"It's OK, Nugget; you're safe now," my sister whispered. "You can stay with us forever."

I wasn't sure if Odran would agree with Ketheria's hospitality.

"Nugget, catch," Theodore said as he swung a chain toward him.

It bounced off Nugget and clanked back and forth. Nugget reached out and grabbed it.

"See? He knows what to do. C'mon, Nugget—we're exploring. Come with us," Ketheria said.

The little alien hesitated until he saw all of us doing the same thing. Gone from his eyes was the meanness I had seen when he used to order us around Weegin's World. Weegin must have abandoned him—or worse, Weegin was dead.

"Wait," Nugget barked. He turned back to the hole. "Inal!"

"What's he saying?" Theodore said.

"I don't know," I replied.

"There is someone with Nugget," Ketheria said.

A small creature with fierce blue eyes and patches of white whiskers poked out from under the same spot where Nugget had been hiding.

"Friends, Inal," Nugget said.

"I don't remember being Nugget's friend," Theodore said.

Inal was the same size as Nugget and had feet like hands. The alien was wrapped in a soiled rag, but his Guarantor's skin was still visible. Inal was a knudnik.

He looked at us cautiously without saying a word, then he asked, "Do you have food?"

"No, we don't. I'm sorry," I told the alien.

"Do you know where any is?"

"Come with us," Ketheria offered. "We'll get you some food."

"Food!" Nugget yelped. "I want food."

"I don't know if this is a good idea, JT," Theodore complained.

I thought the same thing. Inal had obviously escaped from his Guarantor. Someone must being looking for him. I just didn't know what he was doing with Nugget.

"I found another tunnel!" Max shouted. She was three meters below us, swinging wildly on her chain. I looked at Inal.

"Come with us, Inal. We'll find you some food," I said.

"And how do we get over there, Max?" Theodore shouted down the tunnel to her.

"Like this." Max swung on her chain slowly, picking up momentum as she neared the hole. Ketheria did the same.

"Be careful!" I warned.

Max grabbed a grate above the tunnel and let go of the chain, dangling above the opening, and over the huge hole below us. With a swing and a jerk, she landed on the edge of the opening—the very edge. She waved her arms to steady herself and then safely slipped inside.

"Come on—swing over, Ketheria. I'll grab you."

"You *are* crazy," Theodore told her.

"I'm here, aren't I?" she said, proud of what she was doing. She caught Ketheria's chain on the first attempt and helped Ketheria into the tunnel. It was just like the one we left, a hundred meters above us.

"Push Nugget's chain," Ketheria ordered Theodore. The alien leaped at Ketheria well before he should have.

"Nugget!"

He knocked Ketheria flat on her back, but he was safe. Inal was much more graceful than Nugget. He leaped from the hold and shimmied down the chain all in one motion.

"I don't think that was the first time he's done that," Theodore whispered, but Inal still heard him.

"I am a female. Can you not tell?"

Actually I couldn't, but I didn't say anything. Instead, Theodore and I followed Inal into the opening, and soon we were all heading down another tunnel. This one sloped upward, but the light that had followed us in the other tunnel did not turn on. Max shone her light along the tunnel walls.

Scratched onto the walls were circular symbols and spirals. Some drawings looked like waves, while others looked like the markings I'd seen on the faces of Nagools.

"Someone's been here," Max said.

"I've never seen stuff like this before," Theodore said.

I had, on the walls in Toll Town. Circles and sketches made by those waiting—bored or burdened with the desire to leave their mark before they left. I wondered if the same aliens hiding in Toll Town had made these.

The tunnel sloped down and then turned to the right. More debris and junk littered the ground, and now the circle drawings completely covered the walls. The tunnel ended with three more choices, just like before.

"Which way do we go?" Theodore asked, and we all looked at Ketheria.

"Why are you looking at me?" she asked.

Nugget yanked on Ketheria arms and pointed to the tunnel on the left. "I'm hungry!" He charged down the tunnel, dragging Ketheria with him.

"Er, nice to have him back, isn't it?" Max said.

Ketheria and Nugget walked ten meters, and then the ground they were walking on simply gave away.

"Ketheria!"

We ran to the hole in the floor. It was covered with garbage.

"Ketheria! Can you hear me? Are you all right?" I shouted down the hole.

"Yeah, I'm fine—just jump!" she shouted back.

"Someone did this," Theodore realized, picking up a piece of plastic just large enough to cover most of the hole.

"I think someone is trying to hide it, too," I added. "And look at that rope."

Tied to a metal ring at the edge of the hole was a red rope, knotted just like the one we had seen tied to the grate at the top of the main tunnel.

"Switzer?" Max wondered aloud.

"Who else?"

"This is not the way," Inal said.

"The way to what?" I asked, but Inal did not respond. She looked at me, her eyes narrowing as if she was searching for something. Inal took my hand and turned it over, examining my palm.

Unsatisfied, she dropped my hand and said, "What are you doing in the tunnels?"

"Looking for our friends," I told her, grabbing Inal's hand. On her palm, cut into her flesh was a circle with a symbol in it—sort of an upside-down letter *V.* I saw this same symbol on the walls in the tunnel. I had also seen it everywhere in Toll Town.

"What does that mean?" Theodore asked, but Inal said nothing. She pulled her hand back, hid it under her clothes, and ran back the way we had come.

"Inal, wait!" Max yelled, but I knew what the symbol meant. She was on her way to Toll Town.

"Let her go," I said.

As I watched Inal running through the tunnel, I realized

that the tunnels must have been some sort of filling or drain-
ing system for the cooling tank at one time. Even now for all
I knew. But I also figured that knudniks like Inal must use
them to find their way to Toll Town. Maybe they followed the
symbols on the walls left by others who had already made the
journey. Inal must have scratched the symbol into her skin so
she would not forget it.

I turned away and jumped into the hole. It was a quick
drop that landed me next to Ketheria and Nugget in a puddle
of stinky water.

"You all right?" I asked.

Ketheria nodded. "I hope that water is not what it smells
like," she mumbled.

"Don't think about that," I said.

"JT!" Max shouted from the top of the hole.

"It's all right. Come on!" I shouted back, and stepped
aside. Max landed hard.

"Eww!"

"Better move," Ketheria said, but it was too late. Theodore
was not going to wait long at the top by himself. He landed
right on top of Max.

"Cute," I said.

Theodore got off Max without ever touching the water.

"You guys stink," he said.

"And you don't?" I said.

"Where are we?" he asked.

"We're back at the beginning," Ketheria replied.

"What do you mean?" Max said.

"Core City," I told her. "This is where Weegin tried to sell us. Those are the waterways we traveled along to the arena Weegin took us to. See?" I pointed in the dark. The water glowed red from the crystals in the walls.

"Then I don't want to stay here very long," Max said.

"*Clack* Inal?" Nugget asked.

"The central computer doesn't work here," Max said.

"She went a different way," I told Nugget, but it was obvious he couldn't understand. "But she said to say good-bye."

Nugget took Ketheria's hand.

"Which way are we gonna go?" Theodore asked.

We all looked at Nugget.

"Nugget, where's the food?" I asked him. The little alien cocked his head, frowning. I opened my mouth and pointed to it. "Food!"

Nugget grabbed Ketheria's hand and stomped through the red shadows.

"Do you think he knows?" Max said.

We followed Nugget until he left the main waterway and slipped through a jagged crack in the moss-covered wall.

"Wait. Where's he going?" I asked.

"C'mon—Nugget knows the way," Ketheria said, and slipped through the crack. We all followed her into a completely dark tunnel.

"Ketheria?" I called out for my sister, feeling my way along the damp wall.

"Right in front. Keep going," she replied.

The tunnel narrowed, and I was forced to duck. Soon I was on my knees, crawling along the damp rock.

"There's no way Switzer came this way," Theodore complained.

The crack opened up, and I found myself standing in an alley behind some buildings in Core City.

"Food!" Nugget yelped, and stormed ahead, dragging Ketheria with him. Along the wall of one building were three pipes running up from the ground and into the building. The center pipe had some sort of entry spout that was capped. Nugget used his thick claws and his teeth to pry it off.

"Nugget!" Max yelled.

The little alien looked up as the sludge from the pipe sprayed out of the seal he had just cracked.

"Nugget, that's garbage," Ketheria said, and tried to coax him away.

"Food," Nugget argued, pointing.

Theodore stuck his finger in the spray. "He's right. It's the same slop Odran feeds us."

Suddenly a door on the building disappeared. A small alien with a wide, sloped forehead stepped through, carrying a box that was far too big for her. She placed it on the ground and looked at Nugget. When she saw what he was doing, she reached into the box and pulled out something that looked like a piece of fruit.

"This tastes better," she whispered, offering the fruit to Nugget.

Before Nugget could take it, though, another alien emerged from the building. It was a Trefaldoor, and its bulk dwarfed the knudnik. The Citizen saw what she was doing and swiped the fruit from her hand.

"How dare you steal from me!" the Trefaldoor growled, and knocked the fruit out of her hand. Then he stomped on it with his huge foot, crushing it under his weight. "Get back inside!" he shouted and struck the knudnik on the back, knocking her to her knees.

"Don't do that," I snapped.

"You're next if you don't get out of here," the alien replied.

"Let's go, JT," Theodore whispered.

"But he's hungry," Ketheria said, pointing at Nugget.

"Why should I care? Go back to your planet and quit steal-ing from me! Filthy knudniks," the Trefaldoor growled.

I stood there and stared at the Citizen. The Trefaldoor snorted and dragged his knudnik back inside. He was a cruel, selfish creature that only used his status to feed off others. The Citizens of the Rings of Orbis had no more right to be here than we did, but they set up the rules first and some-how tricked the rest of the universe to abide. I no longer admired the Citizens of Orbis. Why would anyone want to come here?

"JT, come on," Max pleaded. "No one knows we're here. I don't know what rules we've broken, but I'm sure Odran can name a few."

"How can he say those things?" Ketheria said.

Max grabbed Nugget and darted out to the main corridor.

"Ketheria." I urged my sister to follow us, but she stood and stared at the spot where the Citizen had stood. "Ketheria, come on!"

I grabbed Ketheria's left hand and pulled her toward Max and Theodore. Together the five of us rounded the building and emerged from the alley deep in Core City. A heavy transport vehicle filled with crystal miners rumbled toward us.

Max pointed and hollered, "There they are!"

Just down the street from us, on the opposite side, Switzer was standing outside a small trading chamber talking to the merchant. From where I stood, it looked as if they were arguing about something, but it was impossible to hear over the noise of the transport. Dalton stood behind Switzer, who was still clutching the mystery sack.

"Switzer!" Max yelled. Both he and Dalton looked up at us from across the street. Switzer thrust his hand into the sack and shoved Dalton down the street and away from us.

"Wait!" Max called out, and she darted in front of the transport to the other side of the street. I dragged Ketheria behind her, and Theodore followed. Switzer and Dalton were already moving, but Max was faster. When she was close enough, she grabbed Switzer by the vest.

"What are you doing?" she asked.

"Get off me," Switzer said, pulling his vest out of her grip and stopping to turn toward her. "It's none of your business what I'm doing."

"What's in that bag, then?" she asked.

Switzer ignored her questions. By now we had all caught

up with them. Dalton pointed at Nugget. "Where did you find him?"

"Did you follow us?" Switzer demanded.

"Of course not," I replied.

"Shut up, dumbwire."

"Why won't you tell us what you're doing?" Max said. "We're not going to tell anyone."

"Like I said, it's none of your business."

But Dalton spoke up. "We're trading," he boasted. Switzer rolled his eyes.

"Trading?" Ketheria said.

"Trading what?" Max asked.

Suddenly, Nugget reached out to grab the mysterious sack. Dalton snatched it away just in time and held it above Nugget's head, but just barely. Nugget kept hopping up and down, trying to grab the sack until Nugget finally kicked Dalton in the shins. The bag fell to the ground, its contents scattering everywhere. There were little pieces of stone with drawings on them, wires, and pieces of discarded metal, but not much more. Switzer scrambled to pick them up.

"That's just garbage," Max said.

"That's what you think," Switzer said in their defense.

Dalton rubbed his shins. "We've traded lots of things. Those dumb aliens love the little spiral drawings. We could have made a fortune off the stuff Weegin threw out."

"Shut up, Dalton," Switzer snapped as he finished scooping up their treasures.

"What have you gotten so far?" Max asked them. She sounded genuinely interested.

"Lots of stuff," Switzer said.

I couldn't put my finger on it, but Switzer looked different. He seemed more focused on his little treasures than on trying to insult us. He looked up and saw me staring at him. I waited for his insult, but it didn't come. A small stone with a spiral etched on it lay next to Theodore's foot. I bent down, picked it up, and passed it to Switzer.

"You missed this one," I said.

Switzer just looked at me. No comment. No insult. The kid I hated was gone. For the first time, I saw him as just another alien figuring out how to make Orbis work for him instead of the other way around. I thought of Toll Town. We could go there, all of us, even Switzer. I wanted to tell them, but I remembered my promise and I said nothing.

"Thanks," Switzer said, and put the rock into the bag.

"What kind of stuff, Dalton? We want to know." Max wouldn't give up.

Dalton put his hand in his pocket and pulled out a crystal. We all huddled around. It was smooth, with a smoky-yellow center and a brightly glowing edge. The symbol of Orbis was carved into the surface.

"Whoa!" Theodore remarked, his eyes as wide as I've ever seen them.

"It's beautiful," Ketheria said, and she tried to touch the engraving. Switzer snatched it away.

"Do you have to tell them everything?" he snapped at Dalton.

"We're not going to say anything. Calm down, Switzer," Max said.

"Yeah, don't worry," I tried to assure to him.

"Let us see it again. How much do you think it's worth?" Theodore asked.

Switzer palmed the crystal. It certainly looked expensive. As we stood around staring at it, Nugget suddenly reached out and snatched the crystal away with the speed of light. He was off and running before anyone knew what happened.

"Get him!" Switzer cried. "This is your fault," he growled at Ketheria.

"Nugget, come back!" Ketheria shouted as she ran after Nugget. We all chased after him, but Nugget was fast *and* he knew where he was going.

Switzer's nostrils flared, and his pupils bulged as he sprinted after the alien. I wanted to get to Nugget before Switzer did—who knows what he would do? Nugget darted around the street vendors, through archways, and under trams. The burly aliens relaxing from their shifts in the mines simply watched.

"This way, Ketheria!" Max shouted. "He went this way."

Switzer turned the corner ahead of Ketheria. I was a distant third but just in time to see Nugget scurry through a crack just past two arched doorways and then disappear into the wall. There was no way Switzer was going to fit—or so I thought. He hurled himself straight into the opening and disappeared behind Nugget.

"Switzer!" Ketheria screamed. "Don't hurt him."

Ketheria launched herself at the crack in the wall before I could protest.

Max and Theodore caught up to me. "You first," Theodore said, but I was already going.

The crack was another opening into the system of tunnels underneath Core City. But these tunnels felt even more deserted than the ones we had been in before. They smelled of things long forgotten. These tunnels smelled of death.

"Ketheria?"

The light running along the tunnel wall only flashed sporadically. In the blink of the unnerving blue light, I could see abandoned crates and garbage littering the tunnel. More drawings marked the curved walls, and I caught a faint whiff of the sickly sweet smell of the bio-bots. *We must be close to the cooling tank,* I thought.

"Ketheria!" I shouted

"Up here. Hurry!" she called out.

I heard Max and Theodore behind me. "Wait for us!" they yelled, but I needed to get to my sister. I forced my way through the garbage and some sort of thin, rubbery seal, as if someone had been trying to block off portions of the tunnel. I finally found Ketheria and Switzer.

"Let me through, freak," Switzer ordered her.

"I'll get him," she said.

Ketheria stood facing Switzer. Even though he was two heads taller than Ketheria she would not back down. Ketheria matched Switzer's every move as he dodged back and forth trying to find a way through.

"Leave her alone, Switzer," I said.

"I don't want her," he said. "I want that little rat."

"You want the crystal," I argued.

"I'll get you the crystal," Ketheria said.

"I can get it myself," Switzer spat.

I knew he could get it, but at what cost to Nugget? "I'll get it for you, all right?" I offered him.

"No chance, dumbwire."

"Where is he?" Max asked as she, Theodore, and Dalton caught up with us.

"That rat went in there, and I want what's mine," Switzer said, pointing to the pile of garbage behind Ketheria.

"Help me," I said to Max. "We'll clear this, and Ketheria can get the stupid crystal."

Switzer smirked. "You may think it's stupid, but I get enough of those and I'm off this alien work farm."

"Maybe in a gazillion years," Max scoffed.

"Let's just get this crystal first," I said, and heaved some of the garbage aside. Ketheria remained between Switzer and the pile of rubbish, never taking her eyes off him.

"There's a door back here," Theodore exclaimed, and he tossed a metal container down the tunnel.

"A door?" Max said.

"We find anything, it's mine!" Switzer shouted.

"I don't think so," she replied.

"Then we split it seventy-five–twenty-five. For me," Switzer continued.

"If we find anything, which we won't," I said, "you can have it all, all right?"

"Speak for yourself," Max protested.

"You wouldn't be here if it wasn't for me," Switzer argued.

"You wouldn't be here if it wasn't for Nugget," Ketheria reminded him. "Maybe he should get fifty percent of anything we find."

"That thing? Are you kidding me? He's probably trying to eat the crystal right now. He's too stupid to know what anything is. I'm gonna kill that little creep this time," Switzer said, pushing Ketheria aside and helping remove the garbage in front of the door.

"Maybe *you're* too stupid to know what anything is," Ketheria snapped. We all stopped.

Ketheria wasn't finished.

"It's time he stopped breathing chaos into everything we do. I'm tired of watching everyone live in terror around him. His veiled threats only hide his own selfish fears. The only life he cares about is his own. There is nothing but darkness that clouds his very being. I *wish* I could hate you!" Ketheria yelled.

We all just stood and stared, even Switzer. No one knew what to say. Ketheria had never spoken this much in her whole life. And she never said anything that mean. I actually think Switzer was afraid of her at that moment. Ketheria pushed Switzer back and kicked aside the last bit of rubbish.

She leaned into the door with her shoulder and gave it a shove. It moved just enough for her to squeeze through.

"Nugget, where are you?" we heard her shout from inside.

Max looked at Switzer and then at me. I still didn't know what to think. Dalton nudged Switzer.

"What?" Switzer spat.

"You're not going to let her talk to you like that, are you?" Dalton asked.

"Yes, he is," I said. "If he wants his crystal back."

"JT, look," Max whispered, pointing to a grimy plaque on the door. I could hardly make out the writing as the letters flashed between our language and some alien language.

"The central computer isn't working here either," Dalton said.

"Or maybe the sign is just broken," Switzer said.

"It says F . . . O . . . ." Theodore squinted to see the letters on the rusted plate.

"It says FORM, knudnik. This is a room for Forbidden Off-Ring Materials," Switzer said, and pushed Theodore aside. "Come on, Dalton. There must be a ton of stuff in here. Help me."

They both leaned on the door and shoved.

"Harder. This side—it's on a hinge," Switzer ordered. "Hurry." The door gave way with a loud thump.

It was definitely some sort of storage room, just like the one at Odran's. Rows of items were stored behind thick glass doors. Some items even gave off their own light, casting gold and green shadows around the room. Some things lay dead inside their glass coffins, while others defied description. I saw locked metal boxes, exotic glass jars filled with powder, and strange alien devices that could only be used as weapons, or so I thought.

"Who would leave this stuff behind?" Max asked no one in particular.

"Who cares?" Switzer answered, yanking at one of the glass doors. "Grab something to break this with, Dalton."

Switzer's mind now seemed focused on bigger and better things. Nugget and the tiny crystal were no longer on his agenda.

"Do you really think you should do that, Switzer?" Theodore asked.

"Do you really think you should do that, Switzer?" Switzer repeated mockingly. "Why do you act like such a little one? What's gonna happen to us if we get caught doing something they don't like? Look around you, knudnik. We're already in prison."

"It could be worse," I told him.

Switzer turned on me. "What? They'll *kill* us? Do you really think they would do that? Not with you here. You're their little favorite, always fixing things for them. As much as I figure, we've got a clean ticket thanks to you." Dalton handed Switzer a metal tube, which he immediately swung at the glass. It shattered into a million pieces. "Oh, and by the way, in case I've never said it, thanks. Now get out of the way if you're not going to help. This stuff has to be worth something."

"Here's your crystal back," Ketheria said. Nugget stood behind her, eyeing the crystal in her open hand.

Switzer pulled out a crystalline orb that pulsed in his hands. "You can keep it now. A gift for that little freak leading us here."

"JT, look at this," Theodore called out. I looked across the room to see Theodore pluck a thick, leathery belt out of a drawer.

I watched Theodore's eyes widen as he slipped the discarded treasure around his waist.

"This is one, isn't it, JT?" Theodore whispered, running his fingers along the tiny little compartments embedded in the belt.

I knew what it was; so did Max. We'd both seen one before. Theodore wished for one once, when Weegin received the fake replicator. He fantasized about using it to get off the ring.

"I think it is," I told him.

"Do you know how it works?" Theodore asked me, as if he was talking in his sleep. "It feels like it's alive."

I walked over to him. "Theodore, be careful."

The warning snapped Theodore out of his trance. He slipped the belt off and held it out for me.

"You're right," he said.

I cradled the Space Jumper's belt. Up close it looked like stone but felt as supple as water. The device was damp to the touch.

"Try it, JT. Use it to jump away from here and then come back and take us with you."

"You'd like that, wouldn't you?" Switzer growled. He walked over and snatched the belt away.

"Be careful with that thing," Max warned as Switzer tried it on.

"Shut up," he snapped, and we all backed away from Switzer. Even Dalton moved away.

"Switzer, listen," I said.

"No, you listen. This is the fastest way. This is my chance to get off this stupid ring," he said, pushing at anything he could find on the belt.

"Switzer, don't!" I shouted.

"Don't what?" he spat. "You only want the thing for yourself. Well, I'm the one getting out of here."

"What about me?" Dalton asked.

"Here," he said, and tossed the sack to Dalton. He didn't even hesitate to sell Dalton out. "Sorry, I might need the crystal where I'm going." And he snatched the crystal back from Ketheria.

"You don't know how to work it," Max said.

"Can't be that hard," he replied, caressing the belt.

Dalton stared at the sack Switzer tossed him. His hands shook. Dalton took Switzer's side even when he knew the malf was wrong. Switzer had used him. He looked up and tossed the sack back to Switzer. "Keep it," he mumbled.

"Suit yourself," Switzer replied.

Something inside me told me to make him stop. I *needed* him to stop. It felt wrong; it felt bad. But I didn't know what to say. I thought of Toll Town. I thought of all the aliens, who just like us, wanted away from Orbis. But I also thought of my promise—my promise not to tell anyone. Wouldn't Toll understand if I told them? I had to take that chance.

"There's another way, Switzer," I blurted.

"What other way?" he scoffed.

"What are you talking about? Another way for what?" Max said.

"To get off this ring," I told her. "I know how we can all leave. Right now. Together. And without that thing," I said, pointing to the Space Jumper's belt around Switzer's waist.

"You're lying," he said.

"I'm not. I've seen it. I've been there. Toll took me. He runs this place in the tank where other knudniks can go to escape."

There, I'd said it. I broke my promise.

"What are you talking about?" Max said.

I looked at Ketheria. She stared at me. *What are you saying?* Her eyes seemed to say.

I couldn't take it back now. I had betrayed Toll's trust. Something inside me hardened.

"Where did Toll take you?" Theodore asked.

"How?" Max added.

"But that water almost killed you," Dalton reminded me.

"And now you want us to believe you've been swimming in it? Get out of here. You're just afraid to use this thing," Switzer sneered. "Or maybe you like it here."

Switzer pulled at the belt and pried at its small compartments.

"Switzer, don't. I'm telling you the truth. Toll gave me a special suit to protect me. He took me there, I swear. Look!" I told him, and pulled out the bag of toonbas I'd gotten in Toll Town. "I got these there. Have you ever seen toonbas on Orbis 2?"

"Where did you get those?" Max exclaimed.

"Isn't anyone listening? In the tank. *In Toll Town.* This alien, Tang, already invited me to stay there. He couldn't let everyone come, but maybe we can convince him."

"He's not gonna do it for free," Switzer said. "Why do you think we've been trading for stuff? No one does anything on this ring for free, dumbwire. Look around you." Switzer tapped his finger to his forehead. "Start using it."

Then Switzer found something on the belt—a small blue crystal that glowed when his finger went near it. I froze, staring at him.

"Don't, Switzer," I whispered.

"All Space Jumpers are softwires," Theodore warned him. "You're not a softwire. Let JT try it first."

"You would like that, wouldn't you? Then your friend here can come back and get each of you," Switzer said. "I know you don't like me, Turnbull. I don't like you either, and I'm never going to trust you to come back for me."

Switzer tugged on the belt and went for the crystal imbedded in the alien material.

"Stop!" I yelled, and reached for Switzer with my right arm.

Everything happened very slowly. It was as if time stopped. Even the air ceased moving. The crystal on Switzer's belt sparkled and flashed a bright blue. The light spread out from the crystal and completely surrounded Switzer. My arm was now inside the glowing blue sphere. It went cold and I looked at Switzer. His pupils were dilated, and his mouth was frozen in a scream. For once Switzer really knew he'd done something wrong.

The white from his eyeballs clouded over his pupils, and his neck stiffened. His hair shot straight out and turned gray right before my eyes. I could see my arm, but I could no longer feel it.

Max screamed. Or maybe it was Ketheria. It was a slow-building scream, as if the sound waves took an eternity to reach my ears.

Then Switzer was gone. Completely. Vanished. There wasn't a trace of him. He got his wish. I don't know where he went, but he wasn't here anymore.

And my right arm was gone, too.

There was no pain—at first. Actually, I was shocked to look down my shoulder and not see my elbow or my hand. It was just gone—a perfectly neat slice just below my shoulder.

Then blood.

Then another scream, this time much quicker, much louder. Time rushed back like a rocket.

And then the pain. *Lots* and *lots* of pain. First I thought it couldn't get any worse, but the pain just kept coming.

That familiar blackness rushed forward. It started behind my eyeballs, creeping around the edges. I felt the toonbas slip from my left hand, and my knees went weak as the darkness shut down my brain.

Again?

"You can't begin to imagine the severity of this situation."

"None of this is my fault."

"Everything is your fault. They are your responsibility. Do I need to remind you where my orders come from?"

"We have had this argument before. This is where I remind you whom you are talking to."

"And this is where I tell you I don't care!"

"So the rumors are true?"

"Yes. The tunnels led to a refugee camp inside the crystal-cooling tank. It was quite impressive actually."

"The Council will be pleased."

"The children will have to be put down. They have broken Keeper decree."

"Before the Festival of the Harvest?"

"They were obviously trying to escape. The Council will want to use them as examples. The humans must be destroyed."

"The Softwire, too?"

"I know. It seems like such a waste."

"The big one won't like it."

"Despite what he thinks, it's not for him to like."

"The Softwire was at the camp. Where else would he have gotten these?"

"Candies? You're going to kill them over candies?"

"Keeper decree gives the Citizens full authority for this."

"They're children. And they're humans."

"Humans have yet to be proven useful. Contrary to what some may think, they are workers. Workers on Orbis under Keeper decree, nothing more."

"Are you kidding me? You? What if the Ancients are right? You more than anyone should understand this."

"The children have been questioned. They are the ones who are lying. None of them will explain the tear in the time stream before they were found. I see no alternative."

"The alternative is to fix the Softwire, destroy the camp, and get ready for the Harvest. Those tunnels need to be cleared anyway. Am I not right? . . . Am I not right?"

"The flow . . ."

"You have no intention of releasing the Samirans, do you?"

"We have every—"

"That bucket of bolts has deceived you. You're as bad as the Council."

Johnny Turnbull? Can you hear me?

   Vairocina?

   Yes.

   Where am I?

   Sleep now. It will be over soon.

I dreamed of a wave, like the waves in Toll's tank when they first dragged me out of the water. In my dream I could see everything, hear everything—the rushing water and the people shouting. But the sounds and images faded as I felt a wave of consciousness sweep across my body.

"He's getting stronger," someone said.

"When he's ready, I want all of them stained."

"Absolutely not."

"You have no choice. It's that or death."

"That's ridiculous! It's dangerous to stain them, let alone unfair. These children have done nothing. How can I convince you of that?"

"It has already been decided."

And then the deep, cold darkness took me under again. I dreamed of Toll Town. I dreamed of Tang. I wanted to be with them. People were leaving Orbis, and I wanted to go with them. Everyone was getting ready, even Switzer. I followed Tang through the streets of the underwater shelter. All the other aliens waved at us and smiled.

"Good luck!" one shouted.

"May your journey be guided by cosmic streams of love," a Nagool master said, his arms outstretched as he shuffled beside us.

"Where's Toll?" I asked Tang, but he would not respond. "Tang, where's Toll?"

I ran up next to Tang and reached out for his shoulder. He was cold. I turned him toward me and stepped back. His thin skin was streaked with blue tears, and his eyes glowed from excessive crying.

"This is your fault!" he screamed at me.

"What is?"

"That!"

Tang pointed over my shoulder to the buildings of Toll Town. Giant flying machines systematically destroyed each building. The flying monsters, all metal and bone, swung enormous chains, at the end of which were huge, gnarled spheres. When the balls struck, the building exploded, flinging debris everywhere.

Aliens screamed and ran from the monstrous machines, but Tang marched on through the flying chunks of concrete and metal. Water rushed in as the crystal ceiling cracked, but still I followed Tang.

He led us to the portal where I'd first arrived with Toll.

"There you go. Are you happy?" Tang said, pointing into

the water. But I could not look. I was afraid—afraid of what he was pointing at. Was it Toll? Was he dead? I could only look at Tang.

"Look!" he screamed, but I wouldn't.

"I didn't mean it. I didn't want to break my promise, but Switzer . . ." I looked at Max and Theodore, but they stared into the water; everyone stared into the water.

"JT?"

I couldn't look. *What if it was Toll?* my mind screamed.

"JT? Can you wake up?"

"Vairocina?"

The sound of my friend's voice yanked me out of my nightmare. I opened my eyes. Where was I? This was not my room. Silvery control panels lined the walls of the dimly lit space, and there was a medicinal smell to everything. My sleeper did not have a lid except for a dome that circled the headboard. A row of empty sleepers lined the wall.

I sat up. At least I tried to sit up, but my right arm offered no assistance. It simply lay at my side for a moment before moving, almost as if it possessed a mind of its own, a mind that wasn't paying any attention. A thick metal band of sensors and flickering lights clung to my arm a few centimeters above my elbow. I tugged on the device, but it would not budge.

I attempted to wipe the sweat from my forehead, but my arm felt like it was asleep, prickling before coming awake. And then, as if trying to catch up, my right hand did as I wanted and wiped away the sweat. It took a moment for the wetness on my fingertips to register.

"You are conscious ahead of schedule," a mechanical voice said, but there was no one else in the room. I knew that on the Rings of Orbis that didn't mean I was alone. "Keep the arm moving. That is exactly what you need."

"Who's there?" I said.

The dome that circled the head of my sleeper hummed to life. A thin, pale yellow energy field sprang from the headboard and engulfed my sleeper.

"I am here," a voice said, the energy shield sparkling with each word.

The outline of a round face collected in the field over my head. It darted back and forth as if reading O-dats in some dimension I could not see.

"What are you looking at?" I asked.

"Well, you, of course. I need to know why you are awake."

"My arm isn't," I informed him. "It's like my arm is still asleep. What's this thing around it?"

"That is not your arm," the computer replied.

"What do you mean it's not my arm?" I said.

"I mean . . . it's not *your* arm."

The round alien face in the energy field stopped over the center of my sleeper. Its large eyes looked in different directions at the same time while continuing to search controls I couldn't see. I willed my arm to move. Reluctantly it positioned itself in front of me. It certainly looked like my arm. I compared it to my left arm. It was identical in every detail except, when I held it up to the light, the arm was semitransparent. The light passed through my skin, making it appear grayer and slightly blue. I could see shiny silver bones, flickering lights, and computer hardware. He was right; this wasn't my arm.

"I did a nice job, won't you agree?"

"Who are you?" I demanded.

"Your species, if I have researched correctly, would call me the doctor, or *a* doctor, or even Doc."

"What does your species call you?"

"Oh, no need for flattery. I am a computer. I will give you the best care programmable."

"Did I hurt my arm?"

"You do not remember? One moment please . . . that's right. The incident has been dampened in your cerebral cortex. Your simple brain will take some time before the chemicals wear off. You will remember in time."

What was this computerized first-aid box talking about? The last thing I remember was coming back from . . . Where was I coming back from? I was . . . I couldn't remember.

"That arm, that very expensive arm, is the property of the Rings of Orbis," the computer doctor said.

"Orbis? Where is my real arm then?"

"I am restricted from giving you that information. Three fingers please."

"What?"

I did not understand. Why was my arm (yes, *my* arm—it was attached to *my* body)—why was it acting so weird?

"Please hold up three fingers. I need to run a diagnostic procedure to understand why you are awake."

I did as I was told. "I think my nightmare startled me," I said. I felt a little embarrassed. And then I felt embarrassed for being embarrassed in front of a computer. I tried to shake it off. After a moment my right hand extended three fingers.

"Explain 'nightmare,'" asked the doctor.

"Um . . ." I didn't feel like talking anymore.

"Now two fingers please," the doctor ordered, and my arm responded a little quicker. "Good, it should be normal in no time."

"When . . ."

"Now five fingers."

My hand responded instantly.

"Look at you," the doctor exclaimed. "It's wonderful, isn't it? Just wait until your arm starts doing things before you even realize you thought about it."

"How long have I been asleep?" I asked.

A single moment of time flashed in the front of my forehead before the computer could answer. It was very similar to the effect I feel when I push into a computer. I was standing in a FORM room with Switzer and my friends. Switzer put something around his waist.

"You're starting to remember, are you not?" the doctor asked.

"Yes."

"Good," it replied. "Soon you will remember everything."

"There are some things I need to understand," I said.

"And I will explain them," Charlie said as he entered the room. He clutched a small bag of toonbas in his left hand,

and he was smiling. He'd been gone for a long time, and there were so many questions I wanted to ask. I was glad to see him.

"Hi, Charlie," I said.

"Hey, buddy. How are you feeling?"

Before I could respond, a pain sprang from my fingertips to the very base of my brain. I looked at my new arm. Colored lights of red and yellow flickered just under my skin, pushing shadows across the metal bones. My body stiffened, and my eyes rolled back in my head. It happened so fast I didn't have time to scream.

"My apologies," the computer doctor said. "There were still several neural synaptic tests to perform before you awoke. Most of the hardware is linked using traditional wetwire methods, but it is your softwire capabilities that I must deal with now. I will try and warn you before it happens again."

"What is he talking about, Charlie?" The pain was subsiding.

"Just relax. You've been through a lot, my friend," he said.

"How long have I been unconscious?" I asked him.

"Quite some time, I'm afraid. It was necessary for the repairs they needed to do."

"What repairs? My arm? Tell me what happened to my arm."

"Here, I brought these for you," he said, diverting my question.

Charlie handed me the sack of toonbas.

"It's been a while since you've seen those, hasn't it?" Charlie said, and smiled again. It seemed forced, though. He was fishing for something. I could tell.

And then another flash. The bag of toonbas was in my hand, and I was showing them to Switzer. I was trying to convince him of something. Something we would get in trouble for. I looked back at Charlie. He stared at me. Did he know?

"Of course. They're Ketheria's favorite," I said. "She ate them all the time on Orbis 1."

"You ever seen them here?" Charlie asked.

What was he looking for? Then pain again, only this time stronger, much stronger. The pale yellow energy screen around my sleeper pulsed bright red.

"JT, you all right?" Charlie asked, but I could not answer. My arm was in control now.

"Emergency procedure," the computer announced. "Suspending consciousness immediately."

"Johnny!"

My mind tore away from the light. Blackness engulfed me once more as Charlie and the room slipped into a distant corner of my consciousness. I was alone again. Alone and dreaming.

20

In my dream I stood at the center of a bridge perched high across the thunderous waterfalls of Magna. I knew the Ancients had lived here once but now the Keepers resided underneath the city. I watched the water cascade over cliffs and pour through the streets, defying gravity whenever it pleased. The roar should have been deafening, but it sounded more like music, and the motion calmed me.

"I knew I would find you here," Vairocina said. Only now she wasn't a computer program; she was a real girl.

"Am I dreaming?"

"Oh yes," she said. "But that never stopped me before."

I smiled. I liked her company. "Can you answer some questions for me?" I asked her.

"I'll try."

"What's with my arm?"

"It was destroyed when the unstable time field Switzer activated removed him and your arm from this dimension," she said matter-of-factly.

"Where's Switzer?"

"It is impossible to say, but most likely he is dead. Only softwires can activate a Space Jumper's belt. It is extremely unstable, and no one can predict where a person without softwire abilities will go, if they go anywhere at all. None have come back to tell their story," she said. "I'm afraid your friend is dead, JT."

"He wasn't my friend," I told her. *But then why do I feel so bad?* I wondered. *Switzer's gone? He's dead?* "I'll never see him again, will I?"

"Does this bother you?" she asked.

"There are a lot of things that are bothering me," I said. "All those knudniks in Toll Town for one. So many people came to Orbis wanting something else, something better, and instead found themselves trapped. They'll risk their lives to get out of working in these horrible jobs for people who don't even care about them."

"The Keepers care about you," she said.

"But I don't work for them, do I? I don't think the Keepers know half of what's going on here. You know, coming to the Rings of Orbis was all I ever thought about."

"Me, too."

"But when I see those people, I can't stop asking myself why my parents would come here. And that's another thing. My father! For all I know, my father might *be* from the Rings of

Orbis. I can't even begin to comprehend that. It doesn't compute. And I don't even know who to ask for help with that one. It's driving me crazy, Vairocina."

Vairocina just stared at the waterfalls and said, "Maybe, in time, everything will be revealed to you. And maybe no one will ever know. You will be forced to carry this burden forever. But dwelling on it will not help you deal with the situation at hand. All that you talk about is outside your circle of influence. Your time with your friends, with Ketheria, and every moment you have on Orbis, right now, is what you need to concentrate on. That's all you really have. The rest will come to you when you are ready. It always does."

Switzer won't be coming back, I thought. But there were lots of kids on the *Renaissance* I never saw anymore. I didn't feel the same way about them. But then they weren't . . . dead. Switzer was dead. Why shouldn't I be happy? He conspired to make my life miserable, and he could no longer torment me. I should be celebrating, but I wasn't. My chest felt heavy, and it was hard for me to swallow.

And then I woke up.

Charlie was sitting at the edge of my sleeper.

"Switzer's dead, isn't he?" I asked, and Charlie nodded. "And my arm went with him. This is some fake robot arm. Am I right?" Charlie nodded again.

"But not just any arm," the computer doctor interrupted. "This arm has many advanced features that your species is incapable of. Along with pain, torque, and strength variances, you may upload digital files using your softwire abilities to store for transfer somewhere else. Isn't it wonderful? You are almost like a real, walking computer."

"I'd rather be a real, walking human, thank you," I informed him.

"I can appreciate that, but let me tell you, it was such a unique experience to build the neural net in accordance to your softwire abilities. I should show you—"

"Not now, please," I said to the computer. "Charlie, what does all this mean? What's happening?"

Charlie didn't answer.

"I heard you when they were working on me. I heard you arguing with someone. I heard lots of things, Charlie."

"And that is why we need to talk. Tell me where you got the toonbas, JT."

"So you know?"

"This is serious, Johnny. *Very* serious."

"Is Toll in trouble?"

"Why would Toll be in trouble?" he asked.

Charlie tilted his head slightly, focusing on me and waiting for my response. They were unaware of Toll's role in all of this. *They don't know everything*, I realized. I needed to be very careful with what I said. I knew Max and Theodore would not say a word. I needed to think. I needed to talk to my friends.

"I'm very tired right now, Charlie. Can we talk a little later?"

"But what about the questions you wanted answered," he said.

"I'm not the one asking the questions now," I replied.

Charlie leaned forward, his face warming as he whispered to me. "I'm your friend in all of this, Johnny. Do you understand that?" I nodded. "I'm on your side," he added for emphasis.

As Charlie left the room, I thought, *my side*. I really hated it whenever *sides* were chosen. I leaned back in my sleeper, examining my new arm and buying time until Charlie was well out of range.

"Vairocina?" I whispered.

She answered in my head without appearing. "Yes?"

"Can you get a message to my sister and my friends? Can you get them to come see me as soon as possible?"

The space bent in front of me, and Vairocina gathered into focus.

"They will not come," she said.

"Of course they will."

"They are confined to their quarters until the staining," she said, almost as if warning me.

"Staining?"

"It has been decided that every human child in Odran's possession will be tagged with a genetic stain. Your DNA will be marked with an inert codon—an amino acid that can be tracked by several legal, as well as illegal, devices."

I didn't know which was worse, her emotionless tone or her information.

"Can I remove it? Can I get rid of this stain?"

"Never," she said.

"Is it dangerous?"

"That all depends on who wants to find you."

"I won't let it happen. They can't do this to us. We're human beings," I said. Anger seeped out into my body, even my new arm. "Who do they think we are?"

"You are also their property," she argued.

"I did not need to be reminded of that."

I squeezed the railing of my sleeper and watched my knuckles whiten as the blood was forced from my hand. *There's blood in my new arm?* I squeezed harder, forcing all of the color out of my arm. I pictured the blood being forced out and spraying over an open void. The blood ignited flames that leaped out from some deep, dark part of me.

The railing under my right hand snapped like space-frozen plastic.

Did I do that? I looked at Vairocina. She too stared at the broken railing.

The computer doctor chimed in. "You will need to control the strength output of your new arm. It really is amazing. You have to let me show you how to use your softwire abilities with the interface I installed. Now you have access to pain thresholds, strength, torque, and temperature limits, as well as a host of other unique functions."

I stared at my new arm. *I think I can learn to like this.*

At the beginning of the next cycle, Charlie arrived again. Only this time he was here to escort me back to Odran's.

"Everyone is waiting," he said solemnly.

"To begin the staining?" I said.

"You know?"

"Vairocina told me."

I wanted to ask him if it would hurt, but I was embarrassed. I could take the pain. I could take anything they threw at me, but I still wanted to know if it would hurt.

A private shuttle waited at the steps of the medical building. I never saw anyone use a private shuttle on Orbis, not even Keepers.

"When are you going to tell me who you really are, Charlie?"

He looked at me and smiled but said nothing. Then he patted me on the head. It felt condescending.

"So much for 'sides,'" I replied.

Charlie chuckled as the shuttle pulled away. "You kids are smart," he said. "Smarter than any kids I've ever known. Smarter then they give you credit for."

I sat in silence as the shuttle glided out of the sunlight and into the dark blue shadow the ring cast upon the buildings. Some were tall, some domed, but every one was simply identified by different colored lights and nothing more. There were no frills to these buildings, as you might find at the Center for Wisdom, Culture, and Comprehension on Orbis 1. No, Orbis 2 was all about efficiency. It was a slick machine. A machine built for profit.

I sat and wondered what was going on in those buildings. Were there other knudniks being stained or forced to work for their keep? Were they longing to escape, too? I flexed my right hand. It felt alien. *I* felt alien.

"At the hospital, you asked if Toll was all right. Why? Does he have something to do with this?" Charlie asked, breaking my trance.

"No," I said quickly.

"You wouldn't tell me even if he did, would you?"

"There's nothing to tell," I told him, then accessed the interface the doctor had showed me to work my new arm. The small screen blinked into my mind's eye, and I poked around the controls the way someone would after installing a new program. Everything was automated, linked to my hypothalamus, and there were an amazing array of options at my disposal. I couldn't wait to show Max.

I saw the Samiran Caretaker's building in the distance. The massive dome curved up to the horizon. A rim of yellow light spread out just below the roof of the building.

"Why are you so against us being stained?" I asked Charlie. "I heard you arguing with someone back at that place."

The shuttle came to a stop, and Charlie got out and turned toward me.

"Like any civilization, Orbis has its problems. They are similar to many of the problems that made Earth such a horrible place. Greed, power, blind faith, all of these obsessions make people do things they shouldn't. Once you are stained you can never hide from this. You will forever be a target to those who use others for their own personal gain. I did not want that for you."

"I can look after myself," I told him. "Don't worry about me."

"And sometimes the stain can create problems within your own DNA," Charlie added.

"Like what?"

"Not so much with you but with your generations to come."

"That's what you're worried about. If I have children someday?"

"It's far more complicated than that, JT," he said, and turned up the steps. "Come—they're waiting."

With my questions conveniently avoided once more, I followed Charlie into the great hall and past the mountainous stairs that led to the top of Toll's tank. I looked into the water, eager to see my friend. At least I hoped he was still my friend, but there was no sign of the Samiran.

Skipping across the surface of the tank were ten slope-winged aircraft, each with a trio of rotating searchlights, sifting through every drop of water. My heart sank to my stomach as what I feared most was happening right before my eyes.

"What are they searching for?" I asked Charlie, knowing full well the answer.

"Why don't you tell me?" he said, looking at me for a reply, but I offered none. "We don't have to play this game, you know."

"What game?" I could not break my promise to Toll—not again.

Max and the other kids were waiting behind Odran when we arrived in the dormitory. Six Keepers hovered near a strange device I'd never seen before. Theylor and Drapling were among them and looked up as we arrived.

Ketheria ran up to me the moment she saw me.

"Be still!" Odran shouted, but Ketheria didn't listen. She threw her arms around me and squeezed as hard as she could. Odran glared at us. His bloodshot eyes told me that he was angry. I had failed at my job on Orbis 2, and I didn't think he was going to let me forget it.

"Are you all right?" Ketheria asked.

"I'm fine."

I looked at my sister. There were small scratches and bruises on her face and arms. I looked at the other children. They looked battered and bruised also.

"The work is getting tougher," she whispered. "The Harvest will be here soon."

"Where's Nugget?"

"He's hiding in our room."

"I want to begin," Odran demanded.

Charlie led Ketheria and me back to the group of kids and then stood with the Keepers. He looked at Odran and then turned his back to him as he spoke with Theylor. Odran was forced to move. This was surely an insult to Odran.

Max and Theodore missed all of this. They surrounded me with a barrage of questions. Grace pinched the skin on my right arm.

"Ow!" I yelled.

"Charlie told us," Max said.

"It feels real," Grace said. "I don't believe it. That's his own arm."

"It's true," I replied. "They're not lying." I held my arm up to the light in order to show them the mechanics inside.

"Wow!" Max burst out.

"It looks real, but just like the doctor said—it's not mine," I informed them.

"You mean you have to give it back?" Theodore exclaimed.

"I mean it's alien, made right here on Orbis. It's robotic or something," I said.

Max inspected it closely. "Unbelievable. How do you open it?"

I pulled my arm away in shock.

"I'm just kidding," she said.

"At least you're alive," Ketheria said.

"More than you can say about Switzer," another boy said.

Grace whispered, "He's not the only one who's different."

"Yeah, Dalton's not the same," Theodore added.

I looked at Switzer's best friend. Something *was* missing. His shoulders were slumped forward, and he was staring at the slabs of stone on the floor. I wanted to say something, but what? I knew Dalton only as someone who agreed with the rotten things Switzer said. Dalton saw me looking at him and turned his back to me.

"I think he blames you somehow," Theodore said.

"Me?"

"It's what you didn't do, I think," Grace said.

"I tried to stop him," I protested, but she just shrugged.

"Let him be," Ketheria said, slipping her hand inside mine. "It will pass."

Yet I couldn't help thinking about it. *Why did I feel so responsible for Switzer's death?* I didn't put that belt on him. I didn't push whatever switch he found to make the belt work. Somewhere deep inside my brain, though, I did feel that I could have done more. I could have protected him, but I didn't and now he was dead. Sometimes I felt so completely unprepared for my life.

"Children?" Charlie waved for us to come over to the Keepers.

The other kids shuffled toward Charlie, but I held Ketheria, Max, and Theodore back.

"Did you tell them anything?" I whispered. "About what I told Switzer?"

"About what's in the tank?" Theodore asked.

Ketheria shook her head. "We didn't say anything."

"I can't believe they're still searching for them," I said.

"JT," Max said, putting her hand on my shoulder, "they didn't find *anyone* in the tank. Not a single being."

"That's impossible. I saw them with my own eyes. I spoke with Tang. They asked me to join them."

Theodore shrugged. "Maybe it was a dream."

"It wasn't a dream!"

"Come on, everyone—over here," Charlie ordered.

"Well, it sure got a lot of aliens asking questions around here," Max said.

"Especially at that ceremony thing," Theodore remarked.

I asked him, "What ceremony?"

"Theylor performed an OIO ceremony after Switzer died," Max said.

"To offset the negative energy released into the cosmic

stream because of Switzer's sudden death," Ketheria explained.

"Where do you get this stuff?" Theodore groaned.

"Figures—she helped him." Theodore nodded toward Ketheria.

"It was beautiful," Max said.

"Children, please," Theylor pleaded, and Theodore turned toward the tall alien at the other side of the long room, past our sleepers.

"Wait," I said. "Even if you didn't believe me then you've got to believe me now. When they were fixing me up, I overheard them talking about punishing us for going into Toll Town. They think we were trying to escape."

"But we didn't go to Toll Town," Theodore cried.

"But they found us in the tunnels, and the tunnels led to the place I described to you," I said.

"Is that why they're going to do the staining thing?" Max asked.

"Yes, it's my fault."

"Look, we believe you, JT," Theodore said. "Maybe everyone got out in time."

"I don't know how. There were too many waiting to leave. They could never have gotten everyone out on such short notice," I whispered. "We have to deny everything until I speak with Toll."

"They will find out," Ketheria warned.

"Children: now, please," Theylor interrupted again.

"No, they won't," I said to Ketheria, and I walked over to the staining machine.

Charlie stood near the device just left of Drapling. As usual, Drapling wasted no time in getting started. He pulled a screen scroll from his velvet robe and read aloud.

"In an agreement with the Trading Council and in accordance to Keeper decree 432-888142, all humans in possession of Odran the Centillian shall be forever marked."

"But we didn't do anything," Grace cried out.

"Silence!" Odran shouted.

"Please begin," Drapling instructed the alien attending the stainer. The alien's long, slender hands moved over the controls with the precision of a computer.

The instrument that was going to mark our molecular structure was a steely blue puddle of plasma underneath a mist of bright blue particles similar to the conveyor belts at Weegin's World. The alien controlling the machine sat at the head, surrounded by transparent O-dats. The alien was linked to the device with more than one hardwire. I wondered if he, too, was a slave on Orbis.

Charlie instructed Grace to lie in the mist on top of the plasma. She hesitated and shook her head. Charlie knelt next to her and whispered into Grace's ear, but she could not stop her tears. Then Odran grabbed Grace by the arm and yanked her toward the device. This only made Grace cry out more.

"Stop!" I shouted. "You can't do this, Odran! They did nothing wrong," I said, pointing to everyone else.

"But *you* did," he argued, moving his support glider toward me. "You were in charge. Maybe you should have thought of the consequences before you violated Keeper decree and tried to escape." Odran sloshed in his tank. "How did you find the camp?" He pushed the words through his clenched teeth. They were barely audible. "Who took you there?"

I couldn't answer him. I couldn't break my promise to Toll.

"Worthless knudnik," Odran mumbled under his breath.

I had to say something. "You . . . you made me the controller! I was . . . I was just doing my job. I was looking for Switzer. You can't do this . . ."

"He's lying!" Odran interrupted.

"Put them to death then," another alien shouted. "If they won't be stained, put them down, all of them. That *is* the proper punishment."

"No!" Ketheria insisted, and stepped toward the staining device. She lifted herself onto the machine and positioned herself in the mist. The tiny alien began working the controls at the top of the stainer. I saw Ketheria's eyes roll back, and she instantly fell asleep. Before her eyelids closed, the plasma sprang up and completely engulfed her, creating a semitransparent plasma mold of her body. The bright blue mist faded, and the plasma sparkled as the tiny alien encoded her DNA.

And then it was over. The plasma puddled away, and Ketheria woke up.

"You can get up," Charlie said, and offered her his hand.

"Already?" Ketheria looked around at everyone.

"I told you it was easy."

"We'll do this, Odran. All of us," my sister said, looking at me.

I stared at Ketheria as she shuffled back to us. Her skin was aglow from tiny blue spots that covered her entire body.

"See? It was nothing," she said.

But I couldn't help but stare at her blue skin.

"What's wrong?" she asked.

Ketheria held up her hand and saw the dots. "Oh," she remarked. "I hope this goes away."

"They will disappear before the cycle is over," Theylor informed her.

"This a waste of time," Odran said, snorting up fluid. "Who's paying for this, anyway?"

"That's enough!" Charlie shouted.

"Who is this human to talk to me like that?" he protested. "I could have them put down right now if I wanted to."

Theylor moved in front of Charlie as Drapling moved Max to the staining device. The little alien methodically manipulated the controls as the Keepers led each of us through the process. When it was my turn, the only thing I remembered was lying in the mist and falling asleep. The procedure was painless and over before I knew it even started.

After most of us went through the stainer, data from the device appeared on the O-dats. Our DNA floated across the screens as the little alien ID'd everyone. It was done. We were marked forever.

The doors to our dorm flew open. "You must kill the Softwire!" the intruder shouted.

She was a hairless creature with long, thin arms. As she charged across the room, every muscle and blood vessel flinched under her transparent skin. Clinging between slender bones extending from her spine was skin so taut, it looked liked a sun sail. The alien's skin was forced back from her forehead and gathered around spikes of cartilage protruding from the back of her skull. This thing was ugly, and from the insignia hanging from her neck, I could tell she was a member of the Trading Council.

The alien stomped straight toward me. Her angry face was streaked white with thick shades of burgundy and pink.

"I don't think she likes you," Theodore said.

I couldn't argue. Only Switzer had ever stared at me with that much contempt.

"Do you think she knows?" Max whispered.

"She knows something," I said.

Charlie stepped in her way. "Move out of my way or face my wrath," she hissed, but he stood his ground. From the corner of my eye, I saw the alien that was operating the stainer discussing something on the O-dats with one of the Keepers. The Keeper motioned Theylor over to them.

"These . . . things," the ugly alien said, pointing at me, "have violated Keeper decree. They tried to escape and they must be punished. Why do you let them pollute what we worked so hard to maintain?"

"They do not deserve to die, especially by the hand of greedy profiteers," Charlie argued.

The alien stepped back. Her chin dropped and her eyes widened. "I will not stand for this," she spat, and made a guttural sound with her throat. Instantly two assistants, armed with plasma rifles, entered the dorm and ran in front of her. These aliens looked just like her—hideous.

"What are you doing, Blool?" Drapling demanded. "This has already been arranged with the Council."

"I was never informed. I was on Voror," she cried.

"Drapling?" Theylor called out. Drapling turned, and the Trading Council member stepped toward me. Drapling looked at the screens again and back at us. Both of his heads moved quickly as one of the Keepers ran from the room.

"What's happening, Charlie?" Max said.

"Be still," Charlie responded.

Drapling shouted something. I could not understand what he said. Before anyone could respond, the air in front of us bent and rippled, and four massive Space Jumpers, armed with more than plasma rifles, appeared in front of us.

"Space Jumpers?" Blool skrieked.

"What are they doing here, Charlie?" I said.

The two armed assistants dropped their plasma rifles and shrunk back. "You have just violated a thousand rotations of trust, Drapling," Blool growled.

But Drapling did not seem to care. He darted toward the first Space Jumper and whispered in his ear. All four Jumpers encircled us in response.

"How dare you befoul my dwelling with these creatures!" Odran cried.

The Space Jumpers were taller than anyone in the room. Each brandished a different weapon, and they were all pointed at Blool. No one spoke. The only sound was the Space

Jumpers' labored breathing through their protective face shields.

The Trading Council member hissed at the Space Jumpers.

"You better have an appropriate reason for this, Drapling," Blool said.

"I am protecting the humans," he replied.

"Now you will need to protect yourself," Blool said, and reached for one of the plasma rifles on the ground.

The alien didn't have a chance. The Space Jumpers attacked in unison.

"Stop!" Odran shouted, but it was too late.

The Jumper to my left pointed his weapon at the bodyguards. The one next to him seized Odran, while the remaining two Jumpers sprang upon the ugly alien. They not only moved through space but they seemed to move through time, too. Before I could blink, the alien was disarmed and pinned to the ground.

"You will not live long enough to regret this!" she screamed.

The alien was encased in a green security bubble as everyone watched—except the Keepers. One by one they scurried off, leaving Drapling and Theylor with the staining machine.

"The Keepers don't seem too concerned that she just threatened to kill them," Theodore said.

"But they do seem concerned about something on those O-dats," I replied.

21

Drapling and Theylor whispered in the shadows as Charlie calmed the kids still upset from the failed attack. The Space Jumpers held Blool's bodyguards while Odran demanded to speak with the Keepers.

"The damage done this cycle is irreparable," he shouted, trying to maneuver around the Space Jumpers, but no one was listening to him.

"Charlie, what's going on?" Max asked.

"Shhh. Nothing. Nothing is going on," he said, staring at the Keepers who were still whispering with the little alien tied to the stainer's controls.

"I demand a hearing!" Odran objected.

Finally Theylor walked over to Odran. His right head smiled at us as he passed, while his left head remained focused on Odran.

"Silence," Theylor demanded. "There will be no tribunal. There will be no panic. There will simply be a return to your responsibilities. The Harvest is of the utmost priority at this time. The Crystal of Life will be upon us in two cycles."

"It is impossible to stay calm," Odran said, dipping in and out of the sludge in his tank and spitting against the glass as he spoke. "You have let Space Jumpers into my domain. You have brought them to Orbis! The Trading Council must be informed."

Drapling joined the discussion. "If you do not heed our warning, then everything you have here," he said, gesturing with his long, thin arms, "will be gone."

"You can't do that," Odran growled.

"The property of the crystal moons is ours. This facility is ours. Even those children are ours," Drapling said, pointing to us. "If you insist on continuing with this line of reasoning, I will personally see to it that you are left with nothing, not even that disgusting bucket you reside in.

"May I remind you that you were given many rotations to find a solution to cool the core crystal before the Samirans were released? And your results have been dramatically disappointing. That alone is a troubling matter that should be dealt with before anything else."

"I've worked extremely hard. The task is impossible," Odran argued.

"You have done nothing!" Drapling yelled.

"I suggest that you continue with the preparations for

the Harvest and put this incident behind you," Theylor said calmly. "Speak no more if it."

"Or we can have you removed from your post right now," Drapling added, motioning to the Space Jumpers, who inched toward Odran.

Odran glanced at the remaining Space Jumpers. "Fine," he spat. I don't think facing the Space Jumpers was an option Odran was willing to take. "But I do not want those creatures in my . . . in *this* building as long as I'm here."

Drapling waved his arm, and the Space Jumpers touched their belts. The light around them bent, and they jumped to somewhere else in the universe, taking the bodyguards with them. I couldn't help but wonder if Switzer felt anything when he did the same thing and died.

Odran spun his tank around and glided for the door. "Children! We have much work to do."

"They will be along shortly," Theylor said.

I was grateful that I didn't have to go with Odran when he was so angry. Odran sped from the dormitory as Theylor turned his attention to us.

"Thank you. I will contact you shortly," he said to Charlie. Charlie smiled at us before leaving. I didn't want Charlie to go. There were so many things I wanted to ask him.

"Children," Theylor began, "I need you to understand that you did nothing wrong this cycle. You were very brave during the staining."

"Don't talk to us like little ones," Max said. "What happened here?"

I expected Drapling to pounce on Max's rudeness, but he did nothing. The Keeper was looking past us or glancing back at the stainer. What was he thinking about? Was he worried about having summoned the Space Jumpers? I wondered if he had ever done that before. Drapling caught me staring at him, and we both looked away.

"The events of this cycle concern only the Keepers and the Trading Council," Theylor said. "Our relationship with the Trading Council can often result in these outbursts."

That sounded like a lie to me, a diplomatic way to cover something up. How much trouble had the Keepers created for themselves by summoning the Space Jumpers? They broke a treaty that has been in place for one thousand rotations. And they did it to protect us? Why would they jeopardize their relationship with the Trading Council—over knudniks?

"Did something go wrong with the staining?" Max said.

"Not at all. It was performed flawlessly," Theylor replied.

"Except now we're marked forever," I said.

"That is true," Theylor replied. "But I assure you that this is for your own safety. One of your kind died—"

"One of our kind?" Dalton cried. He stepped toward Theylor. "He was a human being, and he was my friend!"

No one said anything. Dalton looked around at each of us as he held back his tears and clenched his jaw.

"I am sorry if I offended you, but we want to make sure this will never happen to you again. We are not used to look-ing after so many . . . children," Theylor said. "Now we will know if you are close to danger, like in those tunnels you found."

"What were those tunnels?" Theodore asked.

"They lead to the ocean on Orbis 2," Theylor informed us. "They were used to fill the cooling tank when it was first built. They are still used occasionally to refresh the tank water. You are lucky you were not in the tunnels when that happened. But that is behind you now. You will continue your work. The Softwire will help prepare Toll for the Crystal of Life, and you will soon enjoy the Festival of the Harvest. It is a wondrous experience. It will be like nothing you have ever seen," he added.

"And after that, after the crystal is cooled, you will let the Samirans go, right?" I said.

"Of course," Drapling said. "It is Keeper decree."

Drapling leaned toward Theylor and whispered something. Drapling left the room, followed by Theylor. No one said another word.

22

The Festival of the Harvest celebrated the arrival of the Crystal of Life, an immensely powerful crystal mined from the center of the moon Ki. It happened only once every seventy rotations. All four rings of Orbis celebrate in their own manner, but the biggest celebration was said to be on Orbis 2. Since the crystal would arrive at Odran's, our home was the center of festivities with every event either starting or finishing at Toll's cooling tank. At least that's what Max found out. She had become obsessed with the arrival of the crystal and began spending every moment talking about it.

"Why do you think Odran hasn't discovered a way to float the crystals yet?" Max asked us. It was just before our sleep spoke, and the three of us were sitting on Max's sleeper.

"I don't know," Theodore said.

"Maybe it's because he doesn't want to," she remarked.

"What do you mean?" I asked.

"I was in his quarters. He has everything he needs. He could build another ring if he wanted to," she whispered.

"So?" Theodore replied.

"If the Samirans were free, then he wouldn't be the Samiran Caretaker anymore," I asserted.

"Exactly," she said.

"And he wouldn't be able to rub elbows with the Trading Council anymore," I said.

"I don't care," Theodore moaned, and slipped off the sleeper. "I'm tired. Can we talk about this next cycle? I'm sure we will."

"What does that mean?" Max said. I think she was slightly offended.

"Nothing," I said, smiling. "C'mon, let's go to sleep." I jumped off the sleeper. "Sleep well, Max."

"You too," she replied.

I knew I needed to speak with Toll. I could feel something was wrong. From the pit of my stomach, I knew that Toll and Smool were going to be stuck here. I knew Odran and the Council were going to keep the Samirans working, dragging those crystals until they died.

Once everyone was in their sleepers, I crept out to the tank to look for Toll. I hid in the shadows to make sure the small flying search crafts I had seen earlier were gone. Once atop the platform, I took the summoning staff that Odran used and struck the button on the deck twice. As the sound rippled through the cooling tank, I panicked. Would Toll even speak to me? I had betrayed him. The anxiety swelled inside me like rising water. When Toll surfaced, I was gagging on it.

"I'm glad to see you are all right," Toll said, and I stood up.

The sight of Toll made me burst out, "I'm sorry about Toll Town. I never thought about the toonbas. I didn't want to tell anyone, but Switzer did something very stupid—"

"Please, Johnny Turnbull, I am not angry with you; its time had come. But please be careful what you say. They cannot understand *me*, but if anyone is listening, they will understand *you*."

"Oh."

"Why don't you go and get the salve. I will have to pull soon, and it will help me. I will wait here."

"Absolutely," I told him, and sped off toward the storage room.

I was so relieved that Toll was not angry with me. I had betrayed my friend. *I will never do that again,* I decided before I reached the storage room. After I gathered the materials I needed, I turned to find Odran blocking the entrance.

"Toll Town," he gurgled. "Such a sweet name, isn't it?"

Odran dipped into his tank. It made his eyes glow yellow and his voice sound thick.

"You were listening?"

He extended his arms through the opening in his tank and produced a small circular device from its base. His actions were slow, and he fumbled with the instrument as he fed on the slop inside the tank once more.

"Brilliant idea—the staining, that is," he remarked. "I

knew you would be upon that big dumb creature the first chance you got." Odran held the device up. I assumed he used it to track me.

"What do you care? I'm sure you make enough profit by stealing from the crystals."

Odran laughed, or at least he tried to. His mouth was overflowing with the goop from his tank. "Is that what you think I do, Softwire?" Odran maneuvered his tank closer to me.

"What do you want?" I asked him. "I'm tending to Toll. He's waiting for me."

Odran sloshed around once more and somehow shut the storage-room door behind him with a clank. A loud click told me I was locked inside with the deranged creature, but I refused to show him fear. I knew most doors at Odran's opened with keys, but if he could close that door from within his tank, then there must be a computer device controlling it. I pushed into the device locking the door. It was a simple program and I manipulated it with ease. A simple nudge with my mind, and the door opened. Odran spun his tank around as I moved toward the exit.

"Just wait and see what I can do with that thing you're floating in," I said, trying to sound as threatening as possible.

"We could have done so much," he mumbled, admiring the open storage-room door.

"I've heard that one before. You aliens love to team up with humans."

"We're not much different, you and I. When I was very young, I left a perfectly good planet just as you did. The

Trading Council promised me life on an oasis where crystals rained down every day and I would no longer have to be poor."

"You seem to be doing quite well for yourself," I interrupted.

"No thanks to them," he replied. "You see, all they wanted were a few rotations of my life in exchange for a lifetime on the Rings of Orbis. What was a young Centillian to do? Work was already scarce, and I received a mere pittance for it on my home planet. So I came to Orbis, where I was assigned to a Guarantor. Do you see how we've led such similar paths?"

"So?"

"But this is where our stories differ slightly." Odran drew closer to me. "Your Guarantor, that imbecile Weegin, made you sort through trash. Mine had me tortured. While the Keepers thought I was laboring inside my Guarantor's factory, he was actually harvesting my skin for fat citizens to wear as jewelry. Expensive jewelry."

"I'm sorry," I said, "but that doesn't—"

Odran thrust his tank toward me, pinning me against the wall.

"Where are they!" he screamed. "Tell me!"

"Who?"

"Ones like *you*." His waterlogged skin slid along the glass. "Freeloaders, knudniks, always trying to retract their agreements when they have it so easy. I had to pay with my flesh, and *they* were going to pay me. But now they're gone, thanks to you."

"Who are you talking about, Odran?"

"The knudniks in Toll Town, you fool. How do you think they got there? They just walked in? *I* put them there! I never wanted you here. I had a perfect setup, until you came along. Now tell me where they went!"

"That's why you put me in the tank. You tried to kill me. Is Toll involved with this?"

"Of course he is. He started it. *I* learned about it when I was a knudnik. Without him, they would never trust me. They love that big buffoon. The Samiran language befogs the prying eyes of the central computer and keeps them concealed until passage off the ring can be obtained. It worked perfectly."

Was it true? Is that why Toll was willing to stay for the Harvest even though his work rule was over? But wouldn't he be upset then, too, now that I had exposed Toll Town?

"I don't believe you," I said to him. "You would never let a knudnik escape."

"Not for free."

"But we don't have money."

"You would be surprised what someone will steal in order to gain their freedom. Your friend would have succeeded if he hadn't been so stupid."

"My friend?"

"The one that died. Why do you think I let him go into Core City and trade those trinkets? How do you think he even found those tunnels?"

"Switzer was trying to buy his way out of here?"

"Just like the rest of them," he said.

"You set him up. We never would have found that FORM room if it weren't for you. You killed Switzer."

"Oh, that's where you're wrong. You had a far greater hand in it than I did. Wasn't it you who informed me how Switzer was so eager to escape the very first cycle you arrived here? How did you say it? *Jump the ring*, wasn't it?"

He was right. I did tell him that. But I didn't cause Switzer's death.

"It wasn't my fault."

"That wasn't very convincing."

"You're to blame. You make them steal from their Guarantors. It's no wonder Citizens hate knudniks. How can anyone blame us for wanting to escape?"

"Tell me!"

"Tell you what? I don't know where they are. When I left Toll Town, everything was fine. I don't have a clue where everyone went. Maybe they escaped."

"Do not lie to me," he growled.

"Or what?" Max said, standing in the open door with Theodore and Ketheria.

Odran jerked his tank toward the door.

"What are you doing here?" he cried. "Get back to your room!"

"We just came to help our friend with his chores," Theodore said.

Ketheria stepped toward Odran and said, "You disappoint me." She stared at Odran.

Odran tried to move away from her as if her glare were causing him physical pain but his tank hit the wall with a clank. He was trapped.

"You play at things you know nothing about. You are an imposter," she said quietly.

Odran slumped in his tank. Ketheria's words seemed to affect Odran deeply. The alien moved his tank to the side, freeing a path for me to leave.

"Go and ready the Samiran," he ordered me. "This is an important cycle."

I grabbed the supplies and slipped out of the storage room with my sister and my friends.

"Thanks," I whispered.

"What were you doing?" Max asked.

"I wanted to talk with Toll. Odran was listening," I told them.

"You better watch out for him now, JT," Ketheria said. "He really doesn't like you."

I told them what Odran said. I told them about how he profited from the knudniks in Toll Town and how Toll was involved.

"And you believe him?" Ketheria asked.

"There's only one way to find out," Max said.

"He's waiting for you, isn't he?" Theodore said.

"Do you mind if I go by myself?" I asked them.

Max shook her head. "No, we'll keep an eye on Odran."

"Be careful," Ketheria warned me.

"I will."

When I returned, Toll was waiting for me. He looked different to me somehow. I didn't know what to say him.

Toll noticed my change immediately and said, "Something's troubling you."

"I ran into Odran."

"He's wondering where everyone went, isn't he?"

"So you know? You *are* involved with him. You're making these aliens steal from their Guarantors so they can hide out in Toll Town. Were you going to charge me? I bet you said that stuff about my father just to hook me in. Well, I don't believe you."

"Are you going to get on?" he asked me.

"That's your response? No, I'm not. I don't want anything to do with you anymore."

I threw the oversize applicator to the ground and turned back down the steps.

"Johnny. Come back. Please let me explain."

So he could twist it and make me believe everything was all right? So he could lie to me like everyone else? I was tired of it, yet how *could* I just believe Odran—over my friend? Didn't he have the right to defend the accusations? I certainly hadn't liked it when I had been accused on Orbis and no one gave me a chance to tell my side of the story. Then I thought of the digi—the picture of Toll with my father. I turned back toward Toll to listen one more time.

"Get on," he instructed me. "And please be careful what you say."

Reluctantly, I picked up the pail and the brush and stepped onto the platform harnessed to the side of Toll. I stood in front of the large crevice gouged into his skin and applied the salve with the brush. I didn't say a word.

"You must understand the environment in which you work, my young friend. After the War of Ten Thousand Rotations, after the Keepers made their deal with the Trading Council, the society on the Rings of Orbis began to change. When the Trading Council became the productive class on Orbis, their appetites grew larger and they insisted on their wants until they were satisfied. The Keepers, who have no care for material gain, stepped aside and let the Council create enormous profits from the crystal moons. At first the Keepers did not mind. Now they were better equipped to continue their work and the senseless loss of lives was stopped.

"But once the Trading Council was in control of the economy, money became the dominant force on Orbis and thus the richest became the most powerful. That was Odran's goal, to buy his way onto the Council. But what made matters even worse was that the Source within the people of the society began to deteriorate."

"You're talking about OIO, " I said. "I don't know much about it."

"You do. It is the guiding force within the universe. It *is* all around you. It *is* you. But that is a discussion for later. Let me continue. Unlike hunger or even your longing for freedom, greed at least understands the necessity for discipline. The Trading Council, no matter how anxious, no matter how corrupt, worked as a unifying force and brilliantly mapped out long-term plans for its survival. But greed can rule a society only by fulfilling it's own goals first, no matter what the cost. As generations of Trading Council members were born into this society without any ability to rule or the capacity for self-examination, they grew fat feasting off greed. There are some on Orbis who have created such enormous wealth that they could never spend everything they have in a thousand lifetimes—and they still want more.

"Understand, Johnny, that their greed has no capacity to change. It simply is. With no desire to work on the rings, the Council turned to other worlds to provide the necessary labor force. At first the Keepers opposed this, but the Trading Council persisted. Even the Keepers could see that the Citizens proved more and more useless. Some Keepers, too, were now accustomed to their luxuries on Orbis. They expected it, and they could no longer imagine life without them. Soon they relented, but they insisted on some control and determined which societies should be chosen and what work they would be permitted to do. Some civilizations have it far worse than you do, Johnny Turnbull. The Keepers are lied to, and some people are forced to live certain lives here on Orbis when they would rather die."

"That doesn't justify charging them, forcing them to steal."

"I have never charged anyone. I simply provide them a haven until their eventual escape. Odran is the only one who profits. As I told you, Odran is blinded by the power of the Trading Council. He craves it as a plant craves sunlight."

"That doesn't make it any better."

"Orbis is lost. Even some Keepers are soiled by greed now.

Their pride of this very place degrades the society even further. All that's left of their arrangement with the Trading Council is an agreement to disagree. It is no longer a condition to overcome but a condition accepted by their society."

"I don't understand what you're saying, Toll."

"Odran understands only greed and profit. There is no way an escape can be arranged for these people without money exchanging hands. Odran will not expose Toll Town himself. He profits from it, but what am I to do? Refuse someone who has come to me for help because they stole from their Guarantors to get here? From the very people who have stolen their lives? Without my efforts, Toll Town could not exist. I cannot change society on Orbis. I can only help those that want no part of it."

It was hard to swallow everything Toll said. My understanding of human society was very limited, and he was attempting to explain an alien civilization to me. What answer did I want, anyway? Did I want him to tell me that he was good and Odran was bad? Even I knew life was not that simple.

"So where is everyone?" I asked him.

"They are gone," Toll said.

"You're not going to tell me, are you?"

"As I said, they are gone."

Toll was hiding something, but could I blame him? I had betrayed his trust once already.

"I understand," I said.

"Soon Smool and I will be gone, too. After I pull the

Crystal of Life, our dream of having a family will be fulfilled, and we will swim free once again."

I wanted to tell him what I feared, but I was afraid my suspicions might not be true. "How can you trust them after everything you've seen?" I said.

"The gates to the great ocean have already been prepared. The tunnels will soon be filled, and we will swim from this place guided by the great cosmic currents."

If the gates were ready, then maybe Toll was right. What did I really know, anyway? Theylor said they were leaving, and I was practically unconscious when I'd heard that other stuff. Yet still something told me other things were in store for Toll.

"What if something goes wrong?" I said.

"Nothing will go wrong."

"But what *if*?"

Toll did not hesitate. He said, "Then I will wreak havoc upon these prison walls like nothing they have ever seen. The Citizens will die in a flood of bio-bots. Make sure you are far from this place if that happens, Softwire."

I continued working on Toll's huge wounds in silence. I rolled his warning over in my head as I stared out across the colossal cooling tank. It was a lot of water. When the time came, and I was sure it would, I knew I could not get away fast enough.

"What about the knudniks who still want to leave?" I said. "When you leave, there will be no one to help them."

"Someone will take my place; it always happens. They will find another way. Maybe that person will be you."

23

Early at the start of the next cycle, I received a screen scroll in the dormitory. It was from Odran.

"Why didn't he tell us in person?" Theodore asked.

"Maybe he's too busy getting ready for the arrival of the Crystal of Life," Grace said.

But I knew better. He did not want to face us after the humiliation he received in the storage room. But that worried me even more. *How would Odran retaliate?* I wondered.

Theodore hardwired to the screen scroll and said, "That's a lot of work."

"I'm not doin' any of it," Dalton replied, and slumped onto his sleeper.

Nobody argued with him. It felt strange to see him without Switzer.

"How long do you think he'll be like that?" Theodore said.

"Doesn't it bother you to see him alone?" Max asked him. "You know, with Switzer gone? It feels strange to me."

"Why?" Theodore remarked, "Switzer was a mean person."

"But he was still a person," Ketheria reminded him. She went over and sat next to Dalton. Nugget plopped himself next to her.

"Get that thing away from me," Dalton snapped, but Nugget only snuggled closer to Ketheria.

"Leave them," Max whispered. "Let's start with the shipment of food that's arriving." She headed for the door.

"We'll handle the decorations for the entrance," Grace said. "Come help us when you're done."

Ketheria and Nugget stayed with Dalton. "We'll be over later," she said.

"How long will it take Toll to cool the crystal?" Theodore asked as we followed Max to the receiving bay.

Max looked at him. "Why?"

"Well, there won't be anyone to feed after the crystal is cooled and Toll is gone."

I wanted to say, "Don't count on it," but I didn't have to. When we arrived at the receiving area, there must have been at least fifty crates waiting on the stone floor. The smell of rancid meat was immediate.

"That's an awful lot of food for someone who's leaving," Max remarked.

"Does Toll eat all of this at once?" I asked.

"It would take many phases to eat all of this," Theodore replied.

I looked at the oxygenated crates. What was all this food for? I could hear the little creatures clawing at the walls. *They do seem to know their fate,* I thought. Didn't I know my fate too? Was I ignoring it? I knew the Trading Council was lying—they weren't going to set Toll and Smool free—and Toll would make them pay for it. I would be just as dead as Switzer as soon as the tank was destroyed. *I told you so* wouldn't mean much after everyone was dead.

Max instructed the robots to disperse the crates, leaving two behind.

"You're in for a treat," she said, and maneuvered the first of the two crates near a long, clear chute. I assumed it emptied into the cooling tank.

"Just grab them and stuff them in this chute," Max instructed. "It's easy, but just be fast."

Theodore looked at her, and they both giggled.

When Theodore removed the lid, the frightened creatures huddled in the corners. They were pink with at least eight arms or legs but no eyes. Two long tentacles sprouted from one end of each thing, flickering about in the air. Max thrust her hand in and yanked one out. It twisted and writhed in her grip.

"You have to do it quickly, or they'll die out of the water!" she shouted over the screeching. The little guy flailed his arms about, grabbing at Max's hair and smacking her whenever he got close enough. Theodore grabbed another as Max plunged the thing into the chute and slammed a release button. The "food" scrambled against the current before it was flushed into the cooling tank.

"I think the screaming tells the others what's happening," Max said.

"They start to gang up on you if you wait too long," Theodore added.

I reached in with my right arm and grabbed one. Two other creatures latched on to help their friend. Another jumped from the water, ran up my arm, and punched me in the face. It was more shocking than painful, but their skin was rough and it scratched my cheek. I held the thing as far from my face as possible. *At least they're putting up a fight,* I thought. That was more than what I was doing. But what could I do? Who would help me? Max and Theodore were no better off than me. In fact, everyone in Core City would die if Toll destroyed the cooling tank.

"The vitamin stuff!" Max shouted. "We forgot it."

"I was hoping you wouldn't remember," Theodore mumbled, cracking a sealed crate. The stench burned my nose. That's where the smell of rotting meat was coming from.

"Dunk them in here first. It makes them easier for the Samiran to swallow. Their skin is too rough," she instructed.

"I found that out by myself," I said as I touched the fresh scratch on my cheek.

I managed to dunk the little monster into the stinky stuff and then into the chute. I sent it to its death in the tank and reached for another. This little bugger chomped down on my finger.

"Look, I'm not bleeding," I said, holding up the arm Orbis had given me.

The skin was torn slightly. I felt pain but I did not see blood.

"Let me look," Max said as Theodore flushed the last of Toll's meal into the tank.

"Careful," I told her.

"You baby. You have pain sensors, don't you? Turn them off."

I accessed the interface, located the pain sensor, and turned it off. The pain subsided instantly.

"Done," I said, and Max stuck her finger into the open wound. "Hey!"

"Wow, I can feel some sort of metal under your skin."

I yanked my arm away. "No, don't even think about it. It's my arm."

Max put one hand on her hip. "Relax. I have no intentions of taking your arm apart, but doesn't it make you wonder? If they can make something like your arm, why can't they figure out a way to float those crystals?"

"Maybe they don't want to."

"Well, it's stupid," Max said, shaking her head. She walked away, deep in thought.

"Where are you going?" Theodore called out to her.

"To help with the decorations. To see what this festival is all about."

At the entrance to the great hall, the other children had finished unpacking the enormous crystal sculptures that depicted the first arrival of the Samirans and the harvesting of the Crystal of Life. A small locator was attached to the wall, and flying cart-bots guided the sculptures to their resting place high above our heads. The crystals sprang to life with music and vibrant shades of pink, green, and purple that danced about, enacting a different story around each crystal.

"They're golden, aren't they?" exclaimed one girl as another crystal rested on its locator and exploded with color.

By now Dalton was there with my sister, and he too stared with wonder at the light show. I think he even smiled.

We worked late into the cycle finishing all the chores Odran had assigned to us. Even Nugget helped out when Ketheria fell asleep on a huge bolt of Gia silk that we used to drape the steps up to the cooling tank. Small flying robots buzzed around our heads all cycle, flashing images of the way things were supposed to look.

When I finally fell on my sleeper, I was too tired to even say good night. It felt like I wasn't asleep for even a nanosecond when I heard, "You kids are going to sleep the cycle away!" It was Charlie. He was standing in the doorway. "You ready to see the biggest celebration in the universe?"

The lack of sleep was no longer an issue as we eagerly piled out of the dorm behind Charlie.

Our preparations at Odran's paled in comparison to what the people of Core City had done. It was as if someone had scraped off all the neglect and decay and polished the whole city like a magnificent gleaming spaceship. Everyone was dressed in some sort of costume or elaborate outfit, and every food shop was giving away eats and drinks for free. There were no grumbling mine workers, no cranky shopkeepers, only happy aliens, shouting, dancing, singing, and eating.

"What do we do?" I asked Charlie.

"Have fun. Be kids," he said, smiling.

"Where will you be?" Max asked.

"I'll be right there with Rose and Albert," he said, pointing to a group of small tables surrounding a street vendor giving away drinks.

"Hey, kids!" Rose and Albert shouted, waving at us.

I hadn't seen them since the Earth News Café on Orbis 1.

"What are they doing here?" I said.

"Best festival's on Orbis 2; everyone knows that," Charlie replied.

I was torn between seeing my old friends and exploring the Festival. Some of the other kids had already disappeared into the crowd.

"Go on," Charlie told us. "You can visit later."

Max, Ketheria, Theodore, and I ran into the crowd. Shop owners who didn't sell food had imported delicacies from the other rings and were generously handing them out. Ketheria immediately found someone giving out toonbas and parked herself in front of the shopkeeper.

"Don't be greedy," I whispered.

"There's enough for the whole galaxy," the shopkeeper exclaimed. "You never get to see these on Orbis 2." He gave her another pouch to carry.

I paused before popping one in my mouth. I thought about how these Trefaldoorian treats had betrayed Toll Town.

"It wasn't your fault," my sister said. "Let's have fun, all right?"

"All right."

We ran through the streets, tasting every food we could stomach. Theodore sniffed each treat before he put it in his mouth, while Max tried everything that was handed to her without a thought. The sweet and spicy smells of foods cooking open in the streets filled the air. It made me light-headed. It wasn't long before we were laughing and dancing with everyone in Core City, and any thoughts of Switzer, Toll Town, or Odran were replaced with a giddy sensation that I never felt before.

"This is better than any Birth Day, ever!" Max declared.

In one open quad, Max pointed to a child of a Citizen strapped in a metallic chair that skipped across a large reservoir of yellowish-green water like that in the cooling tank. An alien dressed in festive purple and green silks presented the proud parents with a hologram that depicted their child pulling the Crystal of Life as he dipped in and out of the water.

"Just like Toll," the child cried, reaching up for the holo with three of his arms. He used his free arm to stuff his face with something yellow, stringy, and slimy.

Theodore stopped below another hologram and said, "Look, free use of tetrascopes. You can link into the mind of another being and experience whatever they are doing. It's as if you are them. We can actually be *in* the parade with one of these." He scoured the list of people selling themselves as riders.

"I want to be a miner loading the Crystal of Life," said a small alien clone, pulling on the skirt of its mother or father (I couldn't tell).

"Forget it," Max told Theodore, and pointed at another screen. "No humans. Says so right there."

A large screen floated over the vendor's head. It read:

Due to the addictive nature of tetrascopes,
Keeper decree mandates that the following species
are forbidden from using these devices.

Right there, fifth on the list, were humans.

"I guess tetrascopes are addictive," I said.

"Let's try anyway!" Theodore insisted, and the tall alien in charge only grunted and pointed at the screen, pushing Theodore aside.

"So much for being friendly," I mumbled.

"So much for reading the sign," the alien replied.

"Come on, Theodore. There are better things here than tetrascopes," I said, leading my friends down the street and into a crowd of dancing aliens.

"Yeah, like that!" Max cried, pointing to something that looked like one of the chairs in the water, only this was floating in the air above our heads.

One short, stubby alien dancing by himself told us, "They're for the parade. You don't want to miss a good spot. You'd better get one."

"But we don't have any chits or crystals," I said.

He laughed and said, "No one needs money this cycle."

We raced through the crowd and found a long line forming in front of a shuttle cart that was handing out the flying chairs. Max snuck to the front of the line with us in tow.

"How do they work?" she asked a gruff, stocky alien with a scar around his bald head.

"They are simple," he showed us. "Up, down, forward, and back. Stabilizers will keep you from tipping."

"Golden!" Max shrieked, and jumped on the metal and plastic device.

It looked more like a saddle than a chair except for the armrest that housed the controls. In an instant we were soaring above the crowd, zipping in and out of the aliens already waiting for the parade.

"This is better than Ring Defenders," Theodore shouted as we chased each other back and forth over Core City.

"Try and catch me!" Ketheria yelled. Nugget hung on the back of her flying chair. His big feet were locked into the machine and he waved his hands in the air while whooping.

We caught Ketheria easily when she was stopped by a security-bot.

"Your behavior has forfeited your seats. Please hand them over immediately," it informed us.

"Certainly," I said, and pushed into the flying robot. The computer chip was so simple. I manipulated its programming and trashed its memory of the last report.

"Thank you for complying," it said, and raced away, leaving us with our flying chairs.

"Perfect!" Max cried.

"Do you think you should have done that?" Theodore asked, worried as usual.

"Yes, I do," I told him, and grabbed his toonbas before I raced away. Everyone chased after me.

This was the Orbis promised to me on the *Renaissance*. This was what our parents sacrificed their lives to achieve. This felt good. I squashed my feelings of bitterness, of being cheated, and ignored the fact that this affluent and sophisticated world was not responsible for my happiness.

I saw thousands of aliens below me, and many were already in place to get the best view of the parade.

"Look—there's Charlie!" Max shouted, pointing to the spot we left him.

I waved as small bolts of light shot up from the ground and exploded into images of Toll or the Orbis insignia. As the ring fell into shadow, the lights in each building flickered on, pulsing with different colors for the Festival. More and more glowing images were fired into the air. Some displayed images of OIO symbols, while others displayed images of home planets. It made me want to launch one for Earth.

"This is fun," Nugget said as Ketheria pulled next to me.

"The parade is going to start soon," she informed us.

"Let's find the best place," Max said, and dove into the crowd already forming above the main street.

Every seat was a good seat. Aliens tucked in and around each other, leaving enough room for everyone to see. A lot of people had stayed on the ground, and from where we floated

I could see almost the whole parade below me. A horn blasted, and the crowd roared. The first participants of the parade stepped onto the street.

"It's Theylor!" Theodore shouted. My friend, along with another sixty Keepers, advanced down the street. He carried a carved, golden staff with the insignia of Orbis high above their heads. It was a metallic-colored hologram of the four rings surrounding a blazing wormhole.

Drapling followed them with another group of Keepers, maybe twenty altogether. I immediately recognized them as the Descendants of the Light. Their robes were decorated with long silver and yellow vests, and the staff Drapling carried bore the OIO symbol—a vibrant, shining circle atop a silver staff. It lit up the whole street.

Each Keeper was dressed in a crown of crystals that fit over both of their heads.

"Theylor!" I shouted, and both of his heads looked up and smiled.

Behind the Keepers were small flying aliens that shot streams of colored lights over the parade watchers. The lights bounced off buildings or rained down upon the spectators. I watched Theodore turn completely pink as one of the flying light balls landed on him.

Everyone was shouting over the music and cheering. I saw aliens changing forms as they walked along the parade, and I saw gigantic metallic beasts enacting battle scenes with aliens from their home planets. Creatures I had never seen on Orbis before danced through the parade decorated in costumes of metal, light, and crystals. Small Citizen children darted through the spectators wearing holographic masks of Keepers, Trading Council members, and even Toll. I didn't remember ever being so happy.

"There it is!" someone above me shouted.

"Oh, I can't believe how lucky we are," another alien cried.

I moved my chair up to see what they were talking about.

"What do you see?" I asked the alien.

The slender creature pointed down the street with its long, black claws. "See them?"

I squinted to see better, but long, red ribbons tumbling through the air blocked my view. When they cleared, I caught a glimpse of something large and shiny.

"What is it?" Max shouted over the noise.

"I don't know!" I yelled back. Then I saw ten small aliens with thick arms carrying a silver bit and harness like the one Toll used to pull the crystals.

"Wow! But Toll already has one," I told the alien.

"Not that," the alien snapped, then pointed farther down the street. "That!"

Past the first harness was another identical harness, only slightly smaller, perfect for Smool. I assumed that, with all this pageantry, they must use these shiny, new harnesses to pull the Crystal of Life. But when I saw what was behind the second metal bit, my heart dropped faster than a human in the cooling tank.

"What is it?" Theodore asked.

I looked at it again. It couldn't be, could it?

"Watch my chair!" I shouted, and I dove to the street. I jumped off my seat and ran into the crowd. I pushed past an alien dressed in long, green robes and stood at the edge of the parade. A stately Citizen's belt was visible under the alien's robe.

"It's wonderful, isn't it?" the Citizen gushed. "I mean what a sacrifice they're making for Orbis. I couldn't do it."

I couldn't believe it. Directly behind the new bit and harness for Smool, three small aliens carried a third bit—a bit small enough for a Samiran child.

"They wouldn't," I cried.

The alien in green looked at me and said, "Oh yes, Toll and Smool have given their child to us so we may continue harvesting the crystals. The Centillian made the announcement at the start of the spoke. Isn't that joyous? I mean, we did feed them and care for them for two thousand rotations. If you ask me, I think it's only right," the alien gushed, the last sentence only a whisper but full of arrogance.

I could not stop staring at the miniature bit and harness that was now directly in front of me.

"Are you all right?" I heard the alien ask as I bolted into the street. "Hey, what are you doing?"

I stopped in front of the creatures carrying the baby bit.

"Out of the way," the aliens demanded, pushing me backward as they walked. Their dark, thick skin was crusted and blackened. The noseless creatures looked identical, and they were all the same height as me.

"Where are you taking this?" I asked the one in the middle.

"Are you an idiot? To the cooling tank, where else?"

The other aliens only laughed.

"How long before you get there?" I said.

"When the parade is done?" another said. "This one really is stupid."

More laughter.

"When is the parade done?" I demanded.

"When it is finished," affirmed the third alien, and all three of them were laughing uncontrollably now.

I looked up at Max and waved at them to come down. They bolted straight toward me and hovered just above my head.

"We have to get back to Toll," I said.

"Why?" Theodore asked.

"That bit is for the baby, isn't it?" Max said.

"Yes. That's Odran's solution. Keep the baby Samiran for Orbis. Let Toll go, but keep his child as a slave to pull the crystals," I said.

"Toll will not like that," Nugget said from the back of Ketheria's chair.

"No, he definitely won't like that," I agreed. "He will flood the ring and we'll all be history."

"You have to warn him," Ketheria said.

"Look out!" Theodore shouted as powerful hands clamped down on my arms.

"Let him go!" Max yelled.

I struggled to look over my shoulder, but I already knew who it was. Odran yanked me against his tank, and the metal from his support glider dug into my back.

"Everything was working perfectly until you showed up. My seat on the Trading Council is almost paid for. You will not ruin this for me, you meddlesome brat," Odran gurgled in my ear, squeezing my arm even tighter.

"Stop—you're hurting him, Odran," Ketheria cried.

Max darted forward and pounded on Odran's tank.

"Leave him," I told her.

I'd been in tougher situations than this, and Odran had just given me the advantage—he'd underestimated me.

"Do you actually know how insignificant you are on these rings?" he said. "Can you even begin to comprehend your status on Orbis?"

"That doesn't give you the right to treat us so poorly."

"Just wait to see what I have in store for you," he whispered.

"You're going to steal Toll's child for your own gain, aren't you?"

"Citizens have been doing it for centuries," Odran said. "Security!"

"Not this time," I whispered, and pushed into the computer that ran Odran's glider. I shut the program down, and his tank jerked to the left, tilting wildly. Odran's oily face smashed up against the glass only inches from mine.

"What are you doing?" he screamed.

"I'm not going to let you do this to Toll."

"Security!"

No one in the crowd even noticed us. Our vests told everyone we were knudniks and of little importance. Besides, it was the Festival of the Harvest. The Citizens would never imagine something bad happening now. One more tinker with the computer chip inside Odran's tank and the support glider struck the ground with a loud clank. I yanked myself free and jumped aside. Odran struggled against the tank before it tipped over and slammed onto the street. The glass exploded into a million pieces. The sludge that filled the tank splashed the audience, much to their delight.

Odran dragged his legless torso from the wreckage with the cables and alloy bucket still attached. He clawed at my feet with his waterlogged arms, but I simply stepped aside.

"You will die for this," he gasped, his yellowed eyes ablaze. "You will not see the next cycle! I don't care who you are!"

"I will not let you make a knudnik out of another child," I declared, mounting my flying machine. "Let's go, everyone!"

I leaned forward in the flyer, and it accelerated up and over the parade, straight toward the cooling tank. I looked down, and Core City continued to blossom with color and noise. I saw the Samiran bits turn a corner. All three, even the smallest one, were on their way to the cooling tank.

I could see Charlie below us, too. He shouted, "What are you doing?"

"Nothing, but I need you to slow the parade down!"

"What?"

The cooling tank was located in the largest building ahead of us, so it was the easiest to find. Near the building, on the ring's incline, I could see the bright blue ocean of Orbis 2. The new home Toll longed for was less than a thousand meters from the stadium building that housed his prison. If I didn't get to Toll before he found out what the Citizens had planned for his unborn child, it wouldn't make a difference if that ocean was a zillion kilometers away.

Max put her flyer down smoothly at the entrance of the great hall. About two hundred aliens lined the steps and cheered as we landed.

"We're not with the parade!" Max shouted, to the disappointment of the aliens.

"Hurry, we don't have long," I said, and dismounted the flying machine.

Theodore stopped outside the huge doors. "What about the Crystal of Life?" he asked

"I don't care," I replied.

"But Johnny . . ." Theodore *was* concerned. "Toll may be free, but without the money from the crystals, our lives won't be worth much on Orbis."

"Theodore's right. You will make too many enemies if that crystal is ruined," Ketheria warned.

"There must be something else that can pull those crystals," Max said.

"I think there must be, too," I agreed. "But the Citizens love their pageantry—look at this Festival. They love their old ways, and they love the slavery—it's part of their culture. They don't want a machine to do it."

"I bet you I could whip something up," Max said.

I looked at her. "Are you sure? This isn't like patching up a scavenger-bot."

"You just help Toll and keep him from flooding the ring," she said. "Leave the crystal to me."

We sprinted up the stairs along the tank and used the light chute to jump to the deck. We were not alone. At least ten aliens were putting the final touches on the stands, and even more vendors were getting in place. I grabbed Odran's staff and slammed it on the button. What if Toll wasn't here? I struck the deck again.

The water rippled, and Toll quickly surfaced. "Johnny? There is much work to be done, my friend. There is no time to talk," Toll said.

"We have to," I whispered, and looked around at the aliens staring at us. "But not here."

"There is no time. The crystal will arrive very shortly," he argued, and began to sink into the tank.

"Toll!" I knelt down at the edge. "It's important. More important than the crystal," I said, my eyes fixed carefully on my huge friend.

"Wait here then. I must find enough suits for all of you." Toll dipped into the water as some of the aliens were drifting over to us.

"Suits for what?" Theodore asked.

"To go into the tank," I told him.

"Why do I have to go in there?" he protested. "I saw what it did to you the last time."

"Don't worry—the suit works with the bio-bots in the tank. They'll protect you."

"I don't care; I'm not going in there," Theodore cried,

taking a step back. Nugget, who was listening to everything, followed his lead.

"Theodore, I wore one of the suits. They're fine," I assured him as Toll resurfaced. I jumped onto the Samiran and pulled the suits from the compartment on the harness. "Put them on. They conform to your body."

Max held the suit up, marveling at the technology. "And this will keep the bio-bots from sucking the heat from my body?"

"And killing us?" Theodore added.

"Yes. Now hurry, please!"

Nugget followed Ketheria's lead, and once everyone was dressed, we climbed onto Toll and descended into the tank. In the distance I saw the rock and glass formation that made up Toll Town. This time, however, when Toll emerged inside the air pocket, Tang was not there to greet us. In fact I could see no one. Toll Town was deserted.

"That was unbelievable," Max exclaimed as she jumped off Toll.

"I didn't really believe you before, JT," Theodore said. "But wow!"

Ketheria was all smiles, while Nugget kept sticking his head back in the water to see what else was down there.

"We are safe here, Johnny, but please tell me what is so urgent."

I didn't want to upset Toll. "I don't know where to start," I said. I looked at Max.

"They're going to keep your child to pull the crystals from

now on, after your work rule is done," she blurted out. It was a slap in the face.

"Don't get upset," I said. "I have a plan."

But Toll wouldn't listen. The water rippled around him, his gigantic body shaking. Toll let out a cry that almost cracked our skulls. Everyone clamped their hands to their ears.

"What did he say now?" Theodore shouted over the noise.

"He isn't saying anything," I yelled. "Toll! Toll! Listen to me."

"I will destroy this tank and everything around it before I let them take my child," Toll said, his voice booming off the walls.

"No. You don't have to. We're going to open the tank doors that lead to the ocean. You and Smool can leave before the baby is born," I explained.

"You're gonna do what?" Theodore said,

"You can do that?" Toll asked.

"With a little help," I said, motioning to my friends. "I need you to be ready at the gate."

"But Smool is heavy with the child, Johnny. I am concerned. She will have the child any cycle now."

"Then we have to hurry."

"I need to get back to Odran's," Max said. "Theodore, I need your help."

Theodore nodded. "Of course."

"Toll, can I have a few of these suits?" she asked, and Toll nodded his huge head slightly, imitating our gestures.

"Ketheria, you go with them," I told my sister, but she

shook her head and gave me a look that told me *that* was not an option. "Fine, you can come with me."

"But we have to hurry."

"Wait. We need to take everyone from Toll Town with us," Toll said.

A familiar voice from behind me said, "Everyone is ready, Toll." It was Tang. He crawled out from a hole in the rock high above the water. Another ten or fifteen pairs of eyes peered out from the darkness. "I knew you would be of great help to us one day, Johnny Turnbull," Tang said.

"Tell Tang to call the Linkians," Toll instructed me, and I did. Tang removed a pipe from his pocket and blew on it, then said, "We will meet you at the tank doors."

"What's a Linkian?" I asked.

"You'll see," he replied.

"Toll, you told me that the door to the ocean has been readied. Is there a control room, someplace where this is done?"

"Yes, but it is at the far end of the great tunnel. Near the ocean."

"How are you gonna get there, JT?" Max asked.

"There are power-flow shafts that run the length of the tunnel," Tang said.

"JT, that's not enough," Theodore complained. "You need more than that. What will you do when you're there? This isn't a very good plan."

"It's all we've got," I told him, and turned to Toll. "How can I get to these power-flow shafts?"

"The Linkians will take you there," Toll said as the water next to him began to glow and magnificent purple creatures, with skin like the finest velvet I'd ever seen, broke the surface. The sleek aliens sported four long, identical tentacles that sprang out from the center of their bodies. Two of the thick tentacles swept through the air and stuck to the edge of the pool near my feet.

"Incredible," Max exclaimed.

"Jump on with your sister, Johnny," Toll said. "I'll take the others back to the deck. We'll wait near the main door for your signal."

"Toll will take you back," I said, turning to my friends. "You don't have to do this, you know."

"It's too late for that," Max said.

"Do you know what you're going to do?"

"I just need to get to Odran's quarters, There's something there I remember seeing . . ." she muttered.

"We're doomed," Theodore moaned.

"This is going to work," I assured them. "I'll see you when you're done then."

Max took my hand. "I'm gonna hold you to that, JT."

I stepped onto what I thought must be the head of one of the Linkians, but I could not see eyes or a mouth. I sat with Ketheria holding on to me and Nugget in between us. We nestled into the velvet skin as the creature reshaped itself to keep us snug on its back. I picked up a thick, red chain that wrapped around one of the tentacles, and I grasped it in my hands.

As we dipped into the water, I watched about a hundred aliens crawl out of the rocks and climb onto the backs of the other Linkians. Some needed time with their suits. There was no pushing or shoving, no panic. When four or five Linkians were filled with knudniks, a new batch surfaced. Everything was done in an orderly manner, and Tang stood watch as Toll slipped away with Max and Theodore on his back.

I ran my hand along the skin of the Linkian. "Let's go," I said.

The Linkian then dipped into the water. I was forced to hold on tightly as it took the lead and charged through the tank. The Linkians were graceful beings. They used their thick, velvety tentacles to soar through the water as if they were flying.

"Vairocina?" I said.

"Johnny? Are you all right?" she replied instantly.

"I'm fine," I told her. "But I need your help."

"Someone has alerted security," she said. "They are tracking you now. They are using the staining."

"You must stop them, Vairocina! I can't have anyone know where I am."

"I'm afraid it's too late," she informed me.

"So if someone wanted to, they could tell I was inside the tank right now?" I said.

"Yes," she replied. "The stain allows any Citizen with a tracking device to locate you."

But who would be looking for me? Charlie? Odran? The Trading Council? Probably all of them, I thought.

"Vairocina, you need to tell them I'm fine or stall them, or something. Anything to give me more time."

"What's wrong, Johnny? What are you doing?"

"I'm helping a friend," I said as the Linkian slowed to a stop. Before me were two gigantic columns of rusted metal with tall, thin portals of glass running down between them. *These must be the doors that lead to the escape tunnels,* I thought. On the right side of the doors, just above us, was a grate as large as the tunnels we found running under Orbis 2.

"Through there!" I shouted at the Linkian, pointing to the grate. "That must be the power-flow shaft!"

The Linkian pushed upward with its long tentacles toward the grate.

"Hold on, Ketheria!"

The Linkian rolled on its side as Ketheria and Nugget clutched my waist.

"Duck!"

I lay out flat against the alien as it shot sideways through the narrow slits of the algae-covered grate. We scraped through the opening, and the Linkian bore down against the powerful current trying to suck us back out the grate. It took everything I had to keep from slipping off.

The shaft was narrow and pitch-black except for pools of blue-green light that shone every twenty meters. It ended with another grate, too small for the Linkian to slip through. I saw a thin metal ladder attached to the wall on my left. At the top of the ladder was some sort of hole or door, even blacker than the unlit water. The Linkian sprawled out against the wall and gripped itself against the flat surface. *This must be it,* I thought, and I reached out for the ladder, pulling myself off the Linkian.

Ketheria tried to do the same, but the current was too strong. When she let go of the red chain, the current grabbed hold of her and ripped her from the back of the Linkian. Nugget yelped and reached out for my sister. In an instant the Linkian whipped its tentacle around and grabbed on to Ketheria.

The Linkian brought Ketheria back to the ladder, and I took her from the alien as it gently released her. Nugget was too frightened now to move, so the Linkian picked him up, too, and passed him to me.

"Wait here!" I shouted to the Linkian. I don't know if he heard me, but I used my hands to make him understand I wanted him to wait. The Linkian simply rested against the wall of the tunnel.

At the top of the ladder, I paused in front of the black hole. I tested it with my right arm. There was a little bit of resistance, but my hand went straight through. I stepped in, dragging Ketheria and Nugget with me. The opening led to a small control room, wet and rank with mildew. We peeled our water suits away from our faces, and they shrank back around our shoulders.

A type of stonewort covered everything in the control room, which made it impossible for me to decipher the controls. Ketheria dove in and wiped away the algae with her hands. Nugget followed her lead. They uncovered a long glass portal that gave us a view of the escape tunnel and the enormous doors that led to the ocean—the doors we needed to open.

"Vairocina?" I called for my friend.

The air bent, and Vairocina gathered in front of me. "Yes, Johnny?"

"Can you use my stain to locate where I am?" I asked her as Ketheria glanced at the hologram.

Vairocina said, "You are in the control room for the ocean doors leading to the crystal-cooling tank. What are you doing there?"

"I need to open those doors," I informed her.

"I don't think that is wise, Johnny," she warned.

"It's a must. Can you help me?"

"Of course, but I believe this will attract much attention."

"I'll live with that. But I can't tell what anything is. Everything is covered with this crusty red slime."

"I will fix that."

Four tiny valves opened in the ceiling, and a tangy mist filled the room. The algae clumped and slipped off the controls.

"May I ask why we want to open these doors?" Vairocina said.

"We're going to save a child," I told her.

She smiled. "I always enjoy playing with you, Johnny Turnbull."

"I don't know if I would call this playing."

I stood in front of the controls and pushed into the

computer. I felt the electrons rush across my face and saw the glowing inside of the computer before me. I had to find a lock or file to open the doors. I sped down a corridor, past chunks of data streaming to some unknown destination, and stopped in front of the main portal. Vairocina was already waiting.

"What took you so long?" she teased.

"Reality," I said.

"The ocean doors still need to be opened manually from the control room. There should be a large circular control. Spin it clockwise," she instructed, disappearing through the portal.

I pulled out of the computer and grabbed the wheel. It was about a meter tall with four spokes. It was stuck.

"Help me here," I said.

Ketheria and Nugget joined in. Nugget used his big feet to pound on the spokes.

"Keep going!"

The wheel finally budged.

The instant the wheel began to move, an alarm sounded and a wailing siren filled the air.

"Keep spinning it!" I shouted over the piercing noise.

The wheel spun faster as we turned it, and eventually it was spinning by itself. I watched through the glass portals as the seal on the gigantic doors cracked and separated. Glaring red lights flashed from the top of the doors as the water began to cascade through the growing opening. Huge amounts of water poured in like the waterfalls of Magna. Ketheria and Nugget cheered as the tunnel filled with the ocean water.

"What's that?" I yelled, looking down the tunnel. Something sparkled just out of my sight.

At the back of the room was a small arched doorway. "Through here." I pointed and sprinted through the opening. It led to a railed walkway that stretched the length of the escape tunnel high above the water. The water from the ocean roared past us like a million starships taking off.

Then it stopped.

About one hundred and fifty meters away, a force field, just like the ones that protected Weegin's field portals, held the water back. The tunnel was filling, but only in the section directly below us.

"Vairocina!"

"I see it. The field is a protection device. It was triggered when we opened the doors, which we were not authorized to do."

"Get rid of it," I said.

"I tried. I can't. The water must be removed first. As I said, it's a safety device."

I had to do something. I could see the door to the cooling tank only a few hundred meters away.

"We tried, JT," Ketheria said.

"Don't talk like that. We're not giving up."

"There *is* one way," Vairocina said.

"See?" I looked at Ketheria. "Do it," I told Vairocina.

"The field will fail only when it is breached. Breached by something . . . alive. It's another safety device designed to prevent anyone from being crushed by the water."

"Something alive? Like a person?" I asked.

Nugget jumped up and said, "I will do it. Nugget will help."

"No, you won't," Ketheria argued, grabbing him by his water suit. "Thank you but we'll find another way."

"I'm afraid there isn't one," Vairocina informed us.

"I have an idea," I mumbled, then ran along the balcony toward the blue force field.

Ketheria chased after me. "What are you going to do?"

The flesh around my arm *felt* alive. If I pinched the skin, my arm hurt, although I was able to turn that sensation down. Would the force field detect the difference?

"The chance of death from the crushing water is ninety-eight point nine percent, Johnny," Vairocina announced.

"And from electrocution?" I asked.

"Forty-eight point three."

"That will have to do," I said as I bolted across the long metal walkway. Green and yellow sparks crackled above the waterline as the ocean filled the passageway. It was already more than two-thirds full.

"Johnny, wait," Ketheria begged.

"It's the only way," I told her. "Besides, I'll only stick my arm in. What can that hurt?"

The energy field blocked the entire tunnel and even across the walkway that skimmed above the waterline. I stood in front of the force field, peering through to the doors at the other end.

"We're so close, Ketheria," I said.

I couldn't turn back now, but I was scared. I accessed the

pain sensors in my arm and turned them off. I banged my artificial arm against the railing.

"See? I can't feel a thing," I told her.

"Several terminals have been accessed searching for your whereabouts, Johnny," Vairocina informed me.

"What do you mean?"

"There are many people looking for you right now," she said. "Mostly Citizens and Trading Council members."

I couldn't wait any longer. Soon it would be too late. There was no choice.

I thrust my arm forward and into the energy field.

A lighting bolt of crystal-blue fire shot up my arm and collided with my brain. *So much for the pain sensors*, I thought as I flew backward. At least I was still conscious.

"Johnny!" Ketheria screamed.

The sound of the water thundering down the tunnel was mixed with a crackling that filled my head. Everything I looked at seemed overexposed, and my arm hung numb and lifeless at my side.

"It worked," Vairocina exclaimed.

"Johnny, are you all right?" my sister said. Nugget knelt next to me, too.

"I think so." My voice was thick and the words stuck in my throat. "Give me a moment."

"You don't have one, Johnny. They have reached Odran's," Vairocina informed me, but I wasn't listening. Everything was still foggy.

I looked at my arm. The water suit was torched, and the

flesh on my fingers was fried right down to the metallic bones. They hesitated to move as my mind reconnected with the wiring.

"Remind me to cover these fingers up before Max sees them," I told Ketheria, and chuckled. She wasn't laughing.

"You could have killed yourself!" she screamed at me.

"But I didn't. Come on—we're still not done."

The tank filled quickly. The water gushed past us faster than we could run, faster than the falls of Magna. It hit the door at the end of the tunnel with a thunderous boom. Someone replied with his own boom.

"That must be Toll," I said.

"Hurry, Johnny. They're entering the tank," Vairocina pleaded.

"Who is? Who's entering the tank?"

"The Sea Dragons."

I had no idea what Sea Dragons were, and I didn't want know.

"We can't go this way," Ketheria said as we headed toward the tank doors. "We have to use the Linkian."

"When the tank doors open, Johnny, the remaining part of the tunnel will fill and flush you out to the ocean," Vairocina said. "You cannot stop it. You must leave here."

We raced back along the railing and through the control room. We pulled the water suits over our faces as the material molded to our heads. I moved to the ladder.

"Stop!" Ketheria cried. "Your suit. You can't go back into that water. The suit won't protect you now."

She was right. My suit was gone right up past the wrist.

"You have to wait here," she said.

"But I can't. You heard Vairocana. This whole place will be flooded."

"Pull your arm inside your suit," she ordered.

"What?"

"Just do it. I'll tie it off and we can get out of here."

I tucked my arm back into my suit, and Ketheria tied two knots in the material now hanging at my side. The Linkian never moved from its spot. We climbed carefully onto its back with Nugget between us and charged down the power-flow shafts. The return was much faster. I was ready this time when the Linkian rolled on its side to slip through the grate leading back into the tank.

But I was not ready for what I saw inside.

Circling just below the surface were four creatures with large metallic heads, long, bony bodies, and metal wings made of sharp, curved spikes. Huge searchlights on their undersides penetrated the water. They each had two jointed robotic arms extending from their torsos with long, vicious claws that reached forward as they swam. I could only assume that these were the Sea Dragons. One of the monsters swung two large crystal balls on thick chains as if they were toys on a string. The shining spheres looked as tall as me.

"Vairocina, can you see this?"

"I'm afraid I can."

"What are those spheres?"

"Oh my! Copper-infused crystal bombs. Once detonated, they will destroy all life inside the tank," she said. She sounded defeated. With what I was looking at, I couldn't blame her. Suddenly, I wished I had my other arm back.

I looked back at the doors and I saw Toll. He was out in front protecting the others still on the Linkians. Ketheria pointed to Smool, who was resting near the bottom of the tank. Her belly was very swollen, and all she could do was watch.

In turn each of the Sea Dragons dove deep and charged at Toll. My huge friend was doing his best to hold them back, but each time a Sea Dragon attacked, it slashed Toll with one of the long spikes on its wings.

"We have to stop them!" I shouted. "They're computers. I can simply disable them."

"I'm afraid it's not that easy." Vairocina informed me. "Whoever sent them into the tank knew about your abilities. The brains of the Sea Dragon are real flesh and blood. You will not be able to push into these monsters."

I watched helplessly as two Sea Dragons attacked at once. Toll managed to grab one with his right arm, but the other jabbed his thick flesh with a spike, forcing him to let go.

"They're going to kill him!" Ketheria screamed.

The Sea Dragon with the crystal copper bombs set one down on the floor of the tank and swam to the opposite side to lay down the other.

"They're going to kill us all," I said.

But why would they do that? If they killed the unborn Samiran, then who would pull the crystals? The Trading

Council was not that stupid. The bombs were just an empty threat. A decoy to make us give up.

I leaned close to the Linkian and said, "Let's help them." I felt the Linkian stiffen. "Hold on!" I shouted.

We charged at one of the Sea Dragons and swooped over the monster. The Linkian struck the creature with one of its thick tentacles. The Dragon staggered but thrust out its clawed hand, ripping the Linkian's flesh. Blood from the Linkian and from Toll smeared the water as we darted through the tank.

"What can I do?" I shouted.

"Run!" Vairocina said. "I have bypassed the security controls. Swim to the gate."

The enormous doors of the cooling tank cracked open. I instantly felt the pull as the tank water rushed past to fill the last of the escape tunnel. The other Linkians carrying the knudniks from Toll Town raced toward the opening, but so did the Sea Dragons.

Toll got a lucky break as the rush to the doors distracted an attacking monster. The gigantic Samiran caught the Dragon by the throat. It lashed back and forth inside Toll's grip, but one quick snap from Toll broke the Dragon's back and it sunk to the tank floor.

That's when Toll saw me. His eyes were on fire. Toll was fighting for his life and the life of his family. There was no choice for him; there was no thought of defeat. If this was his last stance, the last moment of his life, he was going to die a Samiran. But I was not going to let that happen.

I saw Toll turn toward the open doors, but a Sea Dragon was already there, waiting to strike.

"Vairocina, I'm going to charge that Sea Dragon. When I do, close the doors to the tank," I told her.

Vairocina resisted. "But . . ."

"Just do it!"

I bolted straight at the Sea Dragon who stood between Toll and his freedom. We dove from the left and distracted the Dragon with a smack of the Linkian's powerful tentacle.

"Now, Vairocina!"

The Sea Dragon was preoccupied with our attack. When it finally realized that the doors were closing, it was too late. The Dragon was pinned between the two doors. It could not swim forward or backward into the tunnel. The Sea Dragon was trapped. The beast flailed and screeched as it was crushed between the giant doors.

"Two down, Vairocina. Open the doors again!"

The Dragon with the crystal copper bombs had planted both devices and was now joining the attack. *Ignore them—they're not real,* I told myself.

Two Linkians, each with about twenty passengers on its back, circled one of the remaining Sea Dragons, slowly tangling it with the wire used to pull the crystals. There was no way the Dragon could break the wire, but that didn't stop it from trying. It pulled hard on the wire, furiously swimming backward and yanking one of the Linkians off balance. The knudniks on the back of the purple alien tumbled to the bottom of the tank. Some tried to swim but most just sank. The

Linkian let go of the rope and dove to retrieve the flailing knudniks, but the last Sea Dragon swooped in, brutally slashing the graceful creature. The Linkian's blood gushed from the wound and engulfed the battered defender.

"No!" Ketheria screamed.

But the Sea Dragon was too much for the Linkian. With one of its tentacles almost completely severed, the dying creature sank to the bottom of the tank with the other knudniks.

The loose wire whipped through the water like a laser cutting plastic, while the Sea Dragon struggled frantically to pull the other Linkian off balance.

"Go!" I shouted.

We dove straight toward them. Our Linkian snared the loose wire with its tentacle and then swam straight up toward the surface, pulling the wire taut. I felt Ketheria lift off the alien, her grip slipping.

"Hold on!" I screamed. I only had one arm to use. "Nugget, hold her tight!"

The Linkian pulled harder on the wire, and I slipped my left arm around the alien's neck rope. *Don't let go.* Nugget wrapped his big feet tighter around my waist.

The Linkian then leveled off and circled the Sea Dragon. The wire caught the fleshless, bony monster around its neck. The Linkian circled the entangled dragon three more times, and we clung to the Linkian as hard as we could. One final pull and the Sea Dragon gave up. The Linkian released the lines, and the metallic beast sank to the bottom of the tank.

I searched the water for the remaining Dragon. I found it attacking Toll near the bottom of the tank. Toll stood between the creature and Smool, who could only lie there. The Samiran's skin was as tough as stone, but the Sea Dragon, with its sharp wing-spikes and bladed claws, continued to hack away.

When my Linkian was directly above the Sea Dragon, I jumped. I didn't think about it. I wasn't scared. I just did it. I couldn't swim, so my body sank. I hit the back of the Sea Dragon just when the tank flashed with a blinding golden light. *The copper bombs,* I thought.

Not knowing how long I had to live, I quickly accessed anything on the Sea Dragon that was controlled by some sort of computer chip. The alien's insides flashed in my mind's eye in bits and pieces. So much of the creature's flesh was entangled with computer parts that I quickly got lost. Whatever I could find I turned off and then stopped.

The water above Smool began to swirl. At least I thought it was above Smool. That's where the gold light seemed to be coming from. Currents of water rushed past me as if guided by some cosmic force. The energy from the light sparkled and danced in the currents. All I could do was stare.

Smool let out a shriek. The sound was both joyful and filled with pain. The energy in the tank came together and flowed through her with one final plunge. And then it was gone. The current stopped, the light snapped off, and the energy disappeared as if someone had sucked everything out of the tank. I closed my eyes and waited for the worst. But nothing more happened.

When I opened my eyes, I saw a new baby Samiran struggling next to its mother. It was about a quarter the size of Smool and much smoother than its father. A Linkian, overloaded with the fallen knudniks, swooped by and plucked me off the disabled Sea Dragon, which was now chasing its own tail.

Toll looked up and smiled at me. His eyes said *thank you.* I didn't need to be a softwire to understand that. The father picked up his newborn treasure and headed for the open waters with Smool close behind and the Linkians moving swiftly ahead. As we slipped through the doors, I saw the copper bombs laying still. They had never detonated. The light had been from the birth of Toll's child.

24

Once we reached the ocean, Toll handed the new baby to Smool and followed our Linkian to the surface.

It was the first time I ever stepped foot on a beach. I immediately noticed the smell, so clean and so bright. I pulled off my water suit as we walked out of the ocean. The sweet smell of the bio-bots was gone, and I knew the water was safe. I stroked the Linkian as it dipped back into the sea.

"You should come with us," Toll said, hoisting himself onto the sand. "It is the only way I can thank you."

I looked across the ocean. Somewhere, out there, was freedom. I thought of Switzer and how he would have relished this moment, but that could never happen now. Ketheria took my hand and for once I felt like I could read *her* mind.

"I can't leave my friends behind, Toll. I hope you understand."

"I do," he said, and bowed his head. "You would have made your father a very proud man, Johnny Turnbull."

Those words caught me unexpected, and I felt my throat tighten. "Thank you," I mumbled.

Toll pushed back into the water, and Ketheria, Nugget, and I watched him swim out into the deep sea.

We were not alone very long when Max, Theodore, and Charlie ran up to us.

"You did it!" Max shrieked. "Toll and Smool are free!"

"So is the baby," I informed her.

"What about the crystal?" Ketheria asked.

"You should have seen Max," Theodore said. "She used the suits and filled them with bio-bots and then used these motors from Odran. It was awesome."

"It was easy," Max said. "Odran *had* been working on something to pull the crystals. I don't think he was ready to use it yet—he wasn't finished renting out Toll. Charlie had to help me to convince them to use my invention, though."

"They didn't have much choice, now, did they?" he said.

"What's going to happen to Odran?" I asked him.

"Don't worry about him. I'm sure they'll find a cozy little place for him at the Center for Science and Research. That's the least that he deserves."

I looked at Charlie. "I'm sorry for not telling you earlier," I told him.

"I'm the one that's sorry. I let you down. We'll have a long talk when we get back, and I promise to tell you everything."

"Everything?" I said.

Charlie smiled. "I'll try."

I sat on the shoreline of the great ocean with Max and Theodore. Charlie stood next to Ketheria while Nugget jumped on his shoulders. We looked out at the water in silence, mesmerized by the sound of the crashing waves. It was like a million people chattering, and I wanted to hear what each one of them had to say.

We stayed and watched Orbis rotate into shadow, and the cool darkness slowly crept across the waves toward us. Somewhere deep in the crystal-blue water was my friend Toll, swimming freely now with his partner, Smool, and their newborn child. It had taken two thousand rotations and a little help from some humans, but they were free. Toll had finally seen his dream come true.

"The ocean is beautiful," I said.

Charlie looked over at me, smiling. "You should have seen the ones on Earth."

"Maybe someday," Ketheria said.